Brink Hudlee

∧∇ - ∧δ - 2∇∇⬠

PART ONE

Dan River Press
PO Box 298
Thomaston, Maine 04861

CHAPTER Λ

It was sun-cool this Firstday, 15, Fourthmonth, 2040. Lawrence Holmes awakened at precisely 06:10. His dawn simulator had started one hour earlier to provide the light his body needed for his correct brain-chemical balance. Because of its high-energy consumption, not everyone could have a dawn simulator. However, those with severe seasonal affective disorders with a minimum disorder rating of plus 7.2 were permitted simulators. Lawrence checked out at 8.1 or higher.

On Firstdays, Lawrence's enclosed glass sleeping box was programmed for a 06:09 change in the humidity and the beginning of a gentle, warm breeze accompanied by Beethoven's "Pastoral" starting at 06:10. "This is the way to be awakened; technology does have advantages," Lawrence mused as he stretched his arms as high as he could. Yesterday's "Tips for Today," which came on each time anyone's computer accessed the planetnet, had the "Stretch when you arise" tip as No. 2.

"Skip sleep report," Lawrence said to Merlin, a paper-thin computer attached to and conformed to the contour of the underside of Lawrence's left arm. Merlin was a strong, but flexible, film that responded to Lawrence's voice, and only Lawrence's. Lawrence didn't even have to hold his arm up to his mouth, unless he was speaking in a whisper. "Comfort Index at 07:25," Lawrence asked Merlin to obtain the beginning thermal setting for his body cover. Lawrence wanted it nice and toasty for when he took his first step outdoors; after which his body cover would automatically adjust to the surrounding temperature and humidity. Wearing body covers was mandated back in Firstmonth, 2029.

Lawrence attached his wrist tube to receive his morning nutrient injection and angled the underside of his wrist towards the wall telling Merlin "Project west" so that today's planet news summary projected onto the wall in front of him. Usually the news was followed by his personal schedule for the day, but this morning he said, "Skip schedule" because he didn't need to be reminded that he was presenting his proposal to the Planet Council today. He quietly smiled at the irony that 15, Fourthmonth used to be the deadline for paying income taxes back in the old days. Lawrence just happened to have set this day as the deadline for presenting his proposal to the Planet Council. Similar to when he filed his income tax reports, here he was making his proposal on the last day of a deadline.

The door to Lawrence's exercise and electrostatic cleansing chamber automatically slid open when Lawrence called out, "Open." Lawrence had wanted to program the door to "Open sesame," but his children thought that was a little too corny especially since Lawrence's Midwestern twang didn't resonate with their image of Ali Baba's voice. The "Pastoral" started up inside the cleansing chamber without having missed a beat from the last note he'd heard earlier. A coil spring mat covered all but a two-meter square area in one corner, which was made of tile with a floor drain. The whole room was seven meters square with frosted glass walls ending two meters below the ceiling to allow air circulation over the walls. The area was large enough for fencing, which Lawrence and his son, Byron, enjoyed about every two weeks. In another corner was an exercise machine, the Integral model, which combined weight lifting, stretching, and bicycling movements by positioning the body appropriately depending on which muscle group was being developed.

A viewing screen standing close to his Integral machine rotated so Lawrence could watch his choice of programs from the position he was in while exercising. Lawrence's favorite program showed scenes of different parts of the world viewed as if you were actually seeing them in person. A walk down Paris's Avenue Champs-Elysees from the Arc de Triomphe de l'Etoile to Place de la Concorde would be shown for the same length of time that it would take a person to actually make that walk. Pictures of a flight over the Grand Canyon in a single engine plane showed as much of the Canyon as the plane could fly over in the time the pictures were shown. Lawrence started his exercise routine using the bicycling set-up of the Integral in rhythm with the music watching a bicycling ride along the coast of Puerto Rico from Rincon north towards the surfing beach. Lawrence was working up to a sixteen-minute work out at a heart rate of one hundred thirty-eight while lifting ten kilograms vertically every eight seconds.

Lawrence didn't have to do the exercises. The only way the Body Functions Department, known as the "BBB" for Big Brother's Bodywatch, could tell if Lawrence had completed his required fifteen minutes was by his monthly physical condition report. Since those reports were monitored remotely, some resourceful guy or gal invented an electronic device that gave the results the BBB expected. The device was available on the black market, and being caught with it was a Level 3.5 offense for which the monetary fine was one day's pay. That wasn't the bad part. Violators had to report bi-weekly to BBB's testing clinic until they met the required physical condition standards.

Lawrence's exercise program was designed for persons with his physical characteristics. He always felt better after his exercises, so he did them willingly. His physical condition test scores placed him in the eighty-ninth percentile for forty-eight year-old white skins, 1.8 meters tall and weighing 72.5 to 75.0 kilograms. Also, Lawrence looked better when he exercised. He was regarded as handsome in a regal way by most of the women he worked with. His hair was still thick and dark enough that the graying was hardly noticeable. He wouldn't admit it, even to himself, but his appearance mattered to him. He finished his work out with stretching exercises.

Lawrence moved to the corner that was tiled and opened his mouth, bent over and with his hands spread his butt cheeks for the mandatory twenty seconds of electrostatic body cleansing. He then said "rinse" for an optional water spray installed only on units owned by persons old enough to have taken showers before cleansing chambers became mandatory in 2024. The rinse added little significant cleansing benefit, but it was such a popular, nostalgic luxury that BBB allowed the manufacture of some cleansing chambers with showers and set them to provide a ninety seconds rinsing and thirty seconds air-drying per shower. Lawrence looked forward to his shower routine each day and since the BBB did not monitor the number of showers taken, he had seen to it that his children knew what a shower was. He encouraged them to sing in the shower, but only Byron didn't think the idea ridiculous. It pleased Lawrence to get away with the unauthorized showers.

Lawrence's wife, Laura, had woken to Elvis Presley's "Hard Headed Woman" in her adjoining sleeping box. Although the song's hardheaded woman was "A thorn in her man's side," Elvis loved her anyway. Laura liked that. She was also pleased that she knew the little known fact that Elvis's voice was well suited for ballads and Christmas carols, and that most people, even many Elvis fans, did not know Elvis had recorded seven Christmas songs and several hymns over his career.

Laura stepped into the cleansing chamber as Lawrence stepped out. Slim and straight like a bamboo shoot, auburn-haired more reddish than brown, and with admirable movements, she was a fitness buff and regularly received special award certificates for exceeding the BBB's physical index for 47-year-old white skin women. Lawrence hugged her naked body sliding his hands down and over her hips. She lifted herself up against him and kissed him firmly. "Tonight?" he suggested, and she responded with a warm smile on her broad face that framed full lips.

Laura took another step into the chamber but stopped and turned back. "What kind of reaction do you expect to your presentation today?" Laura asked. Her voice was high-pitched, thin, nervous.

Lawrence answered quickly, "Opinion will be divided, and the differences will be pronounced."

Laura's shoulders stiffened. "Will it get personal?"

"Yes, I think so."

Laura's eyes displayed her fright. She raised her hand to her face. "Will you be in danger?"

Lawrence took her hand in his. "I'm not worried about myself," and, after a pause, "or you, love. But I am worried about Byron and how the whole affair may affect Anne and Kenneth." Lawrence's head dropped slightly as his eyes were cast downward. He let Laura's hand slip from his.

"Is it worth it, I mean, to resist or, or even contend? Look at me, Lawrence."

Lawrence faced Laura. "Everyone has their own nature, love. Life works that way even in a controlled society. My role isn't my choice any more than yours is yours or Byron's is Byron's."

Laura reached out her arm to touch Lawrence's. "But you have made many choices in the past and still do now; your occupation, whether to marry, whether to marry me, having children, how many, accepting an appointment to the Council, what to say or not say. All kinds of choices." Her grip on his arm tightened.

Lawrence placed his hand over hers. "I fail in many ways, but I aspire to be a man of character and follow a code."

Laura backed away. "And your code comes before your family?"

"I've got to have the respect of my family. It's Shakespeare: 'This above all, to thine own self be true, and it must follow as the night the day, that canst not then be false to any man.'"

"And so Laertes, Hamlet and even Polonius who said those words and Ophelia, who, you would probably say, could not help what she was, all died." Laura turned away to leave.

Lawrence stepped towards her. "Laura, Laura. I need your help. At times I feel I'm alone. Except for you, you and Kate, and Byron, without your being there for me, well, I'd be lost."

Laura turned back, looked intently into Lawrence's eyes and moved back into his arms. "Darling, forgive me. Do what you must. I love you; I'm proud of the man you are. It's just my female vibes acting up again." They kissed and as Laura headed back to the cleansing chamber, Lawrence pinched her on her hip. She jumped slightly, turned her head and stuck out her tongue and then slid it from side to side and smiled.

CHAPTER 2

Lawrence dressed quickly pulling on an olive green body cover with green and red accent stripes. Stripes had not been allowed on body covers until Firstmonth, 2038. Although only a minor improvement in the body cover's drabness, they were highly popular. They had been added only because their pattern indicated the occupation and security status of the wearer, but they had lifted everyone's spirits. Each workday Lawrence donned his body cover, he was thankful that he only had to wear it when he left home. He was particularly grateful that Laura's research work for the sports-psychology department of Columbia University could be done at home where she could wear whatever she wanted. "Damn it all to Hell," was Laura's usual response when she had to go to the Columbia campus to give reports or attend departmental meetings and had to wear a body cover. Their younger daughter, Kate, also had to wear a body cover when she was on campus, but since she had grown up under the system, she hardly thought about it.

Lawrence and Laura's older daughter, Anne, was married and a librarian in the branch near her home. Librarians were allowed a greater choice in their clothing while at work. They could wear skirts and smock-like tops that came in practically any color they wanted so long as they had a pocket for their stun gun. Laura suggested that the liberal clothing provisions for librarians was recognition that their work was duller than others, so they had been allowed a little something to make their lives more interesting. Lawrence said he had known some librarians at the University of Missouri who didn't need anything to liven up their lives. Neither Lawrence nor Laura had ever in any way hinted or acknowledged that Anne was dull, but everyone knew it. Lawrence thought Anne felt it more than anyone else did. He thought that her resentment of Kate and Byron was mainly jealousy, so he was especially pleased that Anne was an outstanding artist. She had illustrated several children's books, which were displayed at the entrance to the library under a sign proudly calling attention to the fact that an employee's work had been published.

Kate was the child most like Lawrence. Both were Libra, athletic, prolific readers, efficient, slow to anger, but critical of wasted time, material, or talent. Lawrence, however, had hardly ever been on a horse while Kate was an accomplished equestrian who showed Arabians and had been Top Ten at the Nationals twice. At 21, she was in her last year of advanced academic preparation. She had completed the required six months of physical conditioning between two university semesters, so her occupational evaluation would occur in three months in the middle of Seventhmonth. Kate's marriage designate was Michael Jefferson. Lawrence liked him. The computer-matching program had for one time, at least, apparently worked. Their match rating was 88--well above the 70 required to enter the nine month trial companionship program, which they had completed with an outstanding 96 score. They were due for interviews for acceptance into marriage probation after Kate's occupational evaluation.

Kate's sister, Anne, was also due for interviews. She and her husband, Kenneth Clark, had applied for the disabling of their pregnancy prevention controls that were built into each person's body chip. The first chips with pregnancy controls were inserted on 3 Thirdmonth, 2024 in selected families in India and Africa where population growth was causing famine in several areas. China had provided an example of the benefits of population controls, so when the Planet Council imposed modest restrictions, no organized opposition occurred. Soon more pregnancy restrictions were imposed in more countries. Pope Paul protested the establishment of pregnancy controls, but since no Catholics were being restricted at the time, his objection was ignored. After large declines in their populations, India and parts of Africa lodged strong complaints to the Planet Council causing a majority of the Council to decide it was only fair to extend pregnancy controls to all nations. As frequently happens with governmental programs, the first measures affected few of the middle-class and were hardly noticed by the great majority of citizens. By the time the restrictions were applied to all persons, most everyone had gotten used to their existence and accepted them without significant protest.

Anne had majored in family psychology and written a paper on the importance of "tough love" for babies. She was twenty-four and her marriage had a near perfect mental/psychological rating for eligibility for parenthood. The high rating qualified she and Kenneth for having twins, which required an extra parental training course, because of the unique problems of raising twins. She and Kenneth had also passed their physical suitability and disease-free tests, but they hadn't made a decision on the twin issue. They had decided that their first-born would be a boy. The interviews were the final step. Kenneth had obtained a one-week leave of absence from his banking job to prepare for the toughest section of the interviews--theory of child training. Anne worried that the public scrutiny resulting from Lawrence's membership in the Planet Council might expose his opposition to pregnancy controls and that the interviewers would find that disturbing. She also worried about Byron's association with a group advocating the immediate reversal of many of the personal restrictions in force.

Byron was a rebel. In spirit he was a youthful version of his father, particularly echoing what his father had been like when Lawrence was Byron's age, but Byron didn't know it. In Byron's mind about the only thing they had in common was their singing in the shower. Their songs were different, but both father and son sang just the same. Byron was rebellious even before he learned to walk. Breast-feeding, mandated except in cases where the mother was incapable of supplying sufficient nourishment, was enforced by requiring the mother to obtain prescriptions for formula milk from the baby's pediatrician. A team of pediatricians could not determine why Byron rejected Laura's abundant supply of wholesome milk. Tests showed Byron was not allergic to it. Lawrence had to plead with the lead pediatrician, a long time friend, to have pity on them for the prescription, even though it put his doctor's license in jeopardy.

Later on, Byron resisted pre-school training by refusing to sit during classes.

He wouldn't answer questions and constantly asked his teachers why they wanted to know what they were asking anyway. His teachers put up with his behavior because his test scores were without exception the highest ever recorded in every subject from the first test onward. Byron tested achievement level 34 at the age of fourteen whereas even the best students didn't reach that level until they were nineteen. At level 41 he had started researching advanced studies in several of the subjects he took so he could ask his instructors questions he knew they could not answer. His instructors started asking Byron to answer those questions finding him able to explain very complex concepts in such a way that his classmates could understand the fundamentals. Thus Byron obtained an influential position with his classmates--particularly since he had a way of never putting down even the slowest student. He was kind and helpful except to those in authority.

Byron benefited especially from the Planet Council's educational requirements in regard to classical literature. Starting at age six with a simplified version of the major Shakespearean plays, all students had to complete courses covering the works of the most distinguished authors, including poets, by age sixteen in order to qualify for the highest level training thereafter. At fifteen, Byron published his first collection of poems, which received national awards. He was interviewed on television programs and became known internationally when he and a group of his friends won an award at Cannes Planet film festival for their documentary film on Colin Powell, the Secretary of State under George W. Bush. After Byron finished his advanced academic training, he secured a position with the Cultural Enrichment Bureau and regularly reviewed new books and poems for several leading literary reviews. By 2036 when Byron was 21, he was truly accomplished.

"I'll be leaving in twenty minutes, destination Planet Council Hall; I'm walking to the commuter station; no air scooter," Lawrence said to Merlin. Lawrence went to the dining counter, which also served as a wet bar, selected French Quarter Cajun coffee beans to be ground, four slices of seven grain bread to be toasted dark with light butter and took a seat on the bar stool. The home chef unit told him, "All are ready" when all his selections were done at the same time. He removed them and started eating. Kate came in.

"Morning Dad. This is the day, isn't it?" Kate asked as she took a stool beside his.

Lawrence leaned over to kiss her forehead. "This is it; at least the beginning."

Kate put her arm around Lawrence's shoulder and said, "Even if Anne and Byron won't tell you, we're all proud of you. Good luck today." She reached over with her other arm to snatch a piece of his toast.

"Do you think I'll get anywhere?" Lawrence swung around out of Kate's grasp and moved his plate out of her reach with a smile.

"Tough to say. Your proposal doesn't change the main features of the body chip. Everyone will still be immune to AIDS, won't respond to most all of the illegal drugs or be able to become pregnant or impregnate without approval. But a lot of people still remember Bastille Day 2018. Even my generation understands that when they damaged the Eiffel Tower, civil liberties would give way to worldwide security measures. Some said the French shouldn't have given up their independence to recover their tourists. Since the world has gotten used to being without rights, you may not have many delegates on your side. My generation feels it's time to start back to the way it was, but we're not doing the voting."

"I'm not so sure I won't have substantial support. I'll have the best minds of the Council with me, and they can swing votes."

"You also have Byron for sure." Quick as a wink, she swiped another piece of toast.

"He's ahead of me. Too far, I'm afraid." Lawrence's cast his eyes downward.

"Is he going to Council today?"

"I'm sure he is. But he won't like my proposed time schedule. I haven't told anybody what it is, yet, partly because I just made up my mind yesterday. Some people say that if many think your plan is moving too quickly and many think it is moving too slowly, you have it about right. Well, I got that kind of response from those I tried it out on. So, hopefully it will be considered a good compromise. But compromise is not in Byron's vocabulary."

CHAPTER 3

Byron awoke without any prompting from his sleeping box, said, "Elvira Madigan" for Mozart's Piano Concerto No. 21 in C Major and it started. He listened until it was finished and then climbed down. He then spent the required twenty seconds in the cleansing chamber, but he skipped his exercises and even his shower because he was already running late to make the Planet Council session. Although Byron evaded every mandatory order he could without being caught, he always used the cleansing chamber in part because he did not wish to cause another person any illness by personally infecting them. He had no choice on the cleansing chamber today, anyway, because to gain entrance to the Council Hall, his body would have to pass the screening for an electrostatic residue from a cleansing performed within the last fifteen hours. The same screening occurred at the commuter station, large restaurants, stadiums, airports, and about anywhere else where large groups of people were in close proximity.

He chose a blue body cover thinking it most appropriate for the Council and because Moira liked for him to wear blue. He skipped his nutrients and walked outside to take his air scooter to the commuter station. His scooter's maximum speed of 35 kilometers per hour reminded him that he should ask his friend, Tim, if he could change the governor on it to get at least 45 to 50 kilometers per hour. It was so irritating to be in a hurry and have to poke along just because the Traffic Bureau studies had shown that 35 kilometers per hour was the safest, most efficient speed, and they wanted to encourage use of the high-speed travel units from the commuter stations. It took forever to get across New York City at 35 kilometers per hour. Byron wondered what the penalty might be if he and Tim were caught.

CHAPTER 4

Lawrence left and walked to the commuter station. The bright sun made him feel cheerful and he always enjoyed a walk in cool weather. Several others were walking, and those on air scooters nodded as if to acknowledge that they wished they had chosen to walk too. As he entered the station, the monitor read his identification code from his body chip, screened his electrostatic cleanliness residue and flashed "Admit" on the overhead screen. He watched the screen display his transport assignment to board travel unit No. 25 in six minutes and that it was running ahead of schedule and his expected arrival time at the Planet Conference Hall was 08:02. He had told Merlin to schedule a seat in the relaxation travel unit and was looking forward to a nap in route even though he didn't like putting on the head set with its sleep inducing electrodes. The headsets also controlled the snoring of users so others would not be disturbed if one chose to ride along in silence or read.

Sometimes Lawrence chose the information travel unit because its "Today's Summary" included opinion polls on the Planet Council's actions. More often he chose the unit known as the melting pot which was always crowded with a noisy cross section of the population jabbering, arguing, laughing or whatever. Traveling in the melting pot, he felt, kept him in tune with the populace, and it reminded him of bus trips he'd taken when he first started work in downtown St. Louis. His degree in journalism from the University of Missouri had landed him a job with the St. Louis *Post Dispatch*. Those were the days when everyone could have their own car or cars, if they could afford it. At that time Laura and he had only one car, so he rode the bus almost every workday. The buses were always crowded in the morning. Most of the riders were service workers who seemed as if they rode the same buses every day and genuinely looked forward to the travel time spent with these fellow transit friends. It seemed eerie that every day when the bus reached the riverfront area, the conversations became muted as riders gazed towards the Gateway Arch. The Arch had been blackened when an ex-maintenance worker who had been fired placed a smoke bomb in the observation car that ran inside the arch on 4, Seventhmonth, 2016. Over 10,000 had assembled under the Arch to watch the fireworks display. No one was injured and most of the discoloration was cleansed within a year, but the slight gray that remained was a constant reminder that thousands could have been killed if a different kind of bomb had been used.

Lawrence's headset woke him as No. 25 travel unit slowed to a gentle stop at the Planet Council station. It was a short walk from the station to the Council check-in desk. Many complaints had been made about the appearance of the desk and the check-in procedures. "It looks as if you are entering a prison," was the usual description of the fenced-in area with it's runway lined with tubular railings restricting passage to one-a-breast leading to a heavy, metal desk fully covered with various scanning equipment. As always, there was a long line waiting to be checked in. Even though all delegates had special DNA identification in their body chip, each delegate still had to undergo a voiceprint, fingerprint, and a painless blood test to gain admittance to the Planet Council Hall. The company that developed the scanning machine for blood tests had not only made great profits, they had received a special commendation, which met with worldwide approval. As Lawrence took his place in line, Thomas Baines, one of his best friends and the delegate from Australia, took hold of his shoulder.

"Are you ready?" Thomas asked.

A hint of a smile appeared on Lawrence's face as he turned around. "My grandfather told me about a game he used to play called hide and seek. The one who was 'it' called out to those who had to run and hide, 'Ready or not, here I come.' Well, I'm ready. The question is whether the Council is ready or not for what's coming."

Now Thomas smiled. "Good, but be careful. My grandfather told me, 'If you're out in front of the crowd, watch your backside; it's exposed.' Lawrence, you really are taking on a bearcat. Not just because of what you're proposing, but because of the guaranteed opposition of your own country. With all their political power, you'll be lucky to avoid a veto in the Directorate. Do you have any word on how China and Russia will react?" Lawrence and Thomas were almost through with the check-in.

"I know both will have problems at home if they support a veto, but their delegates want to get along with the U.S., so I don't know how it will come out in the wash. Thanks for your warning. I'll pick places where I can keep my back to the wall."

"Your back will be against the wall when you present your resolution. See you later. I've got a meeting with my Prime Minister." Thomas moved off ahead of Lawrence.

Lawrence took the escalator down to the Great Hall where all sessions of the Planet Council were held. The Council was an outgrowth of the United Nations and took over its headquarters in New York City in 2017. Several international problems, which grew at differing rates, but all of which became severe by the middle of the second decade of the twenty-first century, spurred the movement for the reorganization of the U.N. Violent protests in many parts of the world continued even after the elections in Iraq in 2005, although no large attacks of the magnitude of the 9/11 destruction of the twin towers in New York City occurred. The spread of AIDS in Africa and among dark skins in general reached near epidemic levels and became a serious concern in Russia and China. Nuclear capability in a dozen countries included the ability to manufacture weapons.

The extremists had proved in the Spanish elections of 2004 that they could alter the course of events when their railway attack there resulted in the upset of the party in power. New groups willing to use any means to gain their ends had seen in Iraq that the use of suicide bombers had been very effective. Using improvements in technology and techniques, extremists of varying nationalities and causes were able to create havoc with fewer and fewer of their number being lost. They struck in Russia, the United States, Great Britain, Germany, Israel, Egypt, France, Spain, Indonesia, Saudi Arabia, Canada, Italy and even China from 2007 to 2016.

Muslim fanatics from Arab states organized many of the attacks, but more attacks involved conflicts within a nation and had entirely different motivations from those in Arab countries. Often the goal was to unseat an autocratic regime. The common element in the almost all attacks was the use of bombs, which usually were detonated remotely. Target locations were government installations and heavily populated public places. International travel declined. More and more of the resources of nations were required for security measures, and even with those added measures, it seemed as if each new day brought a new act of violence somewhere in the world. People began to feel that they were not safe anywhere.

Vaccines to prevent AIDS and neutralize the highs from some illegal drugs were developed by 2014. Parents saw to it that their children were vaccinated at the earliest possible age, but those who needed the vaccinations the most, did not take advantage of the subsidized cost and urgings provided by governments throughout the world. International conferences sought methods of finding and immunizing those with AIDS and illegal drug users. The program that Israel established during the second decade of the twenty-first century to prevent suicide bombings drew attention as a possible solution. Israel conducted an extremely thorough door-to-door census to identify all persons living within their boundaries. Then all persons were provided with an identification card complete with a computer chip, which they were required to have in their possession at all times, which could be scanned at numerous locations. Israel added certification of vaccines to the identity information the chip provided so they could easily determine which persons had not been vaccinated when they passed through the scanning stations. Most nations chose to implement the Israeli system for all parts of their country as soon as practical. Others implemented the system region by region within their boundaries based on the difficulty of finding persons in remote areas.

The development of nuclear power was driven by both economic and military considerations. Countries with huge populations, like India, needed to supply the needs of their industries and institutions with the cheapest power possible. At the same time, India as an example, felt it must have parity with Pakistan and any other military threats.

New leadership emerged in both the United States and Great Britain after 2008, which argued that the coalition that conquered Iraq must receive more widespread approval for future military measures to make the world safer. The coalition approached other governments and made many attempts to reach agreement on proposed new anti-violence measurers. As plan after plan failed to halt the bombings and solve the other pressing problems, the situation became so desperate that the U.S., Russia and China met and agreed to form a new political structure as the best way to confront the worldwide crisis. Those three countries persuaded several other countries to join them to force the U.N. to accept a reorganization plan that included an international military force under the control of a world government. France, in particular, opposed the change, but dropped their protest and joined the coalition after their tourist trade dropped sharply when they refused to cooperate. The reluctance of many nations to surrender their sovereignty was overcome partly by their recognition that a stronger security system was needed and partly by economic considerations. The coalition members enjoyed prosperous trade agreements, while non-members struggled to stay afloat.

The reorganization of the U.N. established a Directorate composed of the U.S., Russia and China, the Big Three, as permanent members and two rotating members elected by the other Planet Council members for two-year terms. The Directorate administered the Planet Council. Two Directorate members voting together could veto any decision of the Council, but at least one of the two votes had to be by one of the Big Three.

Lawrence was one of fifteen delegates who were chosen to represent the world population as a whole. They were known as the peoples' advocates. All other delegates represented geographical areas and were selected by the countries they represented. The Council delegates elected the advocates, but could not vote for an advocate from their own country. Advocates were not subject to control by their native country's government. Most of the advocates had reputations as independent thinkers who had at times vigorously opposed actions of their homeland. Seven had published works in the field of human relations. Five were former presidents of renowned universities. They were voting delegates, had their own staff, were provided funds for travel and research, and were highly paid directly by the Council so they could devote all their time to Council affairs. With his high income Lawrence could afford one of the large single-family residences, as well as a private vehicle available for him at all times. Lawrence used the private vehicle only on special occasions so he would better understand the lifestyle of the ordinary citizen.

CHAPTER ⌂

Byron had not made a travel unit reservation and had to wait an extra ten minutes to catch the melting pot unit. At Council sessions, Byron sat with a group of delegates' children in the special section for non-delegate guests and family members. His group closely followed Council proceeding and met often to vent their frustrations with the restrictions controlling their lives. The group called themselves "JD's Seven" after Jimmy Dean, the rebel without a cause from movie fame in the 1950s. They felt, however, that they indeed did have a cause. Lawrence was a hero to the group, but Byron didn't acknowledge it either to them or to his father.

Byron's girlfriend, Moira, the 24-year-old dark skin daughter of John Browning, the delegate from Scotland, was in the group. Lawrence and John became good friends and that had led to frequent invitations to Byron to spend evenings and weekends with the Brownings while he attended Edinburgh University in Scotland. Byron and Moira were together frequently and, as might be expected, became romantically attached. Even though they had not yet formalized their relationship, their friends knew it would happen soon.

Together, Byron and Moira presented an extreme contrast in more than one way. Byron's complexion was light and Moira's very dark. Byron was 1.9 meters tall and Moira 1.6 meters, a difference of one foot in the old U.S. measurement system. Byron was slightly pudgy; Moira was slim as a reed. Byron's arms and hands were in constant motion in keeping with his booming voice while Moira stayed almost motionless and expressed herself quietly, and Byron was ready to act on issues right now while Moira wanted to "think about it."

"Moira, you beat me here," Byron said as he gave her a hug.

"So what's new?" Moira said as she looked up into his face. "I always do, big guy."

"And I did, too," said Anastasia, the 20 year old daughter of Boris and Klavia Gorbachev. Boris was the Russian delegate and, as one of The Big Three, had access to information and services that other delegates only wished for. Moreover, he had power. These Gorbachevs were from the same region as Mikhail Gorbachev, the President of the Soviet Union in 1989 when the Berlin Wall came down. They were not related to Mikhail, but they shared many of his aspirations. Anastasia was seated next to Moira, her best friend.

"O.K., O.K.," Byron said. "But I made it before the session started." He and Moira separated but continued to hold hands. "I want a copy of the planned Council schedule for debate of Dad's resolution. Do you have a copy?"

Moira answered, "I don't know if it's available yet."

"I'll go check," Byron said. "Be right back."

"Is your dad going to support Lawrence?" Anastasia asked Moira her intentness showing in her eyes.

Moira hesitated, then answered quietly, "In the most part I think he will, but there may be other concerns, which, I think, are going to come into play."

"What kind of concerns?"

"Well, a different issue is coming up that's going to complicate things. Don't say anything about this because I'm not supposed to know, but I overheard my dad talking to some of the other leaders of the dark skin caucus. They're going to try to make a deal with Lawrence to trade votes. I couldn't hear well enough to catch just what the trade-off is going to be. Some of the black skin caucus is going to meet with Lawrence after he introduces his resolution." Moira looked around as if to be sure no one overheard her. There was no one close to them.

"I wonder what they're after. I can't think of any important appointments under consideration. Well, anyway, we'll find out when it happens. My dad and his alternate delegate are sympathetic to Lawrence, but I don't know what will happen inside the Directorate. I'm afraid the U.S. will try to get another vote out of the Directorate to veto debate. Lawrence's chances may depend on avoiding the veto."

"Do you think the whole Council will accept Lawrence's proposal if he gets it past a veto in the Directorate?" Moira asked.

"Hard to say. No one has ever proposed any lessening of control. It's always been more and more, and some delegates feel the news media should be monitored more closely. What do you think?" Anastasia's voice was as intense as her eyes.

"I'm worried. This whole thing may split the Council and stir up things all over the world." Moira twisted her scarf she held first one way and then the other.

"Moira, it's Byron you're worried about. Might as well admit it."

Moira looked away and then turned back. "He's so volatile about the whole thing. I'm afraid he'll do something really dangerous if his dad's resolution isn't adopted. And he really wants a whole lot more. Byron sees it as only opening the door a crack--not what he and I think the rest of our group believe many others are going to demand if the ball gets rolling. It's somewhat like the civil rights movement in the U.S. back in the 90's. Progress was made, but that only whetted the appetite. Here I am, the only dark skin in our group, and I'm wanting to go slowly."

"Just because your skin is darker than mine doesn't make you any different. They only set up the dark skin, white skin, tan skin, light skin classifications so there was a simple system to classify all persons."

"I know, and we haven't felt discriminated against for the last fifteen years or so except for allowed birth rates."

"Anyway I'm with those who want to go faster, Moira. It's time for civil rights to be restored. I think JD's Seven represents how everyone under thirty everywhere feels. We aren't old enough to have been through the worst and don't see things the same way as those who went through it do."

Moira's eyes were downcast. Anastasia's voice began to rise. "I remember my grandfather talking about his uncle, Vladimir, who was born in 1929 just before his parents left Russia to go to the U.S., hopeful of getting rich. They arrived a few months before the Great Depression and almost starved to death. But Vladimir was too young to remember the terrible suffering. When he grew up, he thought it sad that his parents didn't enjoy things like expensive vacations. All they could think about was how much it cost."

Moira started to say something, but didn't when she saw Byron at the end of the aisle coming back. "I know there are risks that lessening security might give terrorism a chance to hit again, but I don't want to live the rest of my life in jail," Anastasia said. "When I want to have children, I don't want to wait until some stupid committee says O.K. and tells me how many I can have. Russia has changed. We were held down a long time. We're like the kid on the block who got a new bike that he hardly knew even existed. Just as he got used to riding and almost had his balance, the bike was taken away. That kid still remembers how to ride a bike and wants to ride again."

"What's Anastasia so wound up about?" Byron asked walking up to them.

"You know Anastasia," Moira answered. "She gets excited about everything. It's nothing special. We've been talking about bicycles." Anastasia pinched Moira on the side so Byron couldn't see her do it and just smiled. Byron looked puzzled, but didn't say anything as he took his seat next to Moira.

CHAPTER 6

Lawrence placed his manila folder with a copy of his speech inside on his desk. Of all the delegate's desks, Lawrence's was the shabbiest. The same nostalgic philosophy that permitted personal showers had prevailed at the Council. Some wag had said that to counter the Council's prison-like atmosphere the inmates would be given a choice of desks just as the condemned were given a choice of their last meal. Every delegate was allowed to bring any desk he or she wanted to the Council auditorium for her or his own use. As a demonstration of the higher status of delegates to alternate delegates, only delegates were afforded this privilege. Lawrence's desk was his old desk he had back at the St. Louis *Post Dispatch*. It was a standard gray, metal office-desk that had been used for many years by a columnist who had retired the year after Lawrence started to work and Lawrence had inherited it. Something about its worn, scratched condition had appealed to Lawrence, so he'd kept it even when offered a new contemporary desk thought to be more in keeping with his position, which had steadily grown in stature at the paper. Other delegates had carved wooden desks of oak or mahogany or even solid walnut or cherry. Some desks were shining combinations of stainless steel and glass and the delegate from France had a Louie the Fourteenth antique desk reputed to be worth well more than $ 70,000.

What Lawrence's desk lacked in style was more than made up with his personal objects he kept on the top of his desk. Most of the delegates had pictures of their families or scenes from their homeland or both poised on top of their desks. Lawrence did not have any negative feelings about that practice for others, but for him, pictures of his family on public display felt like an invasion of his personal privacy. So, instead he had asked each of his family members to give him something to place on his desk.

Laura commissioned a silversmith to make him a sterling silver replica of St. Louis's gateway arch with a small statue of a man underneath attached to the silver base. This was in recognition of Lawrence's daily column "Under the Arch," which received publishing awards and was read with interest by almost every alert and knowledgeable individual in the St. Louis area. Lawrence often used his column to poke fun at the foibles of the government, although he frequently included practical suggestions for improvements.

Byron gave his father one of his first poems he had written when he was nine. Byron framed the original copy complete with its misspelling. Byron had written it on his computer but forgot to spell check and didn't catch the error, because he never had been a good speller. The poem read:

Think of me as sunshine bright
Or no less than pale moonlight
On mission to lightin shadows dark
As my mighty pen makes its mark

Kate gave her father the first blue ribbon she won at an Arabian horse show. It came from a class B show in small town near St. Louis named Eureka. The blue had faded and the ribbon was wrinkled. Kate had subsequently won trophies and plaques from much more prestigious shows, but Kate treasured this ribbon the most and now Lawrence did.

Anne, on the other hand struggled over what to give her father. She asked her mother, brother and sister for help, and finally spurred by Byron's suggestion to think of something she knew her dad liked, drew him a picture of a bulldog, which had been Lawrence's favorite breed ever since he had one in grade school named Butch.

Lawrence had arrived early for the session. When he took his seat in the advocates' section only one other advocate was there: James Anderson, a native of New York who was seated at his desk, which was next to Lawrence's. "Lawrence, you know I am not going to support your proposal, but I want you to know it is because I believe those rights guaranteed in the ten amendments to our constitution will more likely be restored and extended to the whole world if the terrorists can be prevented from acting for just a few more years."

Lawrence finished his freshly squeezed orange juice, which was placed on all delegates' desks each morning. "It's been twelve years since any attack has occurred, James. I'm fearful that in a few more years the answer will be the same--just wait a few more years. Now is the time to start the process before we lose the memory of what freedom is."

"Human life is too precious. Reopening the door for bombings, chemical warfare and perhaps even nuclear weapons is too big a risk," James answered leaning towards Lawrence.

"The bigger risk is to let today's small protest movement grow to open rebellion," Lawrence answered. "You have seen the increasing calls for censorship by some delegates. Censorship leads to loss of freedom of the press. If that happens, underground presses will emerge. I have already seen a few subtle, what I think are anti-Council bulletins on the planetnet. They are in the form of routine announcements, but certain words keep getting repeated. I think they are some kind of code between protest groups in different parts of the world. I know the planetnet is monitored for such things, but I believe some are slipping through because they look innocuous."

James sipped his coffee and looked sideways at Lawrence and said, "Do you think you might be a little paranoid, friend? Maybe reading something into innocent communications that isn't there?"

Lawrence smiled. "I hope you're right. And I may be a little uptight, anyway. I've been working long hours on this."

"Well I wouldn't mention the code thing in your presentation, anyway. I'm not for your resolution, but I am for you. People might misunderstand and think you are connected to a protest organization. You're going to be watched closely enough as it is. Don't give them any more ammunition than they have already."

Lawrence leaned close to James and whispered, "Do you really think I'm already on the Internal Security surveillance list?"

James answered in a low voice. "I don't know. I doubt it. You shouldn't be. But there are those who think that if you want security lessened, it's for some sinister purpose. It's ridiculous someone might think that way about you, but the Internal Security Department attracts that mindset. Anyway, be careful."

"You're the second friend that's said the same thing today," Lawrence said.

James turned to the side as several other advocates were headed down the aisle to take their seats. "I see more of our group is coming in. Well, your big moment is coming closer. You've still got time to get ready. Good luck."

A courier from the Council Communications Center was with the advocates coming down the aisle. The courier came up to Lawrence's desk and said, "Special delivery illustrated p-mail for you, Mr. Holmes." Planetnet had a service that had replaced telegrams. Special delivery illustrated p-mails, known as SDIP's, were for those occasions that senders wanted the recipient to experience the pleasure of a personal communication obviously of greater importance than a p-mail or personal letter. The ads for the software for SDIP bragged, "Select from numerous examples the particular illustrated card you want for your personal message. We have the perfect greeting for all occasions. Delivery by courier will make their day." The cost for this service was very reasonable since it was sent by ordinary p-mail to any office worldwide that was equipped with the software package and stationery supplies needed to complete the order. All large companies and most companies with over twenty-five employees were equipped for SDIP, and they used their own employees for the delivery. In rural areas the post offices provided the service, but there was an extra charge, usually $ 25, for the hand delivery. The Council administrative office was, quite naturally considering the importance of the Council, fully equipped to provide the service. Over 7,000 SDIP's were delivered each year to Council delegates and staff members.

Lawrence thanked the courier cordially. Council employees were forbidden to accept tips, because that might lead to inappropriate favored treatment. Lawrence's SDIP was a large card. On the envelope was a golden sun emanating golden rays in all directions. When he saw the sun he knew that the sender most likely knew of Lawrence's seasonal affective disorder and that sunshine, or the best substitute available, was not only vital to his ability to perform at his best, but lifted his spirits as well. The card inside had an even bigger sun with longer rays. The message read:

"May your day in the limelight be bright and sunny and successful.
Your Dad would be especially proud just as I am, to be sure.

Mother

CHAPTER 7

Lawrence gazed at the card from his mother for some moments. Carefully, he returned it to its envelope. He was glad he arrived early for the Council session. He had planned to sit quietly and think through the presentation of his speech; instead, thoughts of his childhood filled his mind. His father, Larry, was born in Lamar, Missouri. When Lawrence thought of Lamar, he always pictured the large sign at its city limits that said, "Birthplace of Harry S. Truman, Thirty-Third President of the United States." While visiting his granddad in Lamar, he had asked him why they didn't have a sign that read, "Birthplace of Lefty Larry Holmes, Best High School Pitcher in Missouri"? In his dad's scrapbook, right there on the first page, was the clipping from the front page of the Kansas City *Star* Sunday sports section. A picture of his Dad winding up to throw was on the left hand side with the headline "Lamar's Lefty Holmes Leads Team To State Title." And below the headline the article's first line read, "Kansas City Royal's scout, Branch Markey, labeled Holmes 'The best high school pitcher in Missouri I've seen, and I've seen them all.'" Lawrence's granddad would look down from his seat on the porch swing and say, "There should be a sign, right by Truman's. Maybe the mayor can put one up. I'll go talk to him about it." But Lawrence guessed that he hadn't talked to the mayor, or the mayor didn't think Larry deserved a sign, since they never did put one up.

Lefty Larry hadn't been lucky after high school. As soon as he graduated from high school he signed with the Kansas City Royals and was assigned to their minor league team at Omaha, Nebraska. His manager there said he had an arm that would get him to the majors after a year or two of seasoning in the minors, and that as handsome as he was, he'd have young women chasing after him when he made the big leagues. Lefty Holmes believed he would have made it to the big leagues if he hadn't been hit by a line drive at the beginning of his second year with the Omaha team. His left arm was broken at the elbow and his career was ended. Larry never complained about his luck. He would say that being a baseball player had gotten him an interview with the sports editor at the Kansas City *Star,* and that had gotten him a good job as assistant sports editor which led to his becoming sports editor fifteen years later.

When Larry got his first job, he decided to rent an apartment in Independence, Missouri near Kansas City. Harry Truman's final residence was in Independence. Larry thought, "If the President started in Lamar and ended in Independence, why shouldn't I do the same?"

Lawrence wished that he had been kinder to his father. When Lawrence was about ten or eleven he began following sports on a national level. Larry was, naturally, a KC Royals fan while Lawrence rooted for the St. Louis Cardinals. Lawrence said it was because he admired Jim Edmonds, the Cardinals former star center fielder, because he could both hit and field. The truth could be found closer to the father-son rivalry so common to fathers and sons who are very different in interests, temperament, ability and, especially, in intellectual aptitude. Lawrence was smarter than his Dad. When major rule changes began to occur in the sports world starting in 2018, they were invariably on opposite sides in discussing the merits of the changes. Baseball had lost out to football in popularity and fan support. The decline in TV revenues became so severe that something had to be done to speed up games and make them more exciting to TV audiences. One of the changes had the batter out on foul balls when he had two strikes. Another change ended games after two extra innings, if it was tied after nine, which resulted in a switch to the professional hockey system of giving the winning team two points for a win and both teams one for a tie. These changes helped, but the TV networks still weren't satisfied. More rules were changed so batters could not step in and out of the batter's box during their at bats and pitchers could throw over to first base only two times per batter. Larry objected to each change arguing they would ruin baseball. He particularly objected that none of the past records would apply with the new system, and there wouldn't be a good way to compare today's players with former ones. Lawrence would answer that rule changes and playing circumstances had changed in the past. When they lengthened the season, it gave hitters like Roger Maris more at bats to break Ruth's record. Lawrence thought baseball was losing the modern day fan; it was a choice of changing or dying. Larry would grimace and say "Son, you just don't understand. If you had played the game in the minors like I did, you would know what I mean." Then Lawrence would answer, "Dad, I know that's the way you feel, but you're just not being logical." Larry would look away, embarrassed because his son could always out argue him. Larry was sure that he was right and that Lawrence just was too young and inexperienced to understand. After their arguments, Lawrence had a bad feeling in his stomach. He knew he had hurt his dad's feelings.

Larry also covered professional football. He had gotten to know several of the Kansas City Chiefs, particularly the linemen. The change he objected to most gave teams three years to transition to a weight limit of 114 kilograms naked weight checked one hour before game time. Larry said, "Our whole line will be out of jobs. There is no way they can lose 50 to 65 pounds and keep it off." Larry had never gotten the metric system into his head; pounds were the only weight he understood. Lawrence didn't follow football closely, but he knew that many players, including the stars, were injured frequently and often seriously, sometimes ending their careers. It made sense to Lawrence to reduce the weight banging into players and to add spring coils to their uniforms and the playing surface. After the changes were made, everyone agreed the game was faster and more exciting. More star players were in more games since disabling injuries decreased each year until they were more rare than common.

Larry said that the job he got through baseball led to something even better-- his meeting Lawrence's mother, Emily. Emily was working her way through college at the University of Missouri-Kansas City. She was an English major training to be a teacher. She loved poetry and liked to think that she got her name from the poet Emily Dickinson. Lawrence thought Emily's mother just let her believe that since her mother happened to mention to him one time when they were alone together that her best friend in high school was named Emily. One of Emily's assignments took her to the Kansas City *Star* to interview the feature editor. When she walked by Larry's little cubbyhole, they noticed each other. The next week Emily told her instructor she needed to go back to complete the interview. Larry was surprised when the head of the sports department said there was a university English major whose assignment was to interview members of the *Star's* staff from various departments and that she was waiting for him in the conference room. Larry made the best of the opportunity. After Emily's graduation a year later, they got married.

Emily wanted her son to be named Byron and hoped he would be a poet. Larry insisted on "Lawrence" and said Emily could name the girls when they came. Although they tried, one child was all they had. Larry expected that his son would be called "Larry, Junior," or just "Junior." But Emily called him "Lawrence," and it caught on.

Emily was very pleased when Lawrence named her grandson Byron. It turned out to be a good name for him. Emily was also pleased when Laura named her older daughter Anne. That was the name of Laura's favorite Aunt, but Emily liked to think that Laura's fondness for Anne Tyler was involved. Likewise Emily hoped Kate was named for Kate Chopin, the St. Louis author of *The Awakening*, because she was Laura's favorite author and that was her favorite book.

Laura was not into poetry. She would read and reread Byron's poems, but quite often she just couldn't figure out a meaning that had significance for her. She didn't want Byron to know that, so before she would pass along her comments to Byron on his latest poem, she would ask Lawrence, "What is the point of this line?" When Lawrence would interpret for her, she would ask, "Why doesn't he just say that in plain words rather than with all these, uh, all these . . . well, I guess they're images?"

Lawrence tried to explain that good poetry could express feelings and describe things better than prose, because of those what she called images. "Poets try to convey vivid and imaginative senses of experience. They use words chosen for their sounds and suggestive power as well as their meanings. But there is more to it than that. There are techniques poets use such as natural cadence and metaphor. It's an art. It's much harder to write a good poem than a good sentence."

"Why make anything hard?" Laura would say. "Why not say it straight out so everyone can understand it?" Then she would put her hands to her head and shake her head gently and say, "I feel like such a dummy. I think that's why I like plain talking better. I always understand Elvis's songs. Maybe it's because my dad was a contractor and mom worked in a clothing store. She wasn't like your mother."

"Love, anyone who reads Kate Chopin, Robert Penn Warren and last year's Noble Prize winner Anna Christine Sheridan is no dummy. You just like stories the same as millions of other readers do. And there are those who think plays, like Shakespeare's, are the best form of writing."

The first weekend of Sixthmonth, 2013 when Lawrence was to graduate from the University of Missouri with his degree in journalism, his dad arranged a special party to celebrate the big event. Lawrence's grandparents from Lamar and his mother's parents from North Kansas City all came. After dinner Emily gave Lawrence a new lap top computer to replace the Mac that dated to Lawrence's junior year in high school. The grandparents had gone together to buy the newest Epson printer to go with the computer. Larry rose from his place at the end of the dinner table. The smile on his face told that he had something special for Lawrence. "Son, I want you to know how proud I am of you. You have not only graduated, you've done it with honors. We all know where your academic skills came from--your mother, of course." Larry's smile slipped away as he said, "I didn't make it to college because of my baseball career, but I would have had a hard time with all those tests. You've done what I never could have done."

Larry paused. He had already made more of a speech than customary. He seemed to want to think through the next thing he had to say carefully, but his smile returned to signal that he was going to enjoy announcing his gift. "But your old man does have some savvy in other ways. I don't want to brag, but the people I work for like me. So I went in to see them last week and told them about you and all your good grades and awards and honors. When I kind of hinted that you might be looking for a job and you had a degree in journalism, well, you would've been proud to hear what they said, son. They said that I had been one of their best, most reliable employees, and that I had never missed a deadline even when we had that big snow, and I had to borrow my neighbor's four wheel drive to get to work and, well, they said a lot of nice things that they hadn't ever said before. But I'm talking too much about myself; you are the one with the good record. To make a long story short, I got them to offer you a job as a reporter. They said they would match any starting salary you could get anywhere in Missouri. I know you've been talking to other newspapers, but this way we could go to work together, and I could help you get acquainted with the higher ups and that can help when you are up for a raise. Anyway, that's my graduation gift, son. It was the best I could do for you. How about that!"

Emily knew by the look on Lawrence's face that this was more than Lawrence could handle. Earlier, Lawrence had told her that he had a great offer from the St. Louis *Post Dispatch*, but didn't know how or when to tell his dad because he knew his dad wanted him to go to work for the Kansas City *Star*, so Lawrence had kept putting off saying anything to his dad about it.

Emily jumped up and said, "Honey, that's wonderful what you did for Lawrence. How thoughtful and the great news is he now has two offers so he can see which will work in best with the training he's gotten. He was waiting to surprise you, but the St. Louis *Post Dispatch* wants him, too. He thought you'd be proud that he had gotten a job all on his own, just like you did with the *Star*. You always taught him that a man has to look out for himself, and he's been trying to do that. Isn't it wonderful how's it all working out?"

Lawrence went over to his Dad and hugged him and said, "Dad, it means a lot that you would go to bat for me. I'll go talk to the *Star* tomorrow and see what kind of writing they would want me to do. Then, I can decide which offer will be best for my career. Thanks for all you did."

Larry looked bewildered but hid his disappointment as best he could, as the other family members came over to say how nice it was that the *Star* thought so much of Larry that they would offer his son a job sight unseen.

CHAPTER 8

James said to Lawrence, "I hate to interrupt your concentration, friend. You have really been in a stupor. But the session is about to begin."

Lawrence looked up with a start and said, "Was I that out of it? I've been thinking about my dad."

"You've been somewhere."

Henri van de Velde, the President of the Planet Council, started towards the podium, but was intercepted by one of his staff who handed him a message. He read the message and returned to his desk that was about two meters away to take a phone call

Van de Velde was a former officer in the Belgian army who was selected as Belgium's youngest representative to the North Atlantic Treaty Organization in 2007. He succeeded to the presidency of NATO's Parliamentary Assembly in 2016. When the Council was established in 2017, the task of organizing the military arm of the Council was assigned to NATO, so Henri acquired the responsibility of creating a Planet armed force. Upon his recommendation, the Council established three standing armies of equal size and equally equipped with headquarters deep underground in secluded mountainous locations. The sites chosen were the Gannett Peak region near Bondurant, Wyoming in the U.S. Rocky Mountains, the Feveroural'sk region in the Ural mountain range in Russia and the Altai mountainous region near Altay, China. The armies were in place by 2019 and universal disarmament commenced. It took two years and a few minor skirmishes to remove all firearms including those for hunting from all individuals except for a few thousand families living in remote areas. All nuclear weapons were destroyed by 2020, and all materials needed to develop anything nuclear were stored in heavily guarded depots. When those materials were requisitioned for peaceful use, their installed locations were monitored continuously. The range of any weapon was limited to 50 kilometers.

A universal military draft law subjected all men and women over twenty to two years of service, but the military pay scale and large bonus for every four years of service was so attractive that no persons had ever been drafted. No military personnel were stationed in their native country and a balance between the numbers of each race in a unit was a priority. Complications in accomplishing this arose when a soldier came from a mixed marriage, but classifying an offspring of a tan skin father (formerly Hispanic) and a light skin mother (formerly Asian) as a "TLS" helped in running a computer program to achieve balance. All personnel, including commanders, were rotated between the three armies' several bases every six months. All armed forces were trained in emergency relief and were dispatched to needed locations immediately. The armies were available to crush any regional uprising, but since their creation, there had been none. Henri's excellent performance led to non-military positions within the Planet Council and eventually the presidency.

Lawrence's desk was between James Anderson's and the desk of Birgitta Borge, the only peoples' advocate from Sweden. Birgitta agreed with Lawrence on almost every political issue that they had discussed, so Lawrence asked her to be one of the insiders for his attempt to revive civil liberties. She had readily accepted. She slid her chair over next to Lawrence's and said, "The eyes of the world are on you today. I'd be nervous if it were me about to shake up the planet."

"I would be, too, if I weren't enjoying the moment so much. I'm just a ham. I like being on stage. Have ever since I played Petruchio in *Taming of the Shrew* in high school. A spirited red head who was great at throwing temper tantrums acted the part of Katherine, the shrew. I loved the scene where I got back at her by sweeping all the dishes off the table. I wanted to use real china, but my drama teacher said she only had enough in the budget for plastic dishes. On the night of our performance, I slipped onto the table two china plates and cups from home. They broke into a thousand pieces. My Katherine about fell over. She was really under my control that night. Most teachers would have been infuriated, but mine was thrilled. Byron did something just like that when he played Falstaff in *Henry 1V* and drank real beer. He was drunk as a hoot owl and wobbled all over the stage. Almost passed out."

"Katharine was just one shrew," Birgitta pointed out. "You have several more to tame here. Good luck"

Van de Velde walked to the podium, apologized for the delay and called the Council to order at 09:20. The minutes of the previous session had been circulated, reviewed by delegates, revised as agreed to by the Directorate and distributed to all delegates. The delegate from Uruguay, Rita Rivera, raised an objection to one of the revisions in the minutes as not being accurate. After a short discussion, the Council agreed to her objection.

The first regular order of business was the reporting of inter-member disputes. The Council encouraged all countries to settle disputes in direct negotiations. Being identified as a disputant so publicly, was intended to portray the parties as unskilled and/or uncooperative--resulting in short dispute lists. The lists were also short because the next step, to which there was no appeal, brought an arbitrary decision by the Directorate issued after only two hours of presentation by each disputant. Most Council members believed that the Directorate's decisions were often wrong, possibly on purpose, and felt it better to make the best deal you could with your opponent rather than risk losing everything to the Directorate's ruling.

James leaned over to Lawrence, "At least they haven't made you go through the dispute procedure with the U.S.," he joked knowing that Lawrence's resolution was not appropriate for that procedure.

"I know that you're not serious, but I can see that my resolution may stir up a lot of disputes within countries," Lawrence said. "Probably because they don't know which delegations are on which side. Except for about half of them, I don't know either."

The next regular business was a summary of security violations and anti-

Council political activities. The summary noted that for the fifth month out of the last seven there had been an increase in minor security violations. Groups in eight different countries had entered restricted zones, withdrawn quickly and then evidently dispersed. No damage was done by the illegal entries, and no messages left to identify the participants or the cause for the disturbances. Likewise, there had been a noticeable increase in the virulence of editorials and letters to the editors criticizing various governmental decisions. The item most frequently mentioned was the restrictions on new births in countries with large Catholic populations. The Council delegates regularly received letters, p-mail, and even personal calls to them from Catholics. Pope Paul O'Sheridan, the first Pope from Ireland and the youngest ever, regularly objected to the pregnancy control feature of the body chip. In the last two years a ground swell of calls had grown steadily calling for increases in births of almost every race, and particularly by those of dark skin heritage. On motion by the Irish delegation, the Council agreed to an impact analysis based on various combinations of lifting of birth restrictions for different races and countries. The vote for the Irish proposal was in favor 128 to 52 with those countries with large dark skin and large Muslim populations voting in opposition. Van de Valde announced that there would be a brief recess before the next order of business.

During the recess, Aziz Nzo, the delegate from South Africa seated in the section next to Lawrence's came over to see Lawrence. Aziz was the leader of the dark skin caucus at the Council. As one of the longest serving delegates, other delegates sought his opinion frequently. He had been one of the first with whom Lawrence consulted after he decided to make his proposal. Aziz had been encouraging, but Lawrence wasn't sure that it had anything to do with the merits of his proposal. The dark skin caucus often had its own agenda. Aziz said, "We decided to oppose Ireland's proposal but not because we are against changes. We didn't like this particular change. I'll stop by and see you after your speech. Some of our caucus members would like to meet with you."

Lawrence said, "Thanks for coming by. I'd like to know why your group voted against the study on birth restrictions. I know it's one of your major concerns."

"We'll talk about that later," Aziz said. Shaking Lawrence's hand he said, "I'm looking forward to your speech." In his usual deliberate manner, he turned slowly and returned to his seat.

As usual, JD's Seven were sitting together at the session and all seven were there. Anastasia and her marriage designate, Eric Nilsson who was the son of the Council's Secretary General, were next to Byron and Moira.

Anastasia was as famous in Russia for ice-skating as Byron was internationally for his poetry. Slim with jet-black hair and sharp facial features, her striking appearance helped her competitively and made her the young darling of Russia. Her goal had always been a place on Russia's Olympic team, and her early successes made the public think she was a shoo-in to be selected. But she knew there were better skaters who deserved the honor more than she did, and when she realized that public pressure and her father's position were going to give her a place on the team anyway, she withdrew from competition. All Russia was shocked and thought she was a quitter, but her answers to the news media's questioning helped them understand her reasoning. Overnight her fame increased to legendary proportions.

Anastasia's father, Boris, was a Russian historian who taught at the university in Novosibirsk. Boris decided to run for a position in Russia's Federation in 2016, because he thought he could help guide Russia through a difficult time. Russia was reluctant to relinquish its sovereignty. Boris and other political analysts made the point that if Russia did not join the U.S. and China with their push for the reorganization of the U.N., they would not be one of The Big Three. By 2017 when the Planet Council was established, Russia's economy had improved greatly, but it was not nearly as strong as that of the U.S. or China. However, because of Russia's large land mass and population and because of their vast natural resources, Russia was eligible to be one of The Big Three.

Boris was elected and reelected to the Congress until 2031 when he ran for President of the Russian Federation. Anastasia was a huge asset in his campaign as she was constantly in the news and appeared with her father at campaign rallies and at news conferences, which Boris held at skating rinks, supposedly so Anastasia could keep up with her practice. The media knew that Boris often positioned himself so that Anastasia could be seen in the background and be shown in the news reports. They didn't mind, because her lively spirit as well as her beauty and grace on the ice charmed them. Name recognition was no problem for a candidate named Gorbachev, and he was easily elected President. From then on Boris could afford the best skating coaches in Europe.

After one term as President, Boris decided his best contribution would be as Russia's delegate to the Planet Council. He was installed as the delegate on the day after his term as President ended.

Anastasia leaned over to Byron and said, "Well, at least they're going to consider a change in birth rates. That's a start."

"More likely the end," Byron replied. "It'll be another month before the report comes back. At best it'll recommend a one percent increase, but it won't include any guidelines for how the increase will be allotted. Imagine the fights over who gets to lay whom. In the end, everyone will get screwed but not in the way that produces babies. They should get rid of all the restrictions and just make each country responsible for their own populations."

"I agree with you Byron, but no one is starving like they were before birth control, and The Big Three will keep reminding delegates of that," Eric said. "But The Big Three isn't going to let it happen for a different reason. I've been following the actions of the birth approval committee ever since Anastasia and I became engaged and made our application for marriage approval. I can't prove it, but I think the committee is against applicants with high I.Q.'s. They favor the middle class with business interests because they're the ones who will acquire enough that their only concern will be not losing it. That type is not going to cause any trouble for authorities. I think the committee's agenda is to prevent future opposition." Anastasia nodded in agreement. Moira looked worried.

Byron said, "You probably know my sister is up for having her body chip adjustment to allow pregnancy. I don't mean to put Anne down or sound superior, and I sure wouldn't want her to know I said this, but you all know Anne; her I.Q. is not as high as mine. If I hear you right, she is going to be allowed children and I'm not. That's idiotic. I guess none of JD's Seven is going to have children." Byron's arms were swirling and his voice loud enough that others nearby were looking over at him.

Eric paused to give Byron time to calm down and then said, "Your sister probably will get to have children because her husband fits the bill. Although on second thought, if they check you out closely enough, they might decide that genes like yours might end up in your nephew or niece. They wouldn't want that."

Byron hesitated, looked down and said, "You mean that I could hurt Anne's chances? I don't want to do that, but I can't help who I am. I can't just go away, can I?"

Moira took Byron's hand and said, "You're a good person, sweet. Your heart's in the right place. You have the right to be the person you are the same as Anne and your father have their right to be who they are."

Byron put his arm around Moira and said, "Thank God someone understands me."

Eric was hesitant, and with worried eyes said to Byron, "Anne's chances might be improved by your Dad's position. But I don't think that even your father's influence will be enough for them to approve you to father a potential dangerous activist."

Byron's face turned red. "If what Eric believes is true, we need to do something now. Time is against us. We have to move before it's too late." Byron sat up straight as he removed his arm from around Moira. Moira slumped down.

"I think we should wait and see how your dad's proposal goes, Byron," Eric said. Maybe he can get the ball rolling and things will loosen up for having children."

Everyone looked to Byron. He said, "I hope it works out that way, but Dad hasn't told me how soon his plan will take effect, and he didn't seem to want to talk about it. I'm afraid that if any changes come about, they'll move too slowly to be of help to us."

Moira reached over to put her hand gently on the back of Byron's neck. "Your dad knows what he's doing. You know he's thinking of us and doing the best he can. We were just born at an unfortunate time in some ways. But the world is safer now."

Byron turned towards Moira, smiled and said, "It's safer, but it should get better, too, before we're ready for euthanasia."

Eric put his arm around Anastasia's and whispered, "My aunt has a plan if Lawrence's resolution doesn't pass that I need to talk to you about. Stay after the session is over."

Anastasia looked puzzled but said, "Sure, O.K."

Van de Velde reconvened the session and announced that the meeting was now open for new business. The delegates who had been milling around during the recess returned to their seats as Lawrence approached the podium. The audience quieted. All eyes were on Lawrence when he reached the podium and paused before addressing the Council.

The Council's assembly auditorium was composed of three large sections for delegates, one for guests and one small section for the peoples' advocates. The walls were composed of fibers designed to resist large explosive charges. Standby generators were in place to provide a complete backup to the electrical system. Supplies to provide for an extended stay of all Council members were stored in a guarded location.

The Planet Council's current membership totaled 165. Just after the turn of the century, the United Nations had grown to 191 members. By the time the reorganization occurred in 2017, consolidation had occurred through mergers of smaller struggling nations and realignment in Russia. Each Council member country had one vote, which was cast by its one delegate or its one alternate delegate. Translation earphones were not necessary, since a universal language, Unifren, had been adopted in 2025. Unifren was predominately French, since French was known as the language of diplomacy because of its large capability of expressing nuances. The language commission that made the choice thought it was easier to learn than English with its fewer exceptions to the rule in construction and was already spoken throughout many parts of the world. Most delegates used their mother tongues within their family and with close friends, but their children were taught only Unifren in school. As a result, all other languages were slowly dying out. Many countries were disturbed by the probability that their heritage was going to be lost, so they promoted activities to maintain the customs of their land.

Lawrence rested his hands on the podium and looked out over his audience. He had made it a point to meet privately with each delegation each year to ask what their goals and concerns were. He knew by name all delegates who had served over a year; many were personal friends. He was reminded of the feeling he had when he had spoken to his college class at their twentieth reunion in 2034. He had been elected a peoples' advocate in January that year, so the University of Missouri named him one of the four outstanding alumni to be honored at the reunion. Many of his friends made it a point to return to see him and hear his speech. The Council included a different set of friends, but the feeling was much the same. He wasn't worried about making a slip up; his friends would forgive him.

But as he looked over these familiar faces, a different thought occurred to him. He wondered would his friendships hold up under the test of this controversial subject? Almost reluctantly as if he didn't want to stir a tranquil pot, Lawrence began his speech.

"Mr. Chairman, fellow delegates and guests of the Council. I am tempted to ask that you 'lend me your ears.' But I want more than that. Lend me also your memories, your minds, your hearts, even your souls. I need the best of you. Our planet needs the best of you." Then, his voice rising, he raised both arms slowly and said, "That is our call and I believe the time is now." Lawrence paused longer than most speakers to let his challenge sink in.

"So, what is my message? What is my mission? Why is this the time?" Then Lawrence punctuated each of the next points he made with his index finger. "My message is this: liberty is dear, it is precious, it is vital, it is human, it is necessary for the spirit of men and women to flourish and," Lawrence paused and with strong emphasis on each word he pronounced, "it is our right."

Lawrence's voice lightened as if he were telling a friend about something he remembered from long ago. "When I was in high school, there was a Broadway show nearing the end of its long, successful run called *The Fantasticks*. Some of you may have seen it when it had a short revival here in New York City about ten years ago. The words of the theme song go like this: 'Try to remember the kind of September when life was slow and oh, so mellow. Try to remember when life was so tender that dreams were kept beside your pillow.' I remember those days before the 9/11 attacks a few blocks from here. Those memories are precious. The song continues: 'Deep in December it's nice to remember the fire of September that made us mellow. Deep in December our hearts will remember and follow, follow, follow.'"

Lawrence paused, looked out at his audience first to one side and then the other. The advocates' seats were directly in front of him. James had nodded encouragement to him several times already. Since Lawrence knew he wasn't going to get his vote, Lawrence especially appreciated James's moral support. The section for guests, which included the families of delegates, was on his far right side. The floor to ceiling walls between sections to provide protection from bombs taking out all of the Council in one blow were transparent, so he could easily see Byron and the rest of JD's Seven. As usual, Laura was not in the audience. She always offered to come anytime he was going to speak, but Lawrence knew she would be on pins and needles the whole time he was at the podium, so he had told her it would make him nervous if she were there. He thought she knew he was saying it for her benefit, not his own.

In a low, serious voice Lawrence said, "We are deep in December. How do we get back to those days of September? A reckless, hurried and imprudent relaxation of the constant vigilance that is the price of freedom could result in the loss of all. So, we must seek a balance." Slowly, he continued, "A balance that is appropriate to our times. A gradual transition that has been earned by the sacrifices that our generation has made for the benefit of the generations to come." Lawrence looked up and tried to quicken his tempo. He was puzzled that he just could not make his words flow like he wanted them to. "Terrorism, overpopulation, AIDS, drug abuse, misuse of firearms and violent conflicts between rival groups forced a major change in our way of life in order to preserve it. We made that change, and it was successful. Terrorist activities have been stopped, there is no armed conflict in the world, our body chips stopped drug abuse and the spread of AIDS and no one is starving. For twelve years, half a generation, no violent attack on our society has occurred. In the second half of this generation, we can carefully move to benefit from the good work of the first half and return to the way it ought to be while retaining safeguards so that all we have achieved will not be jeopardized. This is my message." Applause was loud and from all sections, except from the section where the U.S.'s delegate and several of its close allies sat.

"What is my mission? My mission is to make the case for the gradual restoration of those inalienable rights so well defined in the Declaration of Independence of the United States of America and thereafter reiterated again and again as constitutional law spread throughout the world. This is the right decision at the right time."

Lawrence moved to the side of the podium and walked slowly away a few steps with his head down as if in deep thought. He noticed that he shuffled slightly. He rubbed his chin as he returned to the podium. He looked up and saw that one of the three security squads had stopped in the aisle to listen to his speech. Their guard dog was in stay position and was so still that the dog appeared to be taking in his speech. "Before making any change, it is only right and proper that we assess where we are. We are doing well in many regards. The daily reports prove we are prosperous, we are healthy, literacy is at its highest level ever, we are constantly increasing the physical comforts of life and peace is with us. This begs the question: why change?"

Lawrence stopped; he looked over his audience. It was quiet in anticipation. Some delegates wondered why he had brought up that question. They thought it would have been better to let the opposition raise the question.

"Let's look at another factor—what is the trend of the peoples' response to our present system?" Lawrence paused. "The trend is becoming apparent. It is the trend of all people of all time," and Lawrence paused again, "to take measures to gain more freedom. The reports show a constant increase in protests. Mild protests at this time but nevertheless increasing. The trend is for more protests, more unrest, more dissatisfaction, more resentment, more cries for freedom.

"Every change should be assessed on a risk/reward basis. I believe if the people of the world are not given a promise of a return to basic freedoms, we risk increasing opposition that will escalate into violence. We can meet this threat with our armies. We can stamp out this mounting opponent, but at what cost? We will become a population made up of fewer liberties, fewer freedoms and greater resistance. Such a world is well described in George Orwell's *1984*. Thankfully, that world has not come about. But if we choose the path of suppression of all opposition to the state, Big Brother could become our ruler." The audience was quiet, its somber mood evident to all. Lawrence liked speaking in an auditorium twenty meters below ground covered with a mixture of dirt and reinforced concrete in layers varying from two to three meters thick. No outside noises distracted, so if he spoke softly or paused, he had the audience's attention.

"Increased controls will create a far greater risk to a stable and peaceful future than a partial return to the past, but we must lessen the controls gradually and carefully." Lawrence tried again to pick up his tempo. "And that is why I say the time is now. Now, before opposition increases, we must swim against this rising tide by promising a return to a free society for one and all. The world has experienced the horrors of terrorism and will not collectively agree to endanger the security we have given so much to obtain. People will be patient if we show them their future, and that it will come." Lawrence had slowed down his tempo as he emphasized his last three words. "Humankind will unite in agreement and guard against a relapse to the undesirable aspects of the past. In the early part of the century we were asked to be on the watch for anything that seemed out of the ordinary that might be dangerous. I remember keeping an eye out when I approached government buildings for suspicious vehicles in the vicinity. We have grown complacent because of the efficiency of our security system. As we make a gradual transition to greater freedom, we will have to have greater citizen participation in security measures. This is a small but necessary price to pay."

Again, Lawrence walked away from the podium, head down in deep concentration. As he returned, he looked up above the audience. As he resumed his place behind the podium, he looked straight out at them. With a firm, ringing voice appropriate to proclamations, Lawrence announced, "My proposal is this: Resolved by the Planet Council that starting on 1 Firstmonth, 2041, all citizens of the world aged forty years or more not incarcerated or on trial which could lead to incarceration shall, upon application, obtain the deactivation of the location feature of their body chip. Any citizen who chooses at a subsequent time to have the location feature reactivated for whatever reason will be allowed reactivation as soon as it is practical. Furthermore, that the age at which application can be made will automatically decrease by two years every year thereafter until the age for application reaches twenty-six subject to an annual review of security violations by the Directorate which can suspend or end this practice if conditions warrant it." Lawrence paused and in his regular voice added, "The delay until next Firstmonth, some eight and one half months from now, will give time for the careful review of potential individuals for inclusion on the list of those not eligible for deactivation and to allow for procedures to be established for receiving applications. I hereby move this resolution for adoption by the Planet Council and submit a copy of it to the clerk for filing and placing on the agenda for debate." Lawrence smiled, raised his right hand as if to signal to the audience it was up to them now and stepped back away from the podium.

The applause was strong from some delegations, moderate from others and only a polite tapping of limp hands from some. Many rose to their feet and called out, "Hear, hear." All the people's advocates but one, James Anderson, rose at Lawrence's last words in enthusiastic approval, until James saw that he alone was still seated in the advocate's section, so he too rose and applauded politely. JD's Seven were on their feet and all but Byron were shouting hurrahs. Moira clapped vigorously and studied Byron who stood, pondering, a solemn look on his face. Moira knew he wasn't pleased.

Lawrence returned to his seat where all the advocates and their assistants stood in line to shake his hand. The first was Aziz Nzo who said, "Your call for our best is on the table now, because you delivered your best. That speech had the characteristics of Abraham Lincoln's addresses. He would have admired your message and joined you in your mission if he were alive."

"Now Aziz, you're talking about the greatest American there has ever been. My name doesn't even belong in the same sentence with Lincoln's. But thank you. What do you think of my chances? I won't ask, yet, what your group is going to do."

"As I mentioned earlier, a few of us from the dark skin caucus would like to meet with you as soon as all your admirers have had a chance to show their adulation. Regarding your chances? I think it will come down to the powers that be. I don't know if The Big Three will let the Council have a direct vote on it or not. Maybe so, since they let you introduce it, and this is going to get a lot of attention in the media, everywhere. If The Big Three cut it off without a full debate, the complaining wouldn't stop. I'll see you later."

Once Aziz left, James Anderson stepped up to Lawrence and said, "The fat's in the fire, Lawrence. I hope you don't get burned. I don't think Uncle Sam is going to like being put on the spot by one of his own."

"Fortunately, I'm not on his payroll," Lawrence answered.

"There are other ways they have of operating. Isn't your daughter trying to get approved to start a family?" James said.

"Yes," Lawrence replied. "The Pregnancy Committee is not supposed to be political, but a few of their recent decisions have caused concern. Some applicants are claiming the Committee is trying to preclude future opposition by preventing certain types of parents from having any children. I hope that's not the case. I'm going to look into it."

"Anyway, " James said as he leaned close to Lawrence so as to not be over-heard, "be careful. And tell Byron to quiet down with his young group for now." With that, James left.

A large group of regular delegates came up to Lawrence next, along with all of the other people's advocates forming a reception line of sorts to shake Lawrence's hand and congratulate him on his speech. Not included in the group were del-egates from any of The Big Three, but the official delegates from the two rotating members of the Directorate, Thomas Baines from Australia and Rudolf Spongle from Switzerland were there. Lawrence had known them both for a long time, and Thomas and Rudolf were part of his inner support group. He spent a little more time with them than he spent with other delegates.

Byron and the rest of JD's Seven came by Lawrence's desk after the crowd had cleared. Moira led the way, gave Lawrence a friendly hug and whispered in his ear, "Byron is upset. Watch out! Deep down he is proud of you, but he wants freedom now."

Lawrence returned the hug saying quietly, "Thanks Moira. I appreciate that more than you know. It may appear that father and son aren't close, but Byron is a lot like I was at his age when I gave my dad hell for all kinds of things. The tie between us is not visible, but it is strong."

Carlos Domingo, the son of Argentinean delegate Raul Domingo, was at twenty-eight the oldest of JD's Seven. His opinion carried the most weight with the group not only because he was the oldest, but also because he masked his strong emotions with a calm, deliberate way that was especially influential with young adults. He was next after Moira to greet Lawrence and extended his hand and said, "That was magnificent. I'll remember today for a long time. Some day I'll tell my son that I was here, and that I knew the speaker personally, and that his son was one of my best friends. Is there anything I can do to help?"

"Tell young people to be patient," Lawrence replied. "My supporters and I will do the best that we can, but these things take time."

"And it'll be five years before I can even apply to go where I want without be-ing watched," Byron interjected looking at his father. "And that's only if they pass the damn thing which they probably won't. We deserve to be free now, not when we're starting to fade. Why don't you start it sooner, at least at thirty? "

"Even some of those who are in favor of it, son, think I need to raise it to forty-five or more to have any chance to get it passed," Lawrence answered. "I'd like for all of you to take advantage of it right now, but it just can't happen that fast,"

"If the Council won't change it, we need to change the Council," Byron said. "Or maybe go back to the old system where the people were free."

"And have terrorists on the loose again is what The Big Three will say." Carlos said. "I'm all for what you want, Byron, but your dad's right. The ones in charge don't want to take chances."

"Well, I'm not going to wait around until I'm forty for life to begin. Come on Moira. Let's get out of here," Byron said as he took Moira by the hand and left.

"Don't let it bother you, Mr. Holmes," Carlos said. "Byron doesn't blame you. We all know you're doing all you can for a cause we believe in."

Lawrence's managed a slight smile "Thanks for your support and stopping by to see me. Keep an eye on Byron for me if you will. Now that he's twenty-five and at his job so much, he's not at home too often, and I don't get to see him as much as I would like."

Carlos paused giving thought to what he was going to say. "I don't' want to mislead you to think that we might influence Byron to back off. The truth is we are worried about Byron too. He takes everything so seriously."

"I know, Carlos. I was the same way when I was in my twenties, " Lawrence replied. "At the time I thought the insecurity in the world was the worst situation a young person could have to grow up in. Now I'm not so sure that what we have now isn't as bad."

"Well, you and others are doing your best. Congratulations again on your awesome address. I'll see if I can catch up with Byron and Moira. Goodbye."

Lawrence had stood to greet everyone who came by to see him. But now that JD's Seven had left, everyone had gone, he settled back in his chair, an old recliner style that he had bought at a flea market. He wondered about the reactions to his speech and what he needed to do next, but at the back of his mind was Byron. Lawrence was tired. Instead of returning home on the high-speed commuter, he told Merlin, "Private car in twenty minutes," something he hadn't done in the last month.

As he rose to leave, three dark skin delegates headed his way. Byron's re-marks had upset him so much that he had forgotten that Aziz wanted to meet with him before he went home. The three delegates, walking almost in step, were the unofficial but acknowledged leaders of the dark skins on the Council. One was from Jamaica, Eliha Jordan; one from Kenya, Jomo arap Moi; and the third, Aziz, was the spokesman for the dark skin caucus. Aziz and Jomo were authors whose primary work told of the dark skins' successful struggle in their countries to reach equality. Now that they had it, they were united in efforts to achieve greater population growth for dark skins. Soon after the beginning of pregnancy control in 2024, strict limits had been placed on the number of dark skin births to combat increases in AIDS and overpopulation. The new limits resulted in a sixty per cent decline in dark skin births within a year. Dark skins argued it was now past time for them to be allowed to multiply at a greater rate than others to make up for what they had missed. They also argued that with improved education and health care, their mental capacity was now equal to any other race and their physical capacity was greater than all others."

Aziz's father had been a close friend of Nelson Mandela and instrumental in ending apartheid. Aziz's graduate work was in England and the United States. He had supported the movement to world government as necessary but hopefully temporary.

After friendly handshakes amongst the group Aziz said, "Lawrence, we've always gotten right to the point; we want to make a deal with you. We'll support your proposal if you'll support us on our cause to increase the dark skins' birth rate. We can guarantee you a lot of votes from Africa, Central America and parts of South America. As you know, we also have sympathizers in the U.S., France, and England. We're not demanding a big change—just a start on the right direction."

"Aziz, I may lose votes if I support you. Your proposal singles out just a part of the world population. Mine benefits all."

"But I think you'll gain more votes than you'll lose. You're going to need every vote you can get. We can deliver those votes."

"I will need every vote, but I can't make a commitment now. I'll get back with you. Thanks for coming over."

After the three dark skin delegates left, Antonie van Leeuwenhoek, a newsman from The Netherlands joined Lawrence on his way down the hall to the escalator and asked Lawrence, "How do you feel being one of the first advocates, if not the first, to initiate a proposal on a serious matter? The regular delegates often ask for your opinion, but you have elbowed your way in with the big boys with your resolution."

"It's like the guy who was first in line for the hangman and said, 'Well, somebody's got to go first,'" Lawrence said with a smile.

"You're going to be on the news tonight. The only reason you weren't besieged by the media after your speech was everyone had enough copy to file. I just finished mine. I'd give you 9 + or 10 on your content and 10 + on your delivery. If you have time to read the Amsterdam *Post* tomorrow, I think you'll like what you see."

"I'll take time, Antonie. And thanks for your rating. Maybe I could get a job in TV if the Council tosses me out for the trouble I'm causing."

"No chance of that. You're going to be an advocate for the rest of your life, if you want to be. Your place in history is made."

"Will you come home with me and tell my wife and children that? They put it a different way. They said after my speech, I would be history."

"Love to meet your family, but I have a date with my wife tonight. She's over here for two weeks and then we go back together. Do you think you will have your resolution wrapped up by then?"

"I think it will be vetoed or voted up or down by then. The U.S. will want to get this issue out of the news as soon as possible."

"Well, they're not going to have their way. Greater freedom is today's hot item, and you just turned its temperature up about 100 degrees."

"I've already been told I may get burned by this."

"Seriously, Lawrence, do watch out."

Lawrence paused, extended his hand to Antonie, and with a slight, worried frown, said, "Thanks. I appreciate your concern."

CHAPTER ♀

"I'm sure you did a great job; you always do," Laura said as she and Kate met Lawrence at the door when he got home. Both recognized his fatigue by the way his shoulders slumped, despite his best effort at smiling. Laura attempted to be up-beat and with a hug and reassuring smile said, "You must be tired after all the tension of being the first advocate to initiate what would be a major change."

Kate stood by smiling and watched Lawrence's reaction before she said, "I imagine its relief he feels. I'm always so relieved after a horse show, even when I thought I was going to win."

"Every one, especially Aziz and even some who are against me, thought I gave a great speech except for Byron," Lawrence said with a worried expression and weariness in his voice. "He's very disappointed that I didn't go for a lower starting age and more changes. I know how he feels, but you can't go for the whole ball of wax on the first go-around. Some delegates felt I should have used forty-five years or higher for the start." Lawrence sat down on the closest thing to him, an old-fashioned love seat from their home in St. Louis that Laura had recovered at least three times. The current pattern was a pastel with cream colored swirls. Kate thought they should have left it in St. Louis, but she never mentioned it.

"Dad, Byron just reacts, he doesn't think things through," Kate said. Lawrence and Laura were all too familiar with her exasperation. They had felt the same way many times. "I hope you're not going to let Byron have a part in running the show. He'd blow it for sure. He has the patience of a stallion in the pen with a mare in heat."

"Don't be so hard on him, Kate," Lawrence responded. "Our cause is the same. He's just wound tighter than most."

Laura said, "Your martini is mixed, but I haven't swirled or poured it yet. The lemon is in the bar frig."

"God bless you and what always cures what ails me, a dry martini," Lawrence said as he got up and headed for his favorite room in the house where a long bar served as a breakfast dining area and wet bar for entertainment. "What about you, Kate? Tanqueray and tonic?"

"With a wedge of lime, please," Kate said. "But make it a short one. Mike and I have some studying to do for our marriage application interview."

All three took stools at the bar. The bar back piece included a large mirror framed with carved mahogany that had been in Guffy's tavern in downtown St. Louis, one of Lawrence's favorite places for a drink after a Cardinal baseball game. Lawrence acquired the mirror when Guffy's closed. He also got the brass rail footrest that curved to wrap around the ends of the bar. Friends said that he had built his house around the bar.

"Merlin called with your message that you would be late because you were meeting with some of the dark skin caucus," Kate said. "What did Aziz have to say?

Are they going to go along with you?"

"If the price is right," Lawrence answered. "I'm counting noses to see how I can get the most votes. Aziz thinks he can swing thirty to thirty-five. Many delegates are on the fence. They're waiting to see just how strong U.S. opposition is going to be and what it will cost them if they don't go along with them. I haven't been able to read the Chinese. It may come down to them and the ones who go along with The Big Three when things get tight. I know I'm in for a fight, but we got off to a good start."

"Mom's worried about you, Dad," Kate said. "She thinks some of the powers that be may get rough if you get it passed." Kate took a big sip of her drink and looked at her watch.

"You're right I am worried." Laura said. "I wish you'd pay attention when I have these nervous feelings."

"I know you're concerned, love," Lawrence said. "But no one has made any threats or said anything out of order to me. I have gotten the silent treatment from the U.S. delegates, and even some of my friends from countries dependent on the U.S. have been somewhat avoiding me. I'm sure I'm a problem for them, and when you are the most powerful force in the world, you don't like problems, particularly from your own countrymen. It's going to be embarrassing if I get it passed, and none of The Big Three likes to be embarrassed." Lawrence leaned into his elbows on the bar.

"I'm worried even if you don't get it passed," Laura said. "Everyone knows how persistent you can be when you get your dander up. They know you won't go away. If you don't get it done this session, you'll be back trying again next session. They won't want a thorn in their side that keeps sticking them. They will want it out even if they have to jerk it out."

"Well, unless I get my chip changed so that my location is not known, they can't get rid of the body without it being known where they dumped it," Byron answered, a smile on his face as he sat up straight.

"This is not something to joke about, Lawrence," Laura said. Her tone was critical, and her worry was real.

"I promise not to ride with any strangers in vehicles with tinted windows," Lawrence said, his smile even wider.

"You just won't take this seriously," Laura said. The frown that had been on her face since Kate had brought up the subject deepened.

"Dad's going to be all right, Mom," Kate said as she put her arms around her mother and squeezed her tightly, "Come on, now. Lighten up. I won't let loose until you say 'Uncle.'"

Laura gave Kate a smile as she hugged her back and said, "I won't say 'Uncle,' but I will say 'Thanks.' I know I worry too much, but I just can't help it."

"If you want to worry about anyone, worry about Byron," Kate said as she finished her drink and started towards the door. "You never know what crazy thing he might do. Bye, I'm going to meet Mike."

Laura stood up and took Lawrence's hand. He slipped off his bar stool and put his arm around her as they headed for the dinner table. She looked up at him and said, "Don't forget that this morning you made a date with me for tonight. I plan to wear the same thing I had on this morning when you felt me up. Oh, I almost forgot. You had two calls, one from the news bureau in London and the other from Canada. Evidently your speech has drawn international attention."

CHAPTER Λ∇

Council consideration of Lawrence's proposal, titled Planet Council Resolution 40-1948 and referred to as R-1948 started on Thirdday, 17 Fourth Month. After contentious debate between themselves, the Directorate decided not to block debate on R-1948. The U.S. could not get another member to join them to veto debate because China and Russia had problems at home, and the two rotation members, Switzerland and Australia, were so strongly in favor of a floor debate that they threatened to initiate a Council Petition if debate by the Council was not allowed. Council Petitions were rare. When signed by a large number of delegates, they were powerful, because the media made it into a major story featuring the few big guys versus the many small guys. Russia had been receiving severe criticism from many citizens for siding with the big guys too frequently.

The problem in China related to cultural changes that occurred in the last decade. Economic contact with and investments from democratic countries brought about pressure for personal liberties in China. A challenge to China's authoritarianism arose in 2039 when a new TV program modeled on the "West Wing" show popular in the early 2000's in the U.S. gained high TV ratings in China. The program did not directly criticize the government, but it featured a Chinese government run by a young, charismatic female Martin Sheen who rose to the Presidency of China and ran China from her "West Wing." Women's groups sprang up to watch each episode in theaters followed by parties during which a contest was held for the best look-alike to the Chinese President. Every week a flood of letters and p-mails to government authorities called for an open election of the President of China with several women ready to run. China did not want to stir up more political controversy by being the party to cut off debate on R-1948. U.S. editorials frequently pointed out that a reversal had taken place over the past decade. Now the U.S. had become less sensitive to its population's call for greater freedom than China was to its population's aspirations.

Under the Planet Council rules for proposals, the resolution's sponsor was given the first day to present arguments for passage. Lawrence opened his presentation with a review of terrorist attacks in the past fourteen years to show that they were first slowed and then stopped. He cited how many children had been born since the last attack that had grown up in a peaceful world. These children, Lawrence argued, would not be inclined towards civil violence since they had not experienced it. Then he cited the number of persons in each of the various age groups to show that those younger persons who might have been inclined towards terrorist's activities were much older now. When the body chips were first inserted, the intelligence service had identified potential suspects by their past activities. Their personal profiles and their chips included an extra signaling device that alerted authorities when they entered areas near airports, government facilities and other locations vulnerable to catastrophic attacks. Lawrence showed that the number of people under this special surveillance had decreased substantially, especially those considered potential leaders. He added that a colleague had suggested attaching a clause to his proposal to deny any persons under this special surveillance the right to have their location chip feature deactivated. Lawrence agreed with that suggestion.

Lawrence called on the clerk of the Council to give a detailed report on the frequency and type of protests that had occurred within the past three years. The report showed the number of protests had increased each year as had the seriousness and number of suspected participants. He then asked the clerk to summarize the trend in suicide rates for each continent since 2017. The clerk reported that in the first few years, the rates decreased yearly until 2029, but they had increased each year since and were now at an all time high, twenty-two per cent higher than in 2017. The rates by country varied but showed similar trends.

The Council recessed for lunch. Lawrence had arranged for those who were going to speak in favor of his proposal in the afternoon session to eat together in a private room. Six other delegates from South Africa, Australia, Sweden, Argentina, France, and Switzerland joined Lawrence and took seats at a round table, which normally seated eight. Lawrence greeted the group, glanced towards the empty place at the table and answered the question on everyone's mind. "Neville isn't coming. The pressure from the U.K. was too great. He didn't get the word from London until last night. He feels badly about it and says that we have a lot of support in the Parliament, but there was too much at stake financially. Also, England needs an increase in their population allotment badly. As you know, they are hurting with so many having left for better paying jobs. The development of the ocean fiber electrical generation system has caused a decline in North Sea oil revenues over the last fifteen years. They are more dependent on the U.S. than ever. Anyway, we'll have to go on without Neville's opening speech and I'd like you, Maurice, to lead off. Is that O.K. with you?" Lawrence asked Maurice Padron, France's delegate.

"Certainly," Maurice answered. "I believe that's appropriate anyway since I think you will all have to agree, quite naturally I speak Unifren better than most and at least most will understand our first speech."

Lawrence went over the order for the other speakers and reminded each of the particular point he wanted them to emphasize. "Aziz, you'll sum up for us," Lawrence told him. "I've decided not to make the last speech. I made my plea when I made the proposal. Some have said my speech was obviously inspired and pretty good. I think that meant I did a lot better than they expected I could do. I don't want to mess up now and let everyone see the real me."

Birgitta Borge, the peoples' advocate from Sweden, joined in the laugher and then said, "Lawrence, the real you is so high above the average of the Council delegates that if you were to mess up, no one would notice it." Five heads nodded in agreement.

During lunch Lawrence asked the other delegates what questions they thought would be asked in the next day's session, which under the Planet Council's rules was restricted to posing questions. Lawrence was surprised when his group came up with several serious issues he had not anticipated--another reminder that this was going to be a tough fight.

CHAPTER ⋀⋀

"I really don't want to wear a body cover today," Laura said to herself, as she looked at her naked body in the full-length automated mirror mounted on the sliding door to her clothing chamber. "One meter," she said to see her image from the closest distance the mirror control was equipped to provide. "Ugh, that's too close. I'm beginning to sag. Two meters." The mirror made the adjustment. "That's at least some better. Well, I have to give my report today, so I have to wear a body cover."

"Clean and deliver No. 7," Laura commanded her clothing chamber. She heard the barely audible buzz of the electrostatic cleanser followed by the clicking of the clothing rack drive. The door of the clothing chamber opened silently and No. 7, a light-tan body cover with the dark red stripes, slid slowly on a telescoping track out to within her reach.

Laura's report to her department head was about the psychological impact of major rule changes on professional athletes. She had asked the top five women and top five men tennis players how the raising of the height of the net by twelve centimeters had affected their strategy against taller and shorter players. Laura's report was ready to be given, but she wasn't ready to give it. Verbal presentations were nerve racking to her. Her voice became more highly pitched than normal and sometimes she even stuttered. She had requested that she be allowed to pre-record her report and complement it with visual images. Her former supervisor at Columbia had allowed that and complimented her presentations. But her new supervisor, Stan Donaldson, denied her request saying he wanted to be able to ask questions at any time during reports. Laura felt he liked to have her at his mercy standing in front of him so he could get a good look at her body and enjoy her discomfort as a kind of power trip. "The prick!" she thought as she contemplated the ordeal ahead of her.

Fortunately, Lawrence had come up with a way to prepare for reports. "Have a glass of wine before you leave," was his advice.

"At 08:30 in the morning?" she had responded.

"Try it. If it doesn't work, at least you will have had one pleasure for the day."

Laura tried it and was much more relaxed and gave a better report. As Laura opened an Oregon Pinot Noir from Cherrywood Cellars, she wondered, "Would two glasses be even better?" Better not push it, she decided.

Columbia was not a long trip on the high-speed commuter from her home, but she would have a little time to read on the way. She took *Waiting* from the rack inside her sleeping chamber. It was a play being performed on Playway Boulevard in downtown New York. Byron had reviewed it for *The New Yorker* and given her a copy along with his review. It wasn't her usual reading matter, but since Byron was involved, she wanted to read it. Byron had been struck by the use of plays as characters in *Waiting*. The character-plays were talking to each other on stage while they were waiting for their time to be performed. Some, *Waiting For Godot,* for one, never did get performed.

Laura made a reservation on the relaxation travel unit and headed for the commuter station on her air scooter. The relaxation unit was on time but crowded. At the rear she was able to find a row with two unoccupied seats. She chose the one away from the aisle looking forward to a peaceful opportunity to start reading *Waiting*. As she turned to page two, she noticed a middle-aged man coming down the aisle. One thing that drew her attention was that he wasn't wearing a body cover, although he looked like the well-groomed type that early in the morning would normally be headed for an occupational activity that required wearing a body cover. When he got to within a meter of her, he stopped, looked at the book she held, hesitated and then very softly and politely asked, "Would you mind terribly if I took this seat next to you and asked your opinion of the play you are reading. I have a special interest in *Waiting*."

To Laura the man looked harmless enough. He was dressed in an attractive light gray sweater-coat with a pale blue turtleneck collar. Laura had bought Lawrence three of the sweater-coats that he liked; not, he said, because they were in fashion but because of their comfort. Made to look like a sports coat with lapels and side pockets worn over a shirt, they were one piece with hidden zippers making them easy to take on or off. They looked very trim, but they were actually loose fitting. Various collars could be attached to give either a formal look or a casual look like the collar the stranger asking permission to sit next to her was wearing. The fact that they were very expensive and this man had one, added to the comfort Laura felt in allowing him to sit next to her.

"No, I wouldn't mind," Laura said in a pleasant but in no way sexually inviting voice. "What is your special interest in this play?"

"First, let me introduce myself, so you can be assured that I am, am, well, I don't know exactly how to say it . . ."

"Safe?"

"Yes, thank you. I'm not accustomed to intruding in the private lives of, of, attr . . ., er, women traveling by themselves who might misinterpret my, my . . ."

"Motives?"

"Precisely, thank you again for being so understanding. My name is Bernard Shelley. I am the head of the English Department at Columbia University."

"I know of you, Mr. Shelley. I do research for the Sports Psychology Department and have seen references to you in the university newsletter. I'm Laura Holmes."

"Not by chance connected to two famous men named Holmes, Lawrence and Byron?"

"Yes. Wife and mother."

"I am pleased to meet a member of the family of two men I admire greatly. Now, to explain my connection to *Waiting*. I am the author of one of the plays, *Louise, Which?* who is, as you probably know, a character in the play. My play was waiting to be performed and actually gets to be performed in the play. I have talked to and read the comments of several women critics who have read both my play and

Waiting, but I haven't had an opportunity to get the opinions of, of . . ."

"Ordinary women?"

"Well, I don't think of any women as being 'ordinary,' but I think you understand what I mean. By the way, I thought your son's review of *Waiting* insightful, but, in truth, I was disappointed with his opinion of the merits of *Louise, Which?*"

"Mr. Shelley, I haven't read your play and have just begun *Waiting*, but I will give you my opinion of both after I've read them. Now I'm going to turn the tables on you. I have heard what all the political experts have said about my husband's proposal, which he presented Firstday this week at the Planet Council. Did you read about it?"

"Every thinking person on the planet has."

"I'd like to know what an, don't be offended, ordinary citizen thinks about it."

"I'm no political expert, and I'm not offended by being classified as ordinary in that field. I have mixed feelings about R-1948. On the one hand, I want a return of some of those civil rights we used to have. On the other hand I don't want to return to a proliferation of divorce, abortions, and AIDS. I favor deactivation of some features of the body chip while retaining the chip itself and its beneficial features."

"You still want governmental control over marriage and pregnancy?"

"Yes, I do. And I'm also in favor of euthanasia; it removes the feeling of guilt that families used to have if they did anything to shorten the life of a loved one whose time was obviously up. Now authorities make the decision and the arrangements."

"I'm surprised by what you say. Do you think it will pass?"

"Do you think Byron will win the Nobel Prize in literature?"

"How can I . . .? I see what you mean. There is a good chance, but no way to know."

"You're a smart woman."

The relaxation unit slowed to a halt at the Columbia station. "I'll call your office at Columbia when I've read the plays. By the way, how do you get out of wearing a body cover?"

"I change in my office if I have a meeting I have to attend. Otherwise, being head of the department has some advantages. I'll walk with you to the campus, if that's all right."

"Sure. And maybe I'll apply for a position in the English Department, if you won't make me wear a body cover."

"If you could persuade Byron to come too, it's a deal."

Laura and Bernard walked together to the campus. She wished her supervisor were more like him.

CHAPTER Λ2

"Viva la France; Viva la Canada; Viva la Chile; Viva la Kenya; Viva la Japan; Viva la Bosnia; and Viva la all countries on the Planet," were Maurice's first words as he gave the first speech in favor of R-1948 in perfect French carefully using only words and phrases that were also included in the Unifren language. "To achieve this we had to give up our independent existences and join together under one language, fortunately using as a base the best language of all, under one new numbering system, under one currency, under one government, and for one purpose-- survival. For the past twenty-three years, the Planet Council's dictates superceded the various desires of the many nations; thankfully, we have survived. For over half that time, some twelve years now, the world has been free of the scourges of terrorism, AIDS, drug abuse, overpopulation and unacceptable crime rates that necessitated world government."

Maurice's words were inspiring, but Lawrence, and he was sure most of the other delegates, couldn't help but be distracted by his constant pulling on the sleeves of his body cover. It seemed as if he pulled on one sleeve or the other after every sentence. Perhaps it was the nervousness many speakers suffer when they are participating in historical events. Lawrence had seen Maurice speak on several occasions without any sleeve pulling, but those had concerned more minor issues. Lawrence wished he could do something about it, but he was powerless.

"During this time the great singular characteristics of the many nations have blended and, if the present trend continues, will be lost as the world continues on this road to homogeneity," Maurice continued. "That would be a tragedy. The world would have all the bread it needs, but it would be without flavor. The spices that add spirit to life would be lost forever. Once a nation loses its identity, it loses its soul. So when I say 'Viva la France,' it is not an empty, meaningless salute. Instead it is an alert, a warning that the spirit, particular excellence, culture, style and all the other attributes of the French are in danger. The danger is real and it is with us now. Everyday in France people are born and cast into a world where individuals may never know what it is to be French. I need not tell you the same is true in your country too. You have seen it in your own families, newspapers, entertainment, art, schools, and even starting in your churches."

With his last words about France, Maurice relaxed and his sleeve pulling ceased. In the family section Anastasia leaned over to Eric and said, "I'm glad Maurice has stopped grabbing his sleeves. Reminds me of the way my dad used to rub his neck when he was making important speeches. I would tell him about it, but he just couldn't keep from doing it."

"As the decision-makers for all countries and all their peoples, we must start now to assure that diversity, the great strength of all long-lasting institutions, is maintained," Maurice said. "Now that our world is safe from the outside threat, we must address the threat from within, the decay and inevitable loss of national identity. Lawrence Holmes, a wise, experienced and reasonable man has laid the first stepping stone before us on the path to a better world. A world still secure but one with greater freedom, greater independence and hope for the eventual return to all the rights we have temporarily suspended. Resolution R-1948 does not cause a radical change. It calls for gradual movement in the direction all naturally want to go carefully monitored so that if we misstep, then we pause until the path is clear for us to proceed. I urge you to support this measure. Your children, your grand-children, your country and the whole world will be grateful. You will have done the right thing. Merci bouquet, mon amis."

Many delegates rose to their feet to applaud. Some cried out, "Viva la liberty," and others "Viva la" followed by their country's name. Lawrence had encouraged his supporters to bring their country's flag to the meeting. They spilled out into the aisles waving their flags creating an impromptu parade of flags winding through the aisles. The atmosphere was like that at a political convention. Some delegates even glanced up at the ceiling to see if a balloon release was coming next.

The next four speakers described the changes over the last few years in the peoples' feelings in their particular regions. Rudolph Spongle from Switzerland emphasized how hard it had been for his country to accept allegiance to the Planet Council. His country now wanted to return to its historical neutralist position. Raul Domingo, the delegate from Argentina said his people as well as many oth-ers from South America were like teenagers who had difficulties growing up, but through hard work and sacrifices had achieved success in adulthood. Now that they had stability, they wanted to afford their children the same opportunities that were theirs years ago. It was time to start a careful return to greater freedom. Thomas Baines from Australia reinforced the message of the previous speakers with examples drawn from his country. Birgitta Borge spoke of Sweden's experiences in World War II and the natural inclination of some women to focus on security. She said she agreed with Lawrence that greater safety would come from the Council's start on the return to freedom. The remarks of each of the four were greeted with sustained applause and flag waving.

Aziz Nzo moved slowly to the podium. Lawrence had chosen him to make the concluding speech for several reasons. He was the best known of the many authors who were delegates; he was one of the most popular delegates; he was the acknowledged leader of the dark skin delegates, and he was an accomplished speaker. Echoing Lawrence's stance at the podium, Aziz looked out over the audi-ence spotting and establishing eye contact with his many, long time friends. In a quiet, dignified voice he started, "Mr. Chairman, fellow delegates and guests, and particularly you, the children of delegates including my only child, my son Nel-son, who is here today, I ask you to rise and stand with me." After everyone rose, Aziz lifted both arms above his head and continued, "Please join me in sending a prayer or message, such as it may be. Those who believe in bowing their heads do so. Those who believe in closing their eyes, do so. Those who believe in a God, pray to him. Those who believe in what they call a Creator, send that Creator your thoughts. And those of you who believe in none of these things, I ask only that you listen to my prayer. I would wager that every different organized religion is represented here, but no one religion has a majority."

Aziz bowed his head and closed his eyes. His eighteen-year-old son Nelson, who was seated next to Byron, did the same, but Byron and Moira just lowered their eyes. "I pray for wisdom for myself and all of you who decide the fate of the millions of people on this planet. I pray for understanding among all of us. I pray for sincerity from all of us. And I renew the call from our friend and colleague, Lawrence Holmes, a thoughtful and wise humanitarian, for your best. Nothing less will suffice. We represent one hundred sixty-five different nations. That's one hundred sixty-five different cultures. The decision we are going to make may be the most important one since that decision made twenty-three years ago to establish world government."

John Browning was not in his usual seat at his desk or even in the section for Scotland's delegation. He was with a group of dark skin delegates who had received permission to sit in the center section reserved for the People's Advocates so they could be closer to the podium during their leader's speech. John was in a position to give a thumbs-up gesture to Aziz without it being noticeable to the audience. John also signaled by raising his hand when he thought Aziz should hurry up his presentation and lowering it when it should be slowed down. They had assisted each other in this way for so many years that those in the know would jokingly use those signals in ordinary conversation with either of the two. "I do not know the personal beliefs of most of you in religious matters, but I know we are of different colors, races, interests, occupations and heritages. When subject to the law, we should be equal. Sex, race or religious preferences should have no bearing and when in a courtroom, I believe this is the case today. But the people of the world are not equal in other regards." John signaled to Aziz to speed up his delivery.

"Now, what does all of this have to do with the location feature of our body chip?" Aziz said as he quickened his pace. "Make no mistake, Lawrence and everyone else knows that passage of R-1948 is not the end of the matter. Rather, it is the beginning. I want to place before you what I think should be the second stepping stone towards eventual personal freedom at the highest level consistent with safeguards to assure that the terrors earlier in century never plague this planet again. Why have I chosen this time and place to bring forth a second issue not included directly or indirectly in Lawrence's proposal? I do so in the hopes of helping obtain a majority vote for his proposal. In blunt terms, I am after votes. I talked with Lawrence about this procedure in advance. After careful deliberation and consultation with others, Lawrence has agreed to tie together his proposal and mine in this way. If I and those I influence help pass R-1948, Lawrence has pledged his full support and others that he can influence to pass my proposal. Thus, we are open and above board as we should be." John gave the thumbs up approval.

"Well, you ask, what is my proposal? Lawrence, in his speech introducing R-1948, evoked the thoughts of the music from that long-running play, *The Fantasticks*. Lawrence quoted, 'Try to remember when life was so tender that dreams were kept beside your pillows.' The last twenty-three years we have had to stay awake has not been a time for dreaming. But now we can rest more securely. Most can sleep peaceful and return to dreaming. In the words of a great dark skin man who lost his life fighting for what he believed, 'I have a dream my four children will one day live in a nation where they will not be judged by the color of their skin but by the content of their character.'

"Just like Martin Luther King, I have a dream and this is my dream. One day every family will be able to choose when and how many children to bear. My father's family had seven children, and my family had nine children of which I was the youngest. My father's life was hard. He was in prison with Nelson Mandela. Through all his difficulties, his brothers, sisters and children supplied the support for his wife and children that saw her through the terrible ordeal of life without a husband. My father often said that without that help, neither he nor his wife would have kept their sanity. I grew up without a father for twelve years. My mother, aunts and uncles raised me. My brothers and sisters bonded with me to survive. My family experience made me what I am today. My son should have had brothers and sisters. The least we can do is allow him to have sons and daughters." Byron reached over and placed his hand on Nelson's shoulder and gave it a gentle squeeze. Nelson turned to Byron with an appreciative smile.

"With the advantages of our universal educational opportunities, we dark skins have risen and proven by test scores that mentally we are equal to any other race," Aziz continued. "I am not asking for immediate elimination of birth control. I am asking that the quotas be altered to give dark skins an equal rate with all other races immediately. Within one year the rates for dark skins should transition to higher rates to replenish their depleted ranks. If you based birth quotas on physical attributes, we should have the highest rate. We are not asking for numerical superiority. We just want a chance to catch up and then stay even."

Five of the delegates seated with John joined him in flashing a thumbs up.

"In conclusion, I share the dream Lawrence has for the gradual return of the freedom to come and go without control. And as the second step, I plead for your help to realize my dream for my children and yours to choose the makeup of their family."

As Aziz left the podium, loud applause and shouts of "Amen, Sisters; Amen Brothers" were heard in every part of the hall. Aziz and Lawrence had decided against a second demonstration that might seem as being too contrived, so the applause and standing ovation for Aziz concluded the afternoon's presentation.

As Lawrence took his seat, a messenger from the Council's public relations department handed him a memo that read: "Please come to the media office after adjournment today for interviews with the media representatives from 20 countries." Lawrence was surprised and somewhat pleased. He told the messenger to expect him.

Byron and Moira stood up and Byron shook Nelson's hand. "Well, Nelson," Byron said. "You have celebrity status now. I don't think any offspring of a delegate has ever been recognized by name before in a speech on the Council floor."

"I wish Mom and Dad's sisters and brothers could have been here," Nelson responded. "Dad outdid himself. Mom would have, like it says in the Bible, pondered this in her heart. None of the family could be here because there have been heavy rainstorms in Port Elizabeth, our hometown. My aunts and uncles have been cleaning up and repairing the damage to our house and farm buildings. Things are such a mess that my Mom would like to sell the place. But Dad won't. He likes to mow the fields, mend the fences and, most of all, walk in the woods. Although Dad is a successful author now, the farm got us through for many years, and he feels kind of grateful to it."

Moira said, "Tell your dad we are all proud of him. I thought his allusion to Martin Luther King's dream was perfect. His dream is the dream of all young people everywhere. And many don't see why their dreams shouldn't be possible. If something doesn't give in that direction soon, I think there is going to be disillusionment and trouble."

Byron said, "You're right about that."

After hearty congratulations to Aziz, Lawrence hurried to the pressroom where he found the number of media representatives had grown to twenty-eight. The first question was from a corespondent from London's *Times* who asked, "What does U.S. Delegate William Dulles think about your proposal? And have you heard from the U.S. Secretary of State? Or maybe your President?."

"To answer your second and third question first, and they are the easiest to answer, no," Lawrence replied. "As for your first question, I have had no conversations with Bill Dulles in regard to my proposal, but I expect they don't like it and will oppose it vigorously."

The French representative of *Le Monde* said, "Apparently you have the votes of the countries whose delegates spoke in favor of R-1948 today, and I saw, of course, my country was among them, but how many other votes do you think you can count on? "

"I'd like to correct one impression you have that doesn't always hold true," Lawrence said. "Just because the delegate from a country speaks for a proposal, does not guarantee when the votes are cast, that country's vote will be for the proposal. As you know, the government of each country ultimately instructs their delegation how to vote and things can change during the question and debate sessions that cause a country to change their position. I'm hopeful of having a majority of the votes for my proposal. How many I think are leaning that way now, I would not tell you if I knew. Council politics is a poker game and it's best not to show your hand until you have to."

The representative from Bombay's *Indian Express* spoke next. "We are well aware of your son Byron's feelings about what he called "life breath" in his latest poem *Liberty*. His contention that a person doesn't exist as a person under the restrictions we live under now indicates his agreement with your proposal. What was his role in R-1948?"

"I hesitate to answer personal questions about my family, but your question transcends my family partly because, I'm proud to say, I think my son speaks for his whole generation and not just one individual. With that in mind, I will give this qualified answer. My proposal is intended to benefit my son's generation in general and for my son particularly. And if you'll please excuse me now, my family is expecting me home soon. I will issue a written statement tomorrow and will be available for more questions during the question and debate sessions. Thank you and good evening."

CHAPTER Λ3

"What is your estimate of the number of citizens who will have their location feature of their body chip deactivated each year for the first five years after deactivation is started?" Israeli delegate Abraham Stein asked. It was the first day of the Council's session reserved for questions about R-1948. Stein reminded history buffs of Israel's first Prime Minister David Ben-Gurion. It wasn't just the large head with the flowing white hair common to both; Stein also fit *Time* magazine's description of Ben-Gurion as a "Tight, craggy man with a volcanic temper." Council attendance was usually minimal for question sessions, but since word had gotten around that Stein was going to leadoff the attack on R-1948, almost all delegate seats were occupied.

"We have not made an estimate," Lawrence answered, "Nothing like this has ever happened in recorded history that we are aware of, so we have no basis for making an estimate."

"Is there any plan for locating these potential terrorists once they are freed to roam wherever they want?" Stein asked.

"Since we will have a record of all citizens becoming 'free' as you call it, we will know their physical description, family's names and their locations and what occupation they were engaged in," Lawrence answered. "Should the need arise to locate these people, authorities will have a good start on finding them."

"But if they alter their appearance or disguise themselves, leave their job, leave their home and sever connections with their family, a likely maneuver for a terrorist, no one will know what they look like, where they are, what they are doing, how many of what kind of stolen firearms are in their possession, what other terrorist they have joined, what they are planning and when and where the next attack will be; is that not so?" Stein continued.

"Mr. Stein," Lawrence said, "I believe your statement is as much of an argument as a question. Debate on my resolution will commence after the question session."

"I take that as a 'yes' to my question and will proceed. What additional measures do you and your supporters plan to propose if by some chance R-1948 should be adopted, a likelihood I will be glad to make a wager on privately with anyone who would be interested? That is, what measures in addition to Mr. Aziz Nzo's attempt to increase his people's population, I presume at the expense of others if we are not to return to ruinous overpopulation?"

"We have no other proposals to make at this time. But as has been indicated by those who have spoken for my proposal, we are not trying to delude anyone into thinking R-1948 is the end. Rather, it is the beginning and that is why this is such a serious matter."

A low mummer could be heard in the Council hall. Lawrence could imagine the opposition's opening argument later when the debate began including words like "Fellow delegates, we are being asked to adopt a very dangerous measure that the sponsors themselves admit that they have no idea how extensive the impact of that measure will be and what passage will lead to."

Stein opened his mouth to reply, but said nothing. He gave Lawrence a sour look, nodded to the chairman and returned to his seat. It was not customary to applaud speakers during the question sessions, so the only sound in the hall was the buzz of many conversations between delegates as Stein left the podium. Lawrence didn't like what he would call the tone of the buzz. He felt Abraham Stein had scored.

Three more speakers asked for information including details about the procedures whereby persons would request to have the location feature of their body chips deactivated and then later activated and what qualifications would have to be met for either the deactivation or reactivation. Other details they asked for were the likelihood of other features of the body chips being accidentally deactivated during the procedures brought about by R-1948 and the possible loss of life if important medical data was erased. Similar questions were raised for the remainder of the first day. In almost all cases Lawrence's answer was the same, "We don't know; this kind of thing has never been done before."

The delegate from United Korea, Roh Tae Hwan, led off the second day of questioning asking what methods of locating fugitives in mountainous areas were to be included in the administration of R-1948. He reminded the Council of the difficulties of finding terrorists in the mountains of Afghanistan after the 9/11 attack on the U.S. and described the mountainous terrain and rugged uplands in northern Korea. His concern was not being able to locate possible saboteurs of the very profitable Korean uranium, copper and gold mines that had spurred the reunification of North and South Korea in 2035. Although reunited, elements of discord continued. Lawrence had to answer that no new program had been developed to counter this particular concern.

Just one more question was asked about the probable administrative costs of R-1948 before President van de Velde paused, awaiting additional questions. Apparently none were forthcoming.

"I'm surprised Dulles isn't going to ask questions." Lawrence said to James as he leaned close to his neighboring delegate so that others couldn't overhear his comment." Lawrence and most Council members had anticipated that the U.S. delegate, William Dulles, would conclude the questioning with a long list of hard-to-answer subtle attacks in the form of questions.

"Sorry to have to tell a friend, but my guess is that Dulles feels that an adequate job of undermining support for your resolution has been accomplished," James said. "Either that or he doesn't want to tip his hand before the debate session."

"Sounds as if I'd better gear up for the next round and include a few surprises for Dulles," Lawrence said as van de Velde adjourned the session at a very early 15:00.

CHAPTER A4

"Race you to the fence," Kate said to Michael. Michael knew he didn't have a chance of winning even though his stallion was faster than Kate's mount. But he kicked his heels into his horse's side and yelled the old, but still effective, "Giddyap," and tried to make a contest of it.

"When are you going to learn how to make a horse move out?" Kate asked, punching Michael on the shoulder as they rested their horses side by side at the fence.

"I couldn't keep up with you on a horse if you were eight months pregnant and on an old lesson-horse mare," Michael answered, taking Kate's hand and pulling her and her horse with her towards him so he could lean over and wrap his arm around her.

"Be careful or you'll fall off." Kate gave Michael's horse a slap, and he bolted forward. Michael grabbed the saddle horn and barely stayed on.

"I'll get you." Michael turned his horse around and started after Kate, but she was already three strides ahead of him on her way back to the stables.

"I thought Byron and Moira were coming to ride," Michael shouted to Kate who was several meters ahead of him leading her horse back to his stall while Michael was still dismounting.

"They are. I'm going after a gentle gelding for Byron. That's as much horse as he can handle." Kate waited for Michael to catch up, and they walked their horses together towards the stables. "I'll have Moira ride your stallion. Would you like a gelding, too, to make it a little easier for you?"

"You little devil." Michael pinched Kate hard on her left hip. She jumped and moved out of reach. "Get a gelding for Moira so she won't get too far ahead of Byron. She won't try to show her man up like some women like to do."

"Poor little Mike. You're just jealous. Maybe we'll have a son who can ride with me." Kate paused, suddenly solemn. "If we get to have any children."

"What do you mean, if? There's nothing wrong with us?"

"Nothing except we may be too smart. Byron said that Eric has been monitoring the pregnancy committee's decisions and think that they are against any couples with high I.Q.'s."

"You look serious. Are you?"

"'Fraid so. Eric doubts that he and Anastasia will be accepted for parenthood. Byron is really upset about it and I am too. Byron's up to something. He's been rushing around buying all kinds of unusual stuff like insulated gloves. I'm surprised he could spare the time to come riding today, but he said he wanted to talk to you."

"There's Byron and Moira in the stables. Looks as if they are ready to go.

Moira's got a bridle and even a whip."

"What a good-looking stallion," Moira said as she came up to Kate's horse.

"Mike's is faster," Kate said to Moira. "I was going to put you on Mike's horse, but Mike said you should plod along with Byron, your slow moving man, Mike called him."

"Byron, how did you survive with a sassy sister like Kate?" Michael asked

"It was difficult but good training for trying to deal with Moira." Moira turned towards Byron and tried to swat him with the whip, but he caught her arm, pinned it to her side giving her a hug and said, "I love spirited Scots."

Moira pushed up against Byron trying to get loose but couldn't.

"Hey, hey," Kate said. "No lovemaking in front of the horses. Let's get you saddled up and go riding."

Kate and Michael tied up their horses, led two geldings out of their stalls, and saddled them.

"You gals ride the stallions and get a workout," Byron said. "Mike and I will take the geldings so we can talk while we ride."

Kate and Moira mounted the stallions and rode off. Byron and Michael mounted the geldings and walked them slowly away from the stables. Byron said, "Mike, I need some legal advice. I know you are just pre-law, but I want to keep this private, and I know I can trust you not to say anything about it, not even to Kate."

"What do you need to know?"

"How to make a will in two days that will stand up if anything happens to me."

"This is something important, isn't it?"

"Yes. I don't have much cash now, but I have royalties from my poetry and I've written a novel. It's not published yet, but I've sent it off to a publisher who is interested and thinks it will sell. He believes it might become a movie. I want to bequeath whatever might come of it to Moira, or if anything happens to her, to any child we might have."

"Aren't you getting way ahead of things, Byron? You don't even have permission to get married, much less be parents."

"I can't explain. I just need a will that can't be overturned. Will you do it?"

"Sure. I've had enough training to do that. List what assets you have and those that might come to you and what you want done with them. I'll put it in legal language and have it back to you the same day. You need to have it witnessed by at least two persons who are not beneficiaries. I can be one."

"I'll p-mail you the list and details tomorrow morning. If you can have it ready by tomorrow evening, I'll bring a witness and meet you wherever you want. And, don't tell Moira about this, O.K.?"

"Sure. Are you in some kind of trouble?"

Byron paused. "No, but I need to get some things settled."

Kate and Moira returned and met up with Byron and Mike at the stables. After Byron and Moira left, Kate asked Michael, "What did Byron want to talk to you about?"

Michael didn't answer immediately. Then slowly and carefully he said, "I'm sorry I can't tell you, darling. It's kind of a client-attorney privileged information thing."

CHAPTER ∧⌂

"My friends," Lawrence said, "tell me where you think we are and where you think we should be going. I'd like for you to start, Birgitta."

Lawrence had reserved the Council's small private dining room for his supporters to have dinner together at the end of the questioning session. Since it was too early for dinner, the group ordered h'ors d'oeuvres and drinks instead.

Birgitta didn't hesitate. "I think we are in pretty good shape with the men, but in trouble with some women. Women make up 45 % of the delegates now. For many of them, especially those with children, security is all-important. They have it now and are not as inclined as men to take chances. I'm not saying that they don't have strong feelings about freedom of choice, particularly in regard to having children, but if there is a chance their family could be harmed, they will give up a lot to prevent that. As I said in my speech, I am convinced that R-1948 will bring greater security, but some women I've talked with don't agree. As to what we should be doing, I think we should emphasize that if trouble develops, we will return to where we are now. And we will do it quickly."

"Does anyone disagree, particularly about the feelings of some women delegates?" Lawrence asked. He was nodding during Birgitta's assessment.

"I don't agree with Birgitta," Rudolf Spongle spoke up quickly to say. "Of course, you may think that we Swiss men don't have any idea about the feelings of women, since we were one of the last countries to let them vote. But in the last generation, our women have taken a very strong stand for traditional Swiss causes such as neutrality. My alternate, Sonjia Mende, who you all know is a very capable and strong-willed feminist, will probably replace me in the next session. The women she has talked to are going along with us. As to any change in tactics, we may have to compromise to get this first step passed. Some I have talked with want to delay a few years and others want the age raised to fifty or higher."

"Compromise on the age, we might," said Maurice Gide. "But we should not agree to any delay. If the Council puts off a decision now, they'll just put it off again and again. They would like to take the easy way of avoiding controversy, not stirring up the masses. We can win this thing if we hold firm. The whole world wants freedom. Remember how many joined our parade of flags?"

"I can only speak for Australia," Thomas Baines said as he turned towards Lawrence. "This is my first term and I don't have the feel for the Council that the rest of you do, but I think that we need to concentrate on China and Russia. They hold the reins. Whoever holds the reins, sets the direction the horses go in. The whole Council, the wagon you might say, goes where the horses are led."

"You haven't been here long, Tom, but you've hit the nail on the head," Lawrence said. "If we can't get those two to back us or at least stay neutral, we probably won't make it."

"Unfortunately, I don't think this particular group has any great in with China or Russia," Aziz Nzo said as a follow-up. "Does anyone know how India is going to vote? It borders both China and Russia. Now that India's population is greater than China's, do you think their position will have greater influence? I know they think they should be added to The Big Three. Maybe we could offer them our support in exchange for theirs."

The group looked towards Raul Domingo, the only one who hadn't commented. "Don't look at me, friends," Raul said. "Argentina probably has less influence with any of the The Big Three than any of you."

"Come to think of it, Lawrence, I do have a connection with China through Nelson who has been courting the daughter of their alternate delegate," Aziz said. "But that's not something we should take advantage of."

"I agree we shouldn't try to get our kids to exert any influence, but I'd feel comfortable in asking Anastasia some general question like, 'How you think the vote will come down?' to get an inkling of Russia's thinking," Lawrence said. "Would that be acceptable to the rest of you?"

Aziz paused while he thought over Lawrence's remarks. "Well, yes, if you didn't go any further than a general question. Our children are what this is all about, but I don't want them to feel it's their problem to solve. Our generation and the one before created the society we have. It's our responsibility to make it better."

"I agree," Lawrence said. "I, for sure, don't want to have Byron under any pressure. He's tied into this enough already." Lawrence looked at Merlin to see what time it was. "Thank you for coming and for your support. If you can create a good opportunity to sound out the Chinese and Russian delegates, report to me what you find out. But do it casually. I want all the Council to think we are confident R-1948 will pass. Everyone wants to be on the wining side, and you can get some votes just using that approach. I'll see what I can find out about India's feelings."

After everyone had left, Lawrence stayed for awhile and had a cup of coffee. It wasn't as good as the French Market Cajun that he got at home, but it helped prepare him for the next item on his agenda, the news conference.

"Mr. Holmes, are you aware of the reaction throughout the world your proposal is receiving from universities, churches, news broadcasts, and news print? You are now known internationally and are a hero to many," Nana Iyemitsu, a correspondent from Japan asked to start the news conference. There were at least fifty media representatives on hand.

"I am aware that the issue I have raised is of great interest to many people," Lawrence answered. "I prefer that the focus be on that issue rather than any individual."

"Delegate Holmes, do you think there is any connection between the recent break-ins at hunting camps and the introduction of R-1948?" a correspondent from Israel asked.

"The break-ins at the hunting camps started over two years ago, long before

I even mentioned my proposal to other delegates. The number and seriousness of those incidents has increased. I think they are the way that otherwise law-abiding citizens have chosen to protest current restrictions. We must pay attention to what the citizens of the world are trying to tell us."

Lawrence answered questions for about another half-hour. The questions tried to elicit controversial answers, but Lawrence continued in a non-confrontational way until the correspondents' senior member said, "Thank you Mr. Holmes," and the news conference ended with most media representatives disappointed.

"Isn't it terrible that hoodlums are breaking into our hunting camps?" Stewart Armstrong asked Lawrence who had the seat beside Armstrong's on the melting pot travel unit. Lawrence was on the way home from the news conference and wanted to get his own reading on public opinion about his resolution. He also was curious if he had become a celebrity.

"Why do you think they are breaking in, since they didn't take any firearms?" Lawrence asked.

"Just know-it-alls who don't want anybody to shoot anything. They want the camps closed. Those camps are the only good thing the Planet, uh, what do they call it, oh yeah, Planet Committee has done since it took over from the UN. I objected, of course, when they seized my rifles and shotgun, and I thought the idea that I could only use them at the camps was ridiculous. But now the hunting is better and safer. With that wrist band that they put on you that sounds off as you approach the boundary of the area you are supposed to be hunting in, the number of accidents and deaths have practically gone to zero. There are plenty of all kinds of game, and they adjust the limits to keep the wildlife population in balance. It's a, what was that kind of slogan from that seven something book, uh, win-win deal."

"What do you think of the resolution to let people change their body chip that the Planet Coun . . , er, Committee is considering?"

"What resolution? I only follow the hunting news. Didn't know anything about it. Are they going to let terrorists be on the loose again?"

"I don't think that will happen."

"Well, I'd hope not. By the way, you look very familiar. Have you been on TV?"

"Yes, I have, occasionally," Lawrence admitted with an embarrassed smile. "My name, uh, my name is Lawrence Holmes," Lawrence said thinking that Armstrong may not follow the Council proceedings, but the media representatives were right; he had become known.

"Bet you didn't think I'd recognize you," Armstrong said as he extended his hand. "I'm Stewart Armstrong. I didn't remember your name, but I never forget a face. You are that professional basketball head referee that handled all of the playoffs in the early '30s. I haven't seen you in quite awhile, guess you've retired. It's been years, but I recognized you for sure." Armstrong's broad smile showed how proud he was to have remembered Lawrence after all these years and how excited he was to be talking to a sports figure.

Slightly dejected and not knowing how to respond truthfully without completely disappointing his new acquaintance, Lawrence felt a little white lie wouldn't hurt, so he said, "Thank you very much Stewart, but that was my brother who looks a lot like me."

"Oh. Well, it must be enjoyable to be related to somebody who knows all the famous basketball players personally. You brother is almost a celebrity." Armstrong smiled, but the smile wasn't as broad as before.

"Yes he is. In many ways it's better to have one in the family than being one yourself, because you aren't bothered signing autographs all the time."

"I'm sure it is," Armstrong said without conviction. "Well, this is my stop. Hope to see you again sometime. Please tell your brother that I remember him. He was a damn fine referee."

CHAPTER ∧Ò

When Lawrence got home the house was dark. Inside the door he found a note from Laura telling that Kate, Michael, and she were out looking at everyday china patterns. Kate wanted to select something that Michael liked too. After that they were going to have dinner, and then she and Kate were going to meet with a seamstress at her house who did custom wedding dresses. Laura doubted that they would be home before 22:00 and wasn't sure if Lawrence would have had dinner or not. The note said that roast beef and a baked potato were in the high-speed Home Chef unit and should be cooked at 7.5 for four minutes. "Hope the question session went well. Love, Laura," ended the message.

Lawrence put on an old pair of jeans that had gotten that soft feeling from numerous washings and a flannel shirt that felt the same. He wished he had some popcorn. The popcorn from the Home Chef was pretty good and better than it had been ten or so years ago, but the old style round brass popper with a non-nutritious vegetable oil and an excess of melted butter and well salted was the only popcorn worth the trouble to him. He still had one of those poppers, but, tonight, he didn't want to go to that much trouble. And he always felt obligated to clean up any mess he made, and cleaning the popper was a chore. He just wanted to sit. Sit and not even think.

"Lawrence this is Marge, I've got terrible news," Lawrence heard her say after Merlin signaled an incoming call from the office of Roland Nilsson, the Council General Secretary. When he saw that that there was a call for him from Nilsson's office, Lawrence expected Roland's assistant, Marge Atkins, to give him the schedule for the start of debate on his resolution. Marge's news wasn't about R-1948. "Roland's in extensive care in the hospital after suffering a severe stroke that paralyzed his left side and left him unable to speak."

"What is his capability rating, Marge"?

"It's at 102, and his rate is dropping slowly."

"That's way below the minimum rating!" The alarm in his voice made Lawrence sound hoarse,

"I know. It looks hopeless." Marge's voice broke and in a halting voice she continued. "Everyone is devastated that his rating probably won't improve enough to avoid euthanasia. He's only fifty-seven, for Christ's sake. I've been told that Roland testified for establishing the system of determining if a person's medical condition justified additional treatment or not. If that's so, it's painfully ironic that he's going to die because of it," she spat out.

"He did support euthanasia for persons whose rating stayed below 100 for sixty days, but originally no ratings for stopping treatment were ever done before the age of seventy. It seemed reasonable at the time." Lawrence coughed and tried to clear his throat.

"That was before my time. How the hell did it get lowered?"

"Same way as a lot of things gradually changed to something worse than intended. First, the age was lowered to sixty if the patient's brain scan showed no activity. Then, it became euthanasia for anyone with no brain activity. A study found that only one per cent with a rating of 100 lived over sixty days, so the minimum was raised and a new study was done. The 130 is based on seven per cent living ninety days and none over a year." Lawrence was speaking so quietly that Marge had trouble hearing. "The same thing happened when they started evaluating everyone when they were seventy to determine if they were making a net positive contribution to society."

"Marie is livid. Not just because she's his sister, but as a surgeon. I think she will try something unusual in the thirty days they have. I was with her at the hospital and I could see the wheels turning in her head."

"Marie argued with Roland over his testimony, so I can imagine how she feels. How's the rest of Roland's family doing?"

"Eric is doing the best he can with his mother. His brother and sister are in Sweden, but I'm sure they will be here as soon as possible."

"I'll go see them. Is there anything I can do to help you and the staff?"

"Thanks. Nothing I can think of right now. But I'm not thinking too well. I'll call you if . . . oh, I'm sure debate on your resolution will be delayed, probably two or three days."

"That's not important. Call me if you need my assistance or hear of something his family needs doing."

"I will. It's been a horrible day. Good night, Lawrence."

CHAPTER ∧7

With the debate session about to begin, the excitement in the Council Hall was obvious by the large number of simultaneous conversations that caused more than the usual buzz. Delegates had heard the latest medical report on Roland Nilsson. It wasn't good; his rating had decreased to 94.

The U.S. delegate, William K. Dulles, had been chosen floor leader for the opposition to R-1948 as expected. Dulles had been a federal judge in New York prior to being named U.S. Attorney General in 2032. In 2036 he was named the U.S. delegate to the Planet Council. On 9/11/01 he had been having breakfast in New York City two blocks away from the Trade Center. When the first tower was hit, he ran out the door and started towards the explosion site to see if he could help. He was on the sidewalk when the second tower was hit. From that moment on he became a fanatic about security.

Dulles initiated his attack with a speech by Abraham Stein detailing the suffering Israel endured when they were forced to relocate to the coast of Brazil, because the Middle East was the only region after disarmament where serious warfare continued. "After all we've gone through being moved to a location we didn't choose, we're not about to give up our security to let loose potential terrorists." This was followed by two speakers reminding delegates that Lawrence had answered, "I don't know" to many questions.

William Dulles approached the podium and the hall fell silent. Dulles's tall figure clothed in a body cover that fit tightly around his bony, sparse frame rose above the platform like a wrapped and tied mast above its sailboat's deck. He was all lean. With a raspy, penetrating voice like that of a prosecutor addressing the jury in his opening remarks, Dulles warned the Council, "Delegates of the Planet Council you have a duty to perform. A serious duty. An unwanted duty but an unavoidable duty. You cannot shirk; you cannot dodge; you cannot run away; you cannot hide. You were chosen to perform just such a duty that is now thrust upon you. The sacrifices of the past and the responsibilities of the future are hanging above your heads." Dulles lifted his right arm up and looked up as he finished the sentence as if to touch a heavy blanket to verify that there was a cover over the audience into which lists of sacrifices and responsibilities were woven.

"You are the keeper of the keys for the gates of security. You must not be lax in your duty. You must hold fast to those keys and not let them be taken from you and delivered to hands that might open the gates to catastrophe." Dulles's clenched fists were held up for his audience to see, as if he were holding the keys tightly himself.

"We know what is behind those gates because we witnessed the horrors they wrought before we found a way to lock them out of our lives. Those gates have been successful. For twelve years, half a generation, the forces of hell have not slipped through those gates. We, on the safe side, are well, prosperous and free to pursue our lives without the scourge of starvation, overpopulation, wars, the proliferation of AIDS, drug abuse, millions of abortions, unwanted children, homeless thousands, nursing homes filled with vegetable-like helpless bodies, high unemployment, ruinous business cycles, undeserved excessive compensation and all the other maladies we suffered through before order came into the world." As Dulles paused, murmurs spread across the auditorium.

Dulles took the microphone in his hand and carried it with him as he stepped to the side of the podium and walked to the very edge of the platform to get as close as possible to his audience. "For the sake of this generation and the sake of all those to come, I urge you to do your duty and reject this dangerous, far reaching, unwise breach of our security that can, and I believe would, do incalculable damage. Don't just try to remember, do remember and follow your head to preserve what is dear to the hearts of all--peace and prosperity."

Sustained applause for several minutes followed Dulles's speech. Lawrence had made a practice to time the length of applause given speakers as a way to measure the degree of support for their position. He was distressed with the three minute and forty-five second time Dulles's speech garnered.

CHAPTER ∧8

"Mother, I think that's a great idea, but you should consider that you've got a good position with good pay," Byron said. "You may not be able to get it back if you resign." Laura had asked him to give her a few minutes before he left for the meeting he was having with the chief of the Cultural Enrichment Bureau where he worked four days a week. They were in the exercise chamber.

"I want an English degree," Laura said in between strokes on the Integral machine that was set up for rowing exercises. "I don't understand your poems. I feel ignorant. Besides, my new supervisor is a . . . well, you know what I mean."

"How long will it take you to get a degree?" Byron asked.

"The head of the English department thinks I can do it in two years. Maybe a year and a half if I take classes in the summer." Laura stopped her rowing. She was breathing hard but wasn't exhausted.

"You're really in good shape. When I row it wears me out. I even have unsteady walking after vigorous exercise some times. Have you talked to Dad about your idea yet?"

"He's got so much to handle right now that I didn't want to add anything. That's why I wanted to get your opinion first. If it's not a good idea, I won't bother him about it. Well, in the words of an old TV show I watched when I was about nine, 'What's your final answer?'"

"In your case, go for it. My concern about giving up your job is the same concern I have that women should have a source of income in case they end up on their own. If getting a degree is important to you, that overrides your having a job for the future."

"Do you really approve, or are you just being accommodating because I'm your mother?"

"How could I not advise anyone who is intelligent and wants to get a degree in English not to when I'm devoting my life to literature?"

"Do you think its fair to your dad? He works hard. I hear what you are saying about thinking about the future, and in addition, our income will be less. Class fees for part time students are high."

"Dad's always encouraged you to do anything you're interested in. I'm sure he'll be pleased, and he doesn't have to have your extra income. I don't think I'd start classes until the fall, however. This summer there's a lot going on what with Anne's application and Kate's review not to mention Dad's mammoth undertaking."

"And your courtship. How are things going with you and Moira?"

"Er, uh, just fine. Is that all? I'd better be going or I'll be late for my meeting."

"Thanks. I needed for you to tell me if I were doing something crazy."

"You're not. See you this evening." Byron left and Laura resumed her workout.

"How long have you been at it?" Kate asked her mother as she came into the exercise area of the cleansing chamber. Kate was uncharacteristically serious.

"Long enough. I'm quitting now." With a push up with her legs and an audible grunt, Laura lifted herself from a rowing position and sprawled onto the floor. "I wish I could take a pill to keep in shape, but I have to keep up with your dad; and that's not easy. He actually likes to exercise." Kate joined her by kneeling down and then lying on her back.

Kate paused and then asked, "Do you know what's going on with Byron? He seems distracted, and he's been making unusual purchases."

"Have you asked him why?"

"I did. He evaded the questions. Said something about going camping with JD's Seven sometime this summer."

"Your dad and I noticed it too. We got the same runaround. Oh, by the way, Byron's in favor of my taking English classes too. I didn't tell him that you and Anne approve, because I wanted his independent opinion. I'm going to start in the fall."

"Great, but don't go too intellectual on us." Kate shifted on the floor to a sitting position. She paused so long that Laura shifted to sit up. "Mom, what do you do if the man you're in love with has different values than yours?"

Laura scooted closer to Kate. "Kate, what kind of differences?"

Words came tumbling out quickly, non-stop, "Important ones to me. Mike wants to be a corporate lawyer after he passes the bar. His uncle is high up in a law firm that specializes in defending doctors in malpractice suits. Mike says his uncle can get him a starting position there. He may end up keeping some widow from collecting from a surgeon who made a mistake and killed her husband. I can't see why he shouldn't use his legal skills to help people in trouble. Mike says it might be an innocent doctor who needs help. I just can't make him understand." Kate hung her head.

Laura put her arm around Kate, and slowly in sympathetic tones, she said, "I have trouble understanding the ethics of the legal profession too. But I also didn't like it when your dad wrote articles about Joan O'Brien that probably kept her from becoming the first woman President of the United States. She was really qualified and would have been a good president. Your dad knew that, but the editor of the *Post* assigned him to check on a story about a decision that Joan made when she was the CEO of General Tech. Your dad found out that she had known about the falsifying of test results on a safety device for air scooters, and she didn't see that they were corrected. She later said it concerned minor defects that at the time she didn't think were important. Fifteen people died when the air scooters crashed. I gave your dad hell about his articles and said that a lot of male CEO's did much worse things. But I can see that I was wrong. He was just doing his job. And doing it well." Kate looked up towards Laura. "If Mike does honest work, I think it's his choice."

Kate didn't reply for a few minutes. "I just wish . . ."

Laura interrupted her with, "I know what you mean, sweetheart, but Mike is a good man. He treats you right, and he treats the people he doesn't have to cater to, like sales clerks, right also. My dad told me to notice that, because some day after you're married, that is likely how your mate will treat you. Your dad likes Mike, and your dad is very particular."

Kate stood up and held her hand out to help Laura stand up. "Is this why there are mothers?"

"I don't know. My mother didn't want me to marry your dad. She said he was too much concerned with helping others and wouldn't ever make anything of himself. She expected me to have to return home when he couldn't support me."

"Did you ever tell Dad that?"

"Didn't have to. My mother told him."

Kate put her arm around her mother and smiled as they walked out of the exercise area and said, "Promise you won't talk to Mike."

CHAPTER ᴧ9

The next morning Lawrence checked on the condition of Roland Nilsson. It was about the same, and family members were reconciled to the likely discontinuance of medical treatment in the near future. Lawrence then met with his inner support group in one of the caucus rooms at the Planet Council hall to plan their next steps.

Aziz had a proposition he wanted the group to discuss. The delegate from Afghanistan, Ahmad Abdali, had approached him about joining in the effort to obtain better birth rates for dark skins by adding Muslims to the mix. New births for Muslims in Afghanistan had been restricted for a long time. He thought that if Lawrence would make the same deal with Muslims that he made with dark skins, about 20 votes that were against R-1948 or at best on the fence, could be brought over to Lawrence's side.

Lawrence's group was split on the question of bringing the Muslims in on the deal. Some felt if it would give them enough votes to pass R-1948, it should be done. Others felt it would further cloud the main issue, which already occurred with the dark skin deal, and might result in the Council putting off any decision. Thomas Baines put his hand on Aziz's shoulder to signal that what he had to say should not be taken as critical of the dark skins. He said he was not really in favor of any deals to get votes. He wanted R-1948 to be considered on its merits alone. But he was willing to go along with the trade-off with dark skins, since he thought they had a legitimate claim and that without their votes, R-1948 would probably not make it. He was against a deal with Muslims. He didn't think they had a valid argument.

"I agree with Thomas," Maurice Padron said. "Births in all Muslim countries have not been restricted and some of them may vote with us anyway without a deal."

Lawrence ended the meeting by saying he would check on the birthrates. He asked everyone to think it over.

Meeting with the news media had become an everyday event for Lawrence. He had let them know he would be available just before lunch. The first question was from a newspaper correspondent from Richmond, Virginia. "Mr. Holmes, did you have a part in the organization of the Patrick Henry clubs that are springing up everywhere? Not just here in the U.S. but even in China, Japan, Russia, and, most surprising, England."

Lawrence said, "I did not; however I am not surprised. Almost all nations at one time or another have had movements for greater liberty in their country. I have been invited to speak to a meeting of the presidents of twenty-four clubs in this area. I have been amazed at how quickly the clubs have organized, but evidently the nucleus of such groups have been meeting monthly in many places over the last year. The adding of a common name for the groups was a simple thing that could be done overnight with the planetnet. The point I will be making tomorrow night is that the sacrifice of lives should not be necessary to obtain a reasonable and safe increase in our personal freedom. I absolutely do not condone violence to achieve the change I am advocating."

The correspondent from Sidney, Australia, asked, "Do you consider yourself the Patrick Henry or maybe Paul Revere of today? There are seventeen Patrick Henry clubs in Australia."

"Well, to be compared with either Patrick Henry or Paul Revere is a compliment," Lawrence answered. "Although I welcome the support of the Patrick Henry clubs, what we are about is a serious, far-reaching affair that should be approached with a less emotional attitude than Henry was known for. The Council should move carefully in what are uncharted waters."

"Mr. Holmes," a correspondent from Canada asked, "what was the reasoning behind the alliance you have forged with the dark skin community of the world? Just to get votes?"

"The trouble with news conferences is that you get questions that are hard to answer truthfully without misleading the public. I would vote to change birth rates for dark skins, regardless. They deserve an increase in their population growth. Aziz Nzo came to me to offer support of R-1948 and asked for my support of his cause. I agreed because I am for his cause. Next question."

The commentator for the largest television station in Madrid, Spain asked, "If R-1948 passes and that is followed up by improved birth rates for the dark skins, what do you think will be the next step in the movement towards greater freedom?"

"As you know, delegate William Dulles wants to know the same thing. I do not know what the next step might be, and I do not want to speculate on it. If the sponsors of R-1948 were to discuss succeeding measures, the debate might well shift to those measures. We are proposing a small, safe change. That is the issue and that is what we desire to discuss at this time. And speaking of time, it is time for me to go. I have a lot of work to do before tomorrow's session. Thank you and good afternoon."

"Lawrence, I'd like to walk out with you," Brigitta said as she caught up with Lawrence when he left the press room.

"It'll be my pleasure," Lawrence said. "You didn't say much at our meeting this morning."

"That's because I'm on the fence. I'm beginning to believe we might win without the Muslims, and that's what I want to talk to you about. Of course, I'd sure be sorry if we didn't make a deal with them and then lost." Birgitta stopped and stepped to the side of the corridor. Lawrence followed. "I've had numerous calls from all kinds of Swedish organizations who are thrilled with your resolution. Stockholm's League of Women Voters is raising thousands of dollars for billboards in New York City that delegates will see on their way to Council sessions. Telephone committees to solicit signatures for a massive petition to the Directorate are working hard too. Have you seen the opinion site on p-net that has your resolution as their current question?"

"No, I haven't even checked my p-mail for the last two days."

"It used to be I kept my ear to the ground for public opinion by walking the streets and talking to people. Today, I think the electronic highway is a better avenue to take the pulse of the people. Rallies are organized on planetnet. My God, I didn't know anybody would leave their homes at night to go to a meeting that they didn't have to. I quit attending anything in the evening years ago. Now there is a rally for your resolution somewhere in Sweden practically every night and a summation of it on planet-net an hour after it is over."

Lawrence looked at his watch and ushered Birgitta onto the escalator saying, "Sorry I have to move on. Byron said he wanted to talk to me tonight, probably about what my resolution doesn't do. You know its all been a revelation to me. I had no idea so much would happen so quickly. The media representatives indicated there was a lot of attention being generated, but I'm always skeptical of their reports, because they want the pot to be boiling and will try to ignite a fire if they can."

"This is not a media event. It's genuine. But I'm not sure that even if the huge majority of the world favors R-1948, their governments will instruct their delegates to vote for it. Anyway, take some time to get out and look at billboards, read your p-mail and see if you think I'm right. Ultimately, our support group will want you to make the decision on the Muslims."

"Thanks for your input, Birgitta. I'll do it."

CHAPTER 2∇

When Lawrence got home, Byron was waiting. Laura was out shopping with Kate. Byron held a half-empty glass of white wine and looked nervous. It was a look Lawrence was familiar with, and it made Lawrence nervous too. Lawrence worried that after Byron had his say about the inadequacies of R-1948, he would go storming out, maybe even slinging what was left of his wine into the bar sink on the way; maybe even smashing his glass, too. Lawrence decided to mix himself a martini before the fireworks started.

Lawrence mixed his drink and took a big sip letting the very dry martini trickle slowly down his throat. It warmed his chest nicely. Byron took a gulp of his wine as if he too wanted to be fortified. Then Byron said, "Dad, I have something serious I want to talk to you about."

Lawrence had heard that opening before, but he was surprised at Byron's demeanor. When Byron and he had talked about Council affairs or politics of any kind, Byron had usually had fire in his eyes and followed up with, "Dad, you've got to do something about this." This time Byron was not confrontational. Lawrence surmised this was something personal and very important. He set his glass down on the bar.

Byron said, "I want to get married, but I'm not sure how to go about it."

Lawrence was relieved. "That's wonderful, Byron. Have you asked Moira yet?"

"No, I wanted to talk to you first."

Lawrence paused. "I strongly suspect that she feels the same way about you as you do about her. I'm very pleased and excited about this, and Laura will be too."

"Should I ask Moira's father for her hand?"

"That's the old-fashioned way. That's the way I did it. I think Moira and her parents will be pleased if you ask John first."

"Do I have to have a ring to give her?"

"I didn't. On the night we got engaged, I gave Laura my college graduation ring as, as kind of collateral."

"When do you think I should ask her?"

"What are you doing tonight?"

Byron moved forward and gave his father a warm hug saying, "Thanks, Dad. Don't tell Mom until Moira accepts, if she does." Byron turned to leave, stopped and faced his father. "Dad, I, I want you to know that, that I love you. And, and I'm not saying it now just for your help this evening. It's because, it's because, well, it's just because I wanted you to know. "

Lawrence was so surprised, so stunned that he was speechless. Byron often expressed his feelings that were critical or joyful, but he had not said anything like this to Lawrence since Byron was a small boy. Lawrence looked at Byron not knowing how to respond. He wanted to say, "I love you too," but thought that might in some way lessen the importance of Byron's avowal. Byron seemed to be relieved that he had gotten the words out. Lawrence was still speechless. Afterward he worried he had let Byron down by not replying.

Byron said, "Well, I'm going to call Moira."

As Byron left to call Moira, he was whistling the tune that a music-major classmate of his had composed for Byron's lyric poem *Liberty*. The tune reminded Byron of Beethoven's *Ode to Freedom* from his ninth symphony that was played to celebrate the fall of the Berlin Wall in 1989. His classmate called the song *Liberty by Byron* and had recorded it and given copies to many of Byron's friends.

Kate came into the room as Byron was leaving and joined Lawrence at the bar. "What brought that on?" she said. "I haven't seen Byron so happy and carefree for ages."

"He's got a secret that I can't tell, but I think you will be hearing about it soon," Lawrence said.

"He's finally going to pop the question?"

"You're too smart for me. Don't tell him you know, please. And don't tell your mother. Byron doesn't want her to know until after Moira accepts his proposal."

"I won't. I'm so glad. Byron needs Moira. It'll be tough on her to keep him out of trouble, but he's special and worth it. I worry about him almost as much as you do, Dad. Now we will have a helper he might listen to."

"I wish he had been born in another generation. I have always wished I had been alive in 1776 and been a part of the Continental Congress. But, we have to play the cards dealt us. Byron will have to also."

Kate leaned over to kiss her father on his cheek. He smiled. His eyes were teary. "Caught your soft side, didn't I," Kate said as she followed her kiss with a hug.

Lawrence put his arm around Kate as they walked into the dining room.

CHAPTER 2∧

The next session of the Council was set aside for rebuttals. Delegates approaching the check-in desk to attend were met by a large group of over one thousand demonstrators carrying signs identifying themselves as Patrick Henry club members. The group was split into two parts leaving a pathway for delegates. The signs showed that most clubs were from cities in the U.S., but there were also clubs from Canada, Europe, Asia, Australia and Africa. Many children were on the shoulders of their parents waving the flag of their country. The crowd was orderly but enthusiastic and shouted out, "Vote freedom," as delegates passed by them.

Lawrence had selected Thomas Baines to refute Abraham Stein's speech as the first rebuttal speech. "Abraham, I have looked up and read the minutes of the Council proceedings regarding the decision to move Israel to Brazil. I acknowledge that Israel was treated unfairly, but the Council had to separate the two sides in the centuries old violent conflict, and it was easier to move Israel than all the Arab nations. I also found that Israel refused to meet with the commission to select the new location for them, and Arab countries contributed most of the trillions of dollars that were paid to Israel to relocate and construct what they needed in Brazil. Israel's security system today is tougher than any other country's system, and no violations of it have occurred since their relocation. You have legitimate grievances for actions in the past, but they are irrelevant to the issue of today," Baines said.

Next, Aziz compared the enactment of R-1948 to the first cautious steps a youngster makes into shallow water when he is learning to swim. "Wouldn't it be a shame if children never had a chance to experience the fun and excitement of swimming for fear of making that first step?" Aziz asked. "It's time for the people of the world to take the first step to a better life."

Lawrence came to the podium. The hall became quiet. "You have heard the delegate from the United States, my homeland, the honorable William Dulles charge us with a call to duty. I second that call. I have no hesitation that this body of worthy women and men will respond to that call in the highest fashion. To discharge that duty is why we were chosen to be here. This distinguished assembly of individuals acting on the behalf of all the people includes the best-educated, deepest thinkers and most conscientious spirits of our time. We are here and our time has come." Once again, Lawrence noticed his slowness of speech. Even though he was making an effort to quicken his pace, he just couldn't get the words out faster.

"And what is duty? Duty is defined as 'an act or a course of action that is exacted of one by position; moral obligation; the compulsion felt to meet such obligation.'" Lawrence held up a large book so everyone could see he was going to read from it. "And how is freedom defined? Webster's dictionary: 'Freedom:

the condition of being free of restraints; political independence; possession of civil rights; immunity from the arbitrary exercise of authority; the capacity to exercise choice, free will.'"

Lawrence closed the book and placed it on the podium. "John Stuart Mill stated it this way, 'The only freedom which deserves the name is that of pursuing our own good in our own way.' The people of the world do not have freedom today. We gave up freedom for security out of necessity. And where are we today? What is our need now that we are secure? I say that our need is the return to freedom." Cheers went up all over the hall. Many rose to their feet and shouted, "Freedom now, freedom now."

Lawrence raised his arms for silence, and when the cheers died down, he said, "No, we cannot have the freedom I defined yet. That freedom is but a goal. We must earn our right to that freedom step by step.

"William Dulles has warned us that to open the door to freedom even a small crack is dangerous. He is right, but I reject his definition of dangerous. To open the door to freedom is only dangerous to those who would deny to the people what they rightfully deserve. It is dangerous to them because once the people get a small taste of freedom, they will never again be satisfied with the bitter taste of state control. They will hunger for what is natural for all living beings, the right to pursue our own good in our own way. That is why it is so very important that we only open the door a small crack and see if the people of the world have learned their lesson and are mature enough to deserve the continuation along the path, step by step, to the goal we all yearn for--real freedom.

"William Dulles asked us to follow our heads to preserve what is dear to our hearts--peace and prosperity. Again, I reject his definition. What is dear to my heart is peace, prosperity, and freedom. And the greatest of these is freedom. Life as it should be lived can have no peace of mind or prosperity of value unless there is freedom of the mind, body and soul. Patrick Henry said it best, "Give me liberty or give me death."

The hall erupted in wild enthusiastic shouting, cheering, whistles, and applause. A large number of delegates rose and spilled into the aisles and marched to the front of the hall where they formed three groups calling out, "Freedom is our goal, freedom is our goal, freedom is our goal." But many remained seated and just watched, some in dismay.

CHAPTER 22

As Lawrence left the hall accompanied by many supporters, Byron with his arm around a smiling Moira, came up to him and said, "Dad, you were great. And evidently I did all right too. Moira, and her parents, said yes."

"Congratulations to you, son, and best wishes to you Moira," Lawrence said with a smile as full as Moira's. "This has been a big day for me, but your engagement is a really important event. I'm very happy for you both. Does Laura know yet?"

"Yes," answered Byron. "She and Mr. and Mrs. Browning are going to meet us at their home for champagne. You are the last to know because we didn't want to do anything to distract you before your speech. Hope you don't mind being last."

"That was very considerate of you both," Lawrence said. "I've had a lot going on. Anyway, now that we all know, it's time to celebrate. How about I'll order our personal vehicle to take us to Moira's home?"

When everyone was seated at the Browning's home and holding a glass of champagne, Lawrence proposed a toast. "Here's to Moira and Byron. How lucky we all are to have such as them in our families. They deserve the best. My fondest hope is that my gift to them will be a gift of a brighter, better future. I've been dedicated to the cause before today, but from this time on, I'm going to give everything I've got to achieve that gift. I'd sacrifice, well, I'd sacrifice . . . I guess I'd even put it on the line like Patrick Henry for them and, of course, Kate, Mike, Anne, and Kenneth and all others like them."

Laura's face showed the shock and fear she felt as she said, "Lawrence, don't say things like that. Don't do anything foolish and risk getting hurt. It's important, but life, your life and everyone else's, is too precious to be lost for a, a, . . . " And she broke down sobbing.

Lawrence rushed to Laura's side and took her in his arms. "Darling, I didn't mean to upset you. Nothing's going to happen to me. I just meant I'm really going to give my all for passage of my resolution."

Laura clung to Lawrence, sobbing into his shoulder, and Byron put his arm around his mother and said, "Mom, everything's going to be all right. Dad carried the day at the Council. I can feel it. R-1948 is going to pass. We poets can sense the emotions of others, and I can tell you the Council is in Dad's palm. It was a great day. Here, let me fill your glass. I've got a toast to make. Here's to the two best sets of parents any couple could have."

Laura dried her tears on her sleeve, but a tear dropped in the glass she held.

CHAPTER 23

The Council session for summation speeches started with a medical report on the condition of Roland Nilsson given by his sister Marie. She should have been clothed in a body cover to be in attendance in the Council Hall, but no one objected to the dark gray full-length dress she wore or the single red rose pinned above her breast. "Delegates of the Planet Council and guests, you all know that my brother's condition is what most people regard as hopeless. His capability rating has decreased to 91. Unless he has a miraculous recovery within the time limit set by law, he will be scheduled for euthanasia." Marie paused. Her voice became stronger as she said, "Since this will likely be my last appearance before you, it is my final chance to speak my piece to those with the power over the life and death of all the people on this planet. So I say to you, as a surgeon, I have witnessed several miraculous recoveries. Some have occurred quickly, but others took months. But they did happen; I was the doctor and my patience and care saved their lives."

Hurrying on, Marie said, "This is no longer a patient world. Sad to say, but for all practical purposes we have set a time limit on life. You may argue that the appeal process has prolonged many lives, but the number of successful appeals is insignificant. We have killed many great hearts and minds. My brother's will be next in the interest of cost and convenience. I damn the world for doing it. Politics is not my game, but the love of life and the obsession for freedom and liberty is more than my game or anyone else's--it's what makes life worthwhile. Under Council rules I should not be speaking about an issue before the Council without permission. My brother would have run me off the platform by now if he were here. But damn the rules and damn having to ask Big Brother for permission. For God's sake, for your own sake and that of your children, vote for R-1948."

The response to Marie's words was tremendous. Many delegates jumped up and applauded vigorously. Marie remained behind the podium obviously moved by the audience's reception of her appeal. Only after she had left the platform and delegates gradually took their seats did Council President van de Velde walk slowly to the podium. He announced that U.S. delegate Dulles would give the summary speech for those in opposition.

As William Dulles rose, he nodded in the direction where Marie had taken her seat in the audience and said, "No finer man, no finer citizen of the world has lived in my lifetime than Roland Nilsson. He has given his all for the good of humanity. The Council will recognize his contribution at the appropriate time and in the appropriate way, but I call on all of you to rise in a moment of silence in tribute to Roland and for those of you who, like me, are inclined to pray to their God, ask for a miraculous recovery in time." Dulles bowed his head. Almost all of the audience did the same as they rose and stood in silence. After more than a moment Dulles said, "Amen." The audience resumed their seats.

"It is in tribute to Roland and what he worked for that I ask you to give serious consideration to the continuance of Roland's good work. The Planet Council has built a house." Dulles first raised his arms and then spread them out as he said, "It is a large house with a good foundation. It is not built on sand. It is built on rock. Its walls are sturdy. All the huffing and puffing of evil forces will not blow this house down." Dulles stopped speaking as if he had huffed and puffed and he wanted the audience to notice that nothing had fallen.

"This house is equipped with a very superior alarm system. The alarm will go off if an intruder breaks into this house, but this alarm system is even better than that. This system screens potential intruders before they get through the gate out in the front yard."

Dulles paused and for the first time he smiled. His smile was not a wide, full and joyous smile, but upon his dour face, it made an impression. "Inside the house it is warm. The house is equipped with many conveniences. There is a nice family that lives in the house. Both parents have good jobs at which they can work hard because they exercise and are in good physical condition. When the parents are at home or away, they carry weapons that cannot kill but can temporarily disable another person or animal that threatens their safety. They have two children. Both are healthy and are in good schools. They can quote Shakespeare, Homer, Joyce, and Goethe and many others."

Dulles's face resumed its normal bland expression as he said, "When the children prepare for their future, they will receive assistance to find out and train for the occupation best suited to their abilities. If the children want to marry, they will get help in finding a compatible partner and preparing for a long and happy life with their mate. If after marriage they want to have children, they will get help in determining if they are suitable for parenthood and how to be good parents. When the parents grow too old to work and are tired and are no longer able to perform useful work, they will get assistance in determining whether they should go on, many times in pain or suffering, or whether it is best that they give up their space to younger, healthier men and women. Roland Nilsson helped build this house and arrange for all the good things in it and the help for the people who live in it. I am sure that if Roland were here with us today he would urge us to keep this house just as it is. He would not like for the family inside or the house itself to suffer harm."

Dulles took a drink of water from the glass on the podium as if to let the audience have time to absorb the points he had made before he gave his concluding argument. "It is unusual that proponents and opponents are in agreement about an important aspect of a proposal, and I would not have expected that to be the case with this resolution. But I have listened carefully to the proponents, and I agree with them that this proposal will change the house that the Council has built and the living conditions for those inside considerably. With passage of R-1948 some potential intruders will be able to come near the house and, if skillful, even enter the house undetected. What happens next, the proponents admit they do not know, but they want more changes. Perhaps the next thing might be that the parents can quit exercising resulting in a decline in their productive efforts. Or perhaps the parents decide to try mind-altering drugs or not be diligent in keeping their children drug free. Perhaps one of the children on drugs needs money and

mugs a defenseless older person who no longer carries a stun gun. And...and...
and on and on until terrorists are on the loose again, and the world is back in the
terrible shape it was. Roland Nilsson spent his life to build a house so these things
couldn't happen. Don't let him down."

The applause following Dulles's speech was not so loud as it was long. Many
heads nodded in approval. Marie rose to walk out; Eric, who was seated next to
her, reached out to take her by the arm and said, "Wait until we hear Lawrence's
answer."

Van de Velde announced that Peoples' Advocate Lawrence Holmes would
give the summation speech for the proponents. Lawrence's gait across the platform
was noticeably slow and slightly unsteady. Friends, and perhaps most of the delegates, attributed his unusual pace to his being tired. He paused when he reached
the podium and looked towards the Nilsson family. Lawrence started speaking in a
slow, deliberate voice and said, "Mr. Chairman, fellow delegates, guests, and members of the Nilsson family. I helped build the house the honorable William Dulles
has so well described. I watched when the foundation was laid and when the roof
was put on. Mr. Dulles is right. It is a well-built house and it has served its purpose
well. The family inside was made safe and secure from the many threats to them.
This house is so strong, so well guarded, so secure that you might say it is as safe and
impenetrable as, as . . . the prison buildings we used to have."

Lawrence paused long enough to look from side to side over his audience.
His expression had changed from placid to somber as he spoke of prisons. His tone
gradually changed from somber to grave as he continued. "Lately, some members
of the families inside those houses have become dissatisfied with living in such a
guarded environment. Some have become depressed. More and more of them
have decided to give up trying, give up even the most precious gift of all--life."

Lawrence's face lightened as he said, "What this house needs is sunshine and
fresh air. I don't advocate we unlock the doors and leave the windows open at
night. I suggest we open up the blinds and let the sunshine of limited freedom in
for those whose records indicate they can handle the responsibility that goes with
freedom. And after we open the blinds and before we open anything else, we watch
and see what the results of opening the blinds are. If it doesn't work out, we may
have to close the blinds until some time later. But if it works and the sunshine of
freedom brings joy and life in abundance, we take the next careful step to allow all
the members of the family achieve their highest capabilities." The cheers were loud
and lasted. The Nilsson family joined Lawrence on the platform to express their
appreciation for his message.

CHAPTER 24

"Do you think it'll pass?" Peggy Browning asked her husband as they left the Council Hall. Peggy, unlike Laura, attended most Council sessions without any qualmishness.

"I don't think anyone knows for certain, I sure don't, but if I were betting I would bet it will," John said.

"Moira doesn't seem as anxious about its outcome as I thought she would be. And Byron has been calmer than I expected. I'm glad he congratulated his father after the rebuttal session, especially after what Moira told me he said to him the day Lawrence presented his resolution."

"Lawrence's insistence that his children feel free to express their feelings, even when they are upsetting, has resulted in many turbulent family encounters over the years, I'm sure." John paused, a serious expression on his face, and continued, " Sometimes I wonder if I've someway or other inhibited Moira. From what I've heard from Carlos, she doesn't hesitate to mix it up with Byron, but she's never said a critical word to me even when we've disagreed."

"I don't recall anyone saying that Anne or even Kate have been critical of their father. Maybe this is just a father-son thing. Freud said something about all politics really being just a primal conflict between father and son. He didn't include daughters."

"Freud did say something about women that I've always remembered. It was one of the things my father told me on our wedding day."

"What are you talking about? You've never said anything about it before."

"I've been waiting for a good occasion after we've been married long enough I thought it safe. Freud said, and I quote my father verbatim, 'The great question which I have not been able to answer, despite my thirty years of research into the feminine soul, is what does a woman want?'"

"What's so contentious about that? It doesn't take a Freud to know that men don't understand women. Never have and never will."

"But women, of course, understand men?"

"Obviously, where have you been all your life?"

"In the dark, obviously."

CHAPTER 2♢

On the morning after the summation speeches, Lawrence met with his supporters in a Council Hall caucus room. The afternoon before at the conclusion of his speech he had made assignments to contact every delegate who had not clearly indicated how they stood on R-1948 to count noses for their side. After his supporters picked up coffee and donuts from the serving table, Lawrence asked them to report one by one.

When Maurice reported he was not able to get straight answers, Lawrence said not to count any votes but sure ones in the first tally. The first tally total was seventy-five votes for the resolution out of the one hundred eighty possible. Then the group discussed additional possible votes and decided that ten more were probable to give eighty-five as their highest probable number. The room got quiet. Five short of what was needed was close, but no cigar.

Aziz broke the silence. "Lawrence, I know you don't want to do it, and we may lose a few votes if we do, but there is no choice. We have to make a deal with the Muslims or we're going to lose."

No one said a word as they waited for Lawrence's answer. He bowed his head slightly, closed his eyes and raised his hands to cover his cheeks, as if he wanted to remove himself from the scene. The group was familiar with that pose. Lawrence was thinking it over. After a long pause, he looked up and turned his head to one side and then back to the other to take into his glances all of the group. Then he asked each one, "Do you agree with Aziz?"

Birgitta said she didn't like the deal with the Muslims, but she would go along with it rather than lose. Some of the group made qualifying statements, but each, in essence, agreed with Aziz. "No sense discussing it anymore," Lawrence said. "I'll make the deal today. If I have problems, I'll get back to you. Thanks for your help and honest answers."

Later that afternoon Lawrence called Aziz and told him they had picked up eighteen votes with the deal with the Muslims, so it looked as if they were going to make it. Aziz said he was pleased, but he didn't have time to get more details because he had to return a call from his South African Minister of Foreign Affairs.

CHAPTER 26

When Lawrence got home, Laura was having some of Byron's favorite Chardonnay. As he took a seat at the bar, she put her hand on the side of his face rubbing it gently and said, "Someway or other you look happy and worried at the same time. Or is just happy and tired?"

"You were right the first time. Apparently we have the votes, but for some reason or another I'm uneasy. It may just be that I had to do something that I didn't much want to do. I didn't do anything underhanded or probably even unexpected, but it didn't feel right."

"Did you ask the others how they felt about it?" Laura sipped her wine.

Lawrence helped himself from a bowl of cashews, one of his favorite bar snacks. "I asked them before I did it. There were some misgivings, but all were agreeable to it. I could dodge the responsibility by saying it was a group decision, but it wasn't. No one would have said a word if I hadn't gone along with their recommendation. It was my call."

"Well, are you going to tell me what the big "it" you did was or do I have to see it on the news?" Laura's glass was less than half full.

"It won't be on the news tonight. Or I sure hope it won't. I made a deal with the Muslims to support them in getting higher birth rates in return for their votes for R-1948." Lawrence got up and moved to the backside of the bar, got a wineglass and poured himself a glass of wine.

"What's wrong with that. You made the same deal with the dark skins."

"The higher rate for them is justified. It will just help them get back to even. They were held way down for a long time. The deal with the Muslims is pure politics. They weren't held back except in Afghanistan and Iraq and a little bit in Iran. They just want to have more power through more votes."

"And it looks like they'll get it. If you can get R-1948 passed, then you probably will have the votes to get the rates raised for dark skins and Muslims."

"Well, I can't guarantee all my supporters will go along, but they will be very sympathetic. This is a good Chardonnay. Byron knows his wines."

"Politics does make strange bedfellows." Laura finished her glass of wine and Lawrence filled her glass again, but this time not a full glass.

"Speaking of bedfellows," Lawrence said as he put his arm around Laura's neck and pulled her lips to his. Would you like to be mine after we finish these?"

"Drink up fellow," Laura said as she took a big swallow of her wine and poured the rest into the sink. "I'm ready now."

Lawrence took one more slip of his wine, took Laura's hand and said to the bar light control, "Lights out."

CHAPTER 27

Since the Planet Council vote was not until the following day, Lawrence changed his sleeping chamber schedule to be awakened at 08:00. When he arose, Merlin's sleep report evaluated his resting rating at 17.4. That compared well with his average of 14.1 for the last month and was the high over the last year. The report ended with a recommended time for his entering his sleeping chamber of 22:15 for this evening. Lawrence wondered if he would make it by then because the night before a Council vote was usually a late one for him. He had decided to stay at home in order to be readily available for private calls from supporters who were calling delegates to check on any new developments.

The first call he received was from Thomas Baines. "Have you heard anything from Aziz? I've been trying to get him all morning but haven't gotten through to him or received a call back to my voice message."

"No. That's unusual. It may involve his Minister of Foreign Affairs, the new guy. I can't remember his name. Aziz mentioned that he had to call him back yesterday."

"Who's responsible for Afghanistan? We better be sure they are staying put. By the way, how many of those twenty votes they estimated would we get for sure?"

"I talked to Ahmad yesterday. He said we could count on eighteen and they were solid. I'll give him a call. How about your contacts?"

"My group is still on board, and we will probably get an unexpected vote from New Zealand, unless the U.S. threatens to cancel their order for 28% of their new gold production. I hadn't included them in my nose count because they are so dependent on the U.S., but they're an independent thinking country and want to go with us."

"Thanks for your call. I'll try Aziz." Lawrence disconnected from Tom and told Merlin to call Aziz. Aziz's recorded message said that he was in a meeting and would not be available until later in the day, Merlin reported.

Lawrence told Merlin to call Ahmad Ahdali. Ahmad was in a meeting and would not be available until in the afternoon. "Hmm," Lawrence thought. "I wonder if they are in the same meeting. And if so, with whom?"

Late in the afternoon, Lawrence got his answer when he received a call from Aziz. That Aziz was distressed was obvious. "Lawrence, terrible news. I'm using an outside, secure line because I'm not supposed to be telling you this, so please keep it confidential."

"Are you O.K., Aziz?"

"I'm not going to be fired, but I may resign. My government has double-crossed me and, therefore, you. They have ordered me to vote against R-1948 and take no part in influencing anyone to vote for it. They said I don't have to solicit votes against it; that's probably because they don't want you to know what's going on. I considered resigning on the spot but decided to talk to you first in case it might help you for me to still be a delegate."

"What happened to make them change?"

"They wouldn't tell me, but I know they had a call from Dulles this morning. I think he got wind last night that the Muslims came over to us. He'd know that would give us enough votes, so he figured out some way to switch my country's position. Dulles may be, probably is, working on our other supporters."

"What do you think Dulles could offer or use to threaten South Africa?"

"I don't know and my government wouldn't tell me. They have a lot of respect for you, but someone has gotten to them. And I can't think of any country other than yours that could make them go against something that is so much in their interest. So, I think it must be Dulles doing the dirty work."

"First of all, do what is best for you, your future, your family and all the good causes you have worked for. Don't resign for me no matter how badly you feel about what your government is doing. I'll survive and I think my cause will regardless of how this turns out. South Africa's vote is just one vote. With the Muslim votes, we're still ahead. I appreciate your calling. Of course no one else will ever know from me what you did, not even Laura. You know this in no way changes how I feel about you. Good luck."

"Thanks Lawrence, and good luck to you. You may need it more than I will."

Lawrence called his other supporters and found that their contacts did not indicate any changes in the countries they contacted. Lawrence thought he had better check with another delegate from a dark skin country. He told Merlin, "Contact, Jomo arap Moi, the delegate from Kenya. Jomo was unavailable, Merlin reported. "Try him again in twenty minutes," Lawrence told Merlin.

Lawrence decided to take a walk. He called to Laura and told her where he was going and he'd be back in time for dinner. Walking was a device Lawrence had used when he was with the *Post Dispatch* and was working on a column or story that troubled him. While walking he seemed better able to sort things out. As he headed outside, a gentle breeze fluttered the leaves of the two hard maples in his front yard. So few New Yorkers had a yard, much less beautiful trees, that Lawrence felt ashamed to be disturbed by his concern for his resolution. He had a wonderful, supportive family and so many benefits the average person wouldn't have during their entire life that he felt nothing should upset him that wasn't a vital threat to his family.

Lawrence walked down the street and noticed that a neighbor three houses from his had resodded his lawn, and it looked much better than his own. "I'll tell Laura to take a look at it," Lawrence thought. "We might want to do the same, it's spring time." In the next block, a large barking boxer charged out to the fence in front of his master's home to let Lawrence know he'd better not cause his master any trouble. Lawrence waited patiently for the barking to stop and succeeded in getting to rub behind the boxer's ears.

Lawrence turned back towards his house walking briskly and feeling much better. As he turned into his yard, Merlin signaled an incoming message, "Jomo's now reported as unavailable until tomorrow." Lawrence slowed down as he walked towards his front door.

"Lunch's ready," Laura said as Lawrence came in. She noticed his lifelessness, but didn't say anything until they were seated at the counter.

"What's wrong, darling?" Laura asked as she placed her left hand over his right one.

Lawrence had a roll in his left hand. He had been holding it for several seconds. He put it back on his plate. "I think the big boys have shown why they are the big boys. It reminds me of when my high school basketball team made the state finals. We had a great team, and we beat everyone in our district hands down." Lawrence had been looking down at his plate. He looked up and turned towards Laura. She still held his hand. "Then we went to the state tournament. It was in St. Louis. We had never played in such a big place. A lot of our fans were there, but they didn't look like much among so many people. Our opponents were bigger and taller. We were faster and better shots, but, I realized later, they were better coached. By the first quarter, we were behind twenty points. We did better as the game went along and only lost by ten."

Lawrence's face tightened and the line in his forehead was more noticeable than usual. He stood up and walked around. "I've been an advocate and had some influence on the Council, but this is the first time I've gone up against the powers that be. They are bigger and taller. I'm going to lose."

Laura stood up and moved next to Lawrence. "I thought with the Muslims you had the votes."

"We do, if every body stays in place. But I'm pretty sure that the opposition has made some changes that we'll see when the game starts. You might call them substitutions."

CHAPTER 28

The voting session of the Council was late in starting. The delegates' computer screens indicated why. Twelve delegates and nine alternate delegates had resigned and the credentials of their replacements had to be presented and checked before the session could begin. Lawrence saw that most were from dark skin nations and the rest from Muslim nations. Aziz was on the list as well as his alternate. At 09:50 Henri van de Velde called the Council to order and said he had an announcement to make in regard to Roland Nilsson. The Nilsson family had decided to fly Roland to Sweden and prepare to have euthanasia and the funeral ceremony there, so Roland would have his last days in his homeland. The funeral was scheduled for next week in Stockholm. All who wanted to attend should notify Marie Nilsson.

Van de Velde was ready to announce that the voting on R-1948 would begin when William Dulles rose and said, "Mr. Chairman, I rise to make a substitute motion." At Council sessions only certain parliamentary procedures had privilege over the motion on the floor. A substitute motion was one of those procedures and, if passed, had the same effect as to defeat the main motion. Van de Velde recognized Dulles to make his motion.

As Dulles made his way to the podium, the buzz of dozens of inquiries between delegates asking each other "What's going on?" was so loud that van de Velde gaveled the meeting to order. Even though Lawrence knew that James was planning to vote against him, he scooted his chair closer to James and said, "Looks as if I'm about to find out how the game is played in the big leagues."

James turned to look Lawrence squarely in the face and said, "Lawrence, I can't tell you the details of what is about to happen, but I want you to know that I didn't initiate it, and I spoke against it. It's not fair play in my book. As you know, I have no power over the U.S. delegation. But I do have my own vote, and I'm on your side now. This is an issue of principle with me. Evidently it was with those delegates who resigned, too. You'll soon know that those resignations were in protest to governments directing their delegates to change and vote against you."

Lawrence reached out his hand to shake James's and said, "That means a lot to me regardless of how this turns out. Thank you, James." Before Lawrence could say anything more, Dulles was at the podium.

Dulles waited for quiet and then said, "Mr. Chairman, fellow delegates and guests. The issue before the Council is a serious one, and we of the U.S. delegation have given it our sincere consideration. We cannot support R-1948, but we acknowledge it is time for change and this substitute motion, if passed, will make a change immediately." Dulles held a sheet of paper in front of him and read, 'Resolved, that the Planet Council order the birth rate for all those families classified as dark skin anywhere in the world be changed to allow unlimited births for one year after which the rate will be set at the same rate as that of white Caucasian families residing in the U.S., and furthermore, that the birth rates for Muslim families everywhere be increased by 6 % above the existing rates.' This resolution is to become effective upon passage of this substitute motion."

Shouts of "No, no, no" could be heard above the applause. Many delegates rose to their feet and shook clenched fists in the air. Van de Velde tried to restore order, but he could not. Several delegates left their seats to gather in the aisles. Dulles remained at the podium; he was calm and seemed unperturbed. Dulles turned to van de Velde to indicate he had more to say, but even when van de Velde banged his gavel on his desk, he could not restore order for several minutes.

James turned to Lawrence and said, "Sorry, I couldn't let you know in advance. Yesterday Dulles told me that he had an important point about R-1948 he wanted to get my opinion on, but he would only tell me if I agreed to keep the matter confidential."

Lawrence said, " If I had known, it wouldn't have made any difference. The U.S. gave the dark skins something I couldn't, and that's why their governments overrode their delegates' recommendations. I could only offer hope for better birth rates. This way they'll get something for sure and more than they could hope for with my help. I'm sure increasing the Muslim's rate made it a done deal for Dulles. He wanted to show where the real power is."

"I still believe the real power is with the people," James said. "Sometimes it takes a dramatic event to produce a change, but you have gotten the process moving."

"I hope you're right. Right now, I'm not optimistic."

"Well, I'm on your side now. We won't have the Muslin issue to deal with when we bring it up next time. I think you lost some credibility by the deal you made with the Muslims. Dulles told me about it. I was a little surprised, but I understood why your group felt they had to do it."

"You're right about that, James. I wasn't happy with the Muslim deal, but I thought it was for the 'greater good' as they call it."

"The other side thought they were for the 'greater good' also. That's been a problem throughout history. Obviously, determining the 'greater good' is not that easy. I changed sides over night."

Order was finally restored. Dulles continued, "In addition to the substitute motion, I will make the following proposal if the substitute is passed. 'Resolved that a commission be appointed to study the probable effect of the passage of R-1948 to answer the many questions that were asked during its debate. Data was not available to answer those questions. My resolution will call for the findings of the commission to be reported back to the Council no later than in six months. Thank you Mr. Chairman, I move the question of the substitute motion so we can vote." Dulles walked slowly across the platform to return to his seat.

"I'm sure you can predict who will be appointed to that commission and what their report will recommend--more time to study," James said to Lawrence. "Dulles is throwing you a bone that he hopes will quell the uproar. I think he is underestimating world reaction. 'Don't give up the ship yet, Lawrence."

"I hope you're right. But I wouldn't want there to be any violence to come out of my movement. I don't want any lives sacrificed."

"Lawrence, you know history. For true progress there have always been lives lost. Someone has to make sacrifices. It's often the sacrifice that ignites the cause. Hamilton's duel discredited Burr and his supporters who were a real threat to our young Republic, and it practically ended dueling too. Look at Christianity. Would it have succeeded if Christ hadn't been crucified? Basically, I was for your resolution. I just felt the time wasn't quite right. I think the protests we have seen needed to reach a higher pitch so that the powers that be felt so threatened that they had to loosen the chains. As usually happens, the first reaction to protests is tighten the grip. That's where we are now. But over time I think the changes will come."

Van deVelde announced voting would commence. The delegates signaled their vote from their desk when their name was called, and it was flashed to all delegates on their computer screens. A delegate could pass when their first turn came, but if they passed a second time, they lost their vote on the issue in question. Frequently, countries dependent on other larger countries, usually one of The Big Three, passed until they saw how the vote was going. Several of the countries supporting Lawrence passed until the substitute motion has a majority. When it did, many passed the second time as a method of showing their disdain for the countries whose governments had overridden the judgement of their delegates. Lawrence cast his vote against the substitute motion when his time came. He didn't forgo his vote as a protest, because he had made the same kind of deal to get the Muslim vote as Dulles did. He felt the kettle couldn't call the pot black.

A majority for the substitute resolution was achieved two-thirds of the way through the role call. A few delegates walked out without taking time to record passing on the second round. So many didn't vote that the final vote was ninety-seven for and eighteen against. Russia and China abstained. Sixty-three delegates wanted no part in the action of the Council that day.

After the vote, James turned to Lawrence to express his sorrow, but Lawrence was already on his feet and headed for the aisle. "Got to catch Byron," Lawrence said as he hurried up the aisle.

Lawrence half ran to the family and visitors section, but Byron was gone. Carlos was still there and Lawrence asked him, "How did Byron take it?"

"We had gotten wind of the deal Dulles made with the dark skins and the Muslims through, well, I'd better not say who told us, so Byron was prepared for what happened. He wasn't as infuriated as I would have expected. That intensity he has when he feels strongly about something was there, but he didn't say much. He and Moira left as soon as Dulles made his motion. We all knew how it would turn out. Sorry, Mr. Holmes. You did a great job, but, . . ."

Lawrence interrupted to say, "Thanks Carlos. Do you know where Byron has gone?"

"He, Moira, Eric and Anastasia were going together to the hospital to see Marie. Eric has been taking them to see Marie regularly, and she wanted to talk to them. I guess it's about Roland's funeral."

"Thanks. I'll try to reach him," Lawrence said to Carlos. "How did Moira take it?"

"She is only worried about Byron. I'm glad she's there for him."

"Me, too. I'll try Byron now." Lawrence told Merlin, "Contact Byron on his personal computer. "

Byron's computer answered, "The person you are trying to contact is unavailable at this time. To leave a message, please start recording at the beep." Lawrence for the umpteenth time thought, "After all these years, couldn't they come up with a different, say friendlier message than that." He was glad that Moira was with Byron. It probably helped that he was with the others, too. Lawrence hoped that the group might do something special, which would help relieve the disappointment he knew they were suffering.

As Lawrence was leaving the section for family members and guests, a columnist for the New York *Times*, Wanda Newton, came up to him and said, "Mr. Holmes, I've been looking all over for you. Could you please give me your reaction to the vote?"

"Sure, Wanda," Lawrence answered, "but this will be brief and more like a comment, because those for R-1948 plan to make a statement tomorrow. For now, I am glad that the Directorate allowed my resolution be debated and come to a vote. That, in itself, brought attention here at the Council and throughout the world to the issue I wanted to raise. I am disappointed in the outcome, but I am pleased with the effort we made, and I thank all those who supported me. That's probably not as much as you would like to have, but that's all I have to say this evening."

"Thank you and I understand. There is one more thing that you may not be aware of that has come up in regard to your resolution. After the vote I called my office to get a report on international reactions. Our paper was covering several of the gatherings that the Patrick Henry Clubs organized to watch the Council proceedings including those in Paris, London, Madrid, Moscow and Montreal. At some locations, near rioting broke out even before the final votes were cast. A great deal of damage was done at some places, Madrid for one, but no reports of injuries have been received. Had you thought about the likelihood of this?"

"Not specifically, but I have been alarmed at the growth in protests, especially in the last year, and I have predicted that unless the people of the world are given hope their basic freedoms will be restored, there is going to be trouble. I want to make clear, please include this in your report of this conversation, that I do not condone breaking the law and damaging property. I am glad no one has been hurt. I want any support for my position to be expressed in a non-violent manner. Those who do otherwise harm my cause and can start something that might well bring harm to themselves and all people. My statement tomorrow will emphasize that point. Now, I must be going."

Wanda started to ask another question, but changed her mind and said, "Thank you, Mr. Holmes, and . . ." Wanda's expression was sympathetic, but she didn't finish her sentence.

"Thank you, Wanda. I'll not quote what I saw in your face," Lawrence said with a smile.

CHAPTER 29

When Lawrence got home, Laura met him at the door and put her arms around his neck and said, "Want to go out and hang one on, darling? You sure have a right to. I watched the vote on the Council Continuous channel."

"Maybe, but tell me did you find out today what English classes you'll be taking?" They walked into the media room and sat down on the back row couch that Kate kidded was there for those times when a couple was watching a sexy movie.

"Three basic survey classes, a composition class, a philosophy of teaching class and three electives. I want one of the electives to be in poetry."

"With your ability and Byron as a private tutor, you'll cause a problem for the other regular students." Lawrence was good at poker faces.

"What problem?" Laura's voice expressed more alarm than surprise.

"Your work will set such a high standard for the top grade that other students will have trouble getting a level forty in the course."

"I don't mean to be a problem." Laura looked at Lawrence and caught his slight smile. "Are you kidding me?"

"Yes, love. I want you to ace your classes. We'll all get to see you graduate with honors."

Laura looked down at her folded hands. "I really don't like what Dulles did. It's hard to believe that our own country has changed so much in the last two or three decades. We used to be the leaders for freedom and liberty."

"Don't be so hard on our leaders. They are doing what they think best. It's a huge burden to have the responsibility for the safety of the planet on your shoulders. If they are going to err, they want it to be on the side that protects lives more than rights. Sometimes I almost agree with them. And it's the easy way out, too."

"Don't let Byron hear you say any of that. He is really proud that you have taken the lead."

"Have you heard from him? I tried to get to him as soon as the vote was over, but he left before I got to where he was seated."

"Not a word. I'm glad he's got Moira. I'm sure she's with him, thank God. He may hang one on tonight even if you don't."

"I really couldn't blame him. When I was his age, I would have. And regretted it the next day, but still have done it the next time. Remember when I ranted and raved when the Congress agreed to world government?"

Laura stood up and took Lawrence's hands to have him stand up beside her. "Let's call our private vehicle and go to the most expensive place we can think of. You deserve something special. O.K.?"

"O.K. And to hell with caution tonight." Lawrence slipped his hand inside Laura's blouse as he kissed her.

CHAPTER 3∇

"The undersigned delegates of the Planet Council wish to express their appreciation to the Directorate for permitting R-1948 to be debated and voted on by the full Council," was the opening sentence of the news release, which Lawrence delivered to the Council headquarters late on the morning after the Council vote.

Lawrence had met with his supporters at breakfast earlier that day and asked them, one by one, to recommend what they thought should be included in the news release. Some of the group were so angry they didn't contribute anything but bitter complaints. Cooler heads made constructive suggestions.

The release continued: "We accept the decisions as the will of the Council. We feel that important issues were involved, and the floor of the Council was the proper setting for deliberations on those issues. We are disappointed that R-1948 did not receive a majority vote, but progress has been made. The substitute motion did pass and will result in needful changes in the birth rates. This is the first such change to come about in several years. We look forward to participation in the commission to study the effect of passage of R-1948. In order to assure that the commission fully understand the intent of R-1948, we respectfully request that half of the members of the commission be selected from the attached list of delegates."

The release concluded with: "We regret that consideration of R-1948 evidently played a part in the resignation or replacement of many well-qualified and experienced delegates who have given conscientious service to the Council. We hope that the governments involved will reappoint many of those delegates either now or when new terms begin. Those delegates, in our opinion, acted unselfishly to promote the well-being of their constituents and the peoples of this planet." When Lawrence delivered the statement to the Council headquarters he said that he would be available in the pressroom at 11:30 to answer questions.

At 11:30 Lawrence opened the news conference with an additional statement: "The supporters of R-1948 are concerned about the continuing public disturbances that have resulted in property damage and violations of public safety laws. Our purpose in introducing and urging passage of our resolution was not to trigger these unlawful activities, and they are damaging to our cause. We urge that all persons participating in such activities to cease them immediately and do not renew them. We are starting a fund to reimburse those parties who have suffered property damage. Anyone wishing to contribute to this fund, contact the office of the Planet Council Secretary General which has agreed to receive contributions and hold them in escrow until guidelines are established for proper reimbursements."

"Mr. Holmes, if these what I would call riots, not disturbances, escalate, what additional activities would you anticipate?" a reporter from the London *Times* asked.

Lawrence paused to think through and carefully word his reply. "I have not given your question consideration and am reluctant to name any such activity in the fear that some might say I was calling for them in protest of the defeat of R-1948. Our group is not protesting the decision of the Council. The issue, like others, was considered, debated and then voted on. Proposals are voted either up or down. This one was voted down."

"In light of the tremendous publicity you are receiving, which according to recent polls has established you as the most admired individual in the world, are you considering running for elective office in the United States?" the representative of the weekly *Planet Personalities* asked.

"No. Next question."

"But the polls indicate that you could be elected to anything," the questioner continued.

"Next question."

"What do you plan to do now that your resolution was defeated?" Allen Sturey of the St. Louis *Post Dispatch* asked.

"I'd like to have my old job back, Allen, but I wouldn't like for you to lose yours," Lawrence said with a big smile on his face. "Seriously, I plan to continue as a Peoples' Advocate if the Council still wants someone who has raised such a ruckus."

The concluding questions tried to draw out more confrontational answers but didn't, and the conference ended on a flat note.

After the news conference Lawrence decided to find out for himself what the so-called "average citizen" felt about the defeat of his resolution. So he told Merlin, "Haircut in fifteen minutes. Harry if possible."

As Lawrence walked into Tony's Trim a short distance from the Council Hall on a side street, Tony looked over from his first chair position and nodded to him. Lawrence preferred that Harry rather than Tony cut his hair, because Harry occupied the last chair in the five-chair barbershop and wasn't, like Tony, concerned if his politics offended his customer or not. Lawrence had happened on to Tony's Trim one afternoon when he was looking for a gift for Laura at an antique shop next door to Tony's place. He was surprised to see the red and white barber poll and find a few of the old-time shops still operating. Lawrence's cleansing chamber included hair styling equipment that offered an illustrated selection of hair fashions which were accomplished by use of low power laser beams and a computer controlled blower that removed, curled, waved, or otherwise styled hair in accordance with the input by the customer on the attached keyboard. Like his preference for an unnecessary shower, Lawrence preferred a manual haircut because it made him feel good, and he liked to find out what Harry, his "average citizen," thought about the hot items of the day.

That Harry was available to cut Lawrence's hair on such short notice was not unusual. Harry was not popular with many of Tony's customers and survived financially on the large tips of those who wanted an opinionated New York barber to cut and critique at the same time.

"You got a lot of life insurance?" Harry asked as Lawrence settled himself in chair number five.

"Yes, do you want a piece of it for a price?" Lawrence replied.

"No way. You got a wife and kids. Maybe even a dog, huh?" Harry started snipping away starting with Lawrence's left side around his ear.

"Had a bulldog, but the summer before last was just too hot for him. Bartlett was seven."

"Well, what do ya want to know? I actually have an appointment in fifteen minutes with a big tipper, unlike you. I'll be done in a minute or two with your trim. I don't think you needed a haircut. You just wanted to talk. Go ahead."

"What are the odds on real problems developing because of my resolution? I mean on the violence side."

"I was kidding about your insurance. I don't think they'll hurt you or your family, but I think there will be some who get hurt, maybe bad."

"Some or many?"

Harry didn't answer for a minute while he used an electric razor on the back of Lawrence's neck. "Depends. I heard your speeches. I agree people are getting antsy. They feel it's time things loosened up. If The Big Three tighten the screws too much on these protesters, some are gonna snap. I'll turn you around so you can see if I've trimmed enough."

"What can I do about it?"

"Nothin.' It all depends on what the authorities do, and I don't think you've got much influence with them right now."

"You're right about that."

"I'm right about everything. That's why you keep coming back. I'm done. How do you look?"

"Better than when I came in. Here's all the folding money I've got. I don't want to be a cheapskate."

"I take checks."

"Go on. You won't get a tip that big this month."

"You're right. Just kidding. Thanks for comin' in. Good luck."

Lawrence gave Tony a smaller tip on his way out. He wanted to be sure Tony kept Harry.

PART TWO

CHAPTER Λ

Lawrence was seated in his home office reading Faulkner's T*he Sound and the Fury*. It was one of ten books his college creative writing instructor had recommended for the class. Lawrence made an effort to reread all ten every ten years, one each year. At the same time Lawrence was reading ***Siberian Ire*** (by a professor who was Boris Gorbachev's colleague), a new novel like ***The Sound and the Fury*** about three brothers. Byron came in and Lawrence put his book down and said, "What have you been reading lately? Anything you think I'd like?"

"Moira and I borrowed Eric and Anastasia's manual on engagement probation and have been reading it together. I think you and Mom don't need it."

"Maybe we'll write our own version some day."

"I'd like to read that." Byron took a chair opposite his Dad. His head was bowed and in an uncharacteristic low, soft voice said, "Dad, all the JD's Seven group want you to know how much they appreciate your efforts. We all feel that the U.S. didn't really even consider the merits of your argument. They are blind to what's going on in the world."

Lawrence looked at Byron and was reminded of the time that Byron had protested to his level three teacher that the grading system was unfair. Byron had worked out a new system that he was very excited about, wrote out the plan, and presented it to his teacher. His teacher, according to Byron, just listened to his proposal so he could claim he had given him a fair hearing. The teacher said he would think about it and get back with him, but Byron was sure nothing would change. When Byron came home from school and told about it at dinner that night, his head was bowed at just the same angle that it was now.

"I like your group a lot. I wish I could have gotten it passed. I'm not giving up. I'm just going to change tactics."

"I want to go to Sweden to be with Eric at his father's funeral service which is Fifthday at 14:00," Byron said as he looked up. "I hope to get a discount of my air bus ticket. Eric thinks that Air Sweden gives discounts to close friends of the family if they have student status. I may qualify because of the Canadian literature class I'm taking. Anyway, I'm planning to go and Moira and the rest of JD's Seven are going too. We're leaving day after tomorrow to get there in time for the service."

"I'll make up the difference if you don't get the discount," Lawrence said. "I thought about going to the services, but I feel run down. I've even been unsteady walking, and when I was making my speeches, I couldn't seem to get my words out quickly enough." Lawrence sensed that Byron had some purpose for this visit. He was talking in a casual way, but it wasn't quite natural.

"When was your last full physical? You had better check on those symptoms. That's not like you to be unsteady."

"My last full physical was not too long ago. I called Rex's office for an appointment and told his nurse about my walking and talking problems. She called back and Rex is going to work me in as soon as he can. It's good that your group will be there with Eric. How long do you plan to stay?" Byron hesitated before answering. He seemed nervous.

"Eric is making arrangements for us to stay with friends of the family and wants us to go camping with him afterwards. Probably a week or ten days. I've checked with my bureau chief and he gave me his O.K."

"Do you want to take my small portable heater? It may get cold in the evenings in a tent."

"That would be swell if you're sure you won't need it for awhile. And thanks for the help on the ticket, if I need it, Dad." Byron turned to leave.

Lawrence called out, "Have you told your mother you're going?"

Byron turned back and paused as if he was thinking over how to answer. "Not yet, but I will, unless you want to tell her." Byron looked to the side.

"No, you tell her. I'm sure she'll be pleased and probably will have a lot of questions."

Byron's slight frown puzzled Lawrence. Byron usually told his mother things like this first, and Lawrence heard it from Laura.

Lawrence asked, "Do you want your granddad's old Boy Scout manual, too? You may remember it even tells how to roast an ox. I wonder if they have oxen in the forests of Sweden. I've kept the manual for sentimental reasons. It's hopelessly out of date, but there are some good basic camping tips."

"I picked up the latest version of *Camping Guide*, but I'd like to take your granddad's manual, too. Maybe we'll find a bear to roast." Byron seemed more at ease.

"If you go looking for bear, carry a big stick." Lawrence's smile was embarrassed. He looked as if he wished he could take his joke back.

"Funny, funny, Dad. I think you told me that one when I was six." Byron paused and then smiled at his father. "But I like hearing it, again. We'll be careful."

Relieved, Lawrence smiled back. Their eyes met and Lawrence noticed a softness in Byron's expression he didn't often see.

As they headed out of the room together, Lawrence raised his arm to put it around Byron's shoulder but pulled it back. Byron happened to turn towards him just then and saw Lawrence's gesture. Byron stopped and put his arm around his father's shoulder, and they walked out together.

CHAPTER 2

"Do you have any medications you need to have refilled?" Moira asked Byron. "It'll be a lot more trouble over there." They were in Moira's bedroom at her parents' house. She was sitting on the floor next to a large, dark-blue camping pack that was open. It was nearly full of casual wear including a new lightweight thermal jacket with extra solar sensors and wind-activated mini-generators across the back. Moira was wedging socks and hiking shoes into her pack. Lying next to her was Nina, her Border Collie she had brought with her from Scotland. Nina was nine years old and slowing down, but still independent, well more than that, willful at times. "Smartest dog I ever had, and I've had lots of dogs," was how Moira described her.

"I need to take some of my nutrient so I can get a match for it when we get to Sweden. If we need any new prescriptions, Eric can get them through his aunt. I'm glad Eric is pre-med. And he has been camping with his dad and brother."

"Anastasia's mother was a nurse in pediatrics. Medically speaking, we should be O.K. By the way, did you have an eye doctor look at your eyes? They still have a tinge of yellow."

"Eric mentioned that, too. I'll have Marie look at it." Byron looked down at the clothes in the pack. "Has your mother asked about what you're going to wear at Roland's funeral? Mine has."

"I told her I was going to get a dress in Sweden so I wouldn't have to carry it on the plane. What did you say?"

Byron sat down beside Moira and put his arm around her. Nina didn't protest, but she raised her head and kept a close watch on Byron. "About the same. I told her I was going to get you to pick something out for me when we got there. She said we would be hurried and why didn't I just pack at least a conservative suit coat. She's asked me a jillion questions. I better go over my answers with you so we back each other up."

"How did your dad take the Council's voting down his resolution?" Moira was slipping sunglasses, sun block lotion, and a small flashlight into the side pockets of the pack.

"Dad didn't say much. He was more tired than usual. Somewhat depressed. Did you notice he shuffled a little going up to the podium? There was a slowness of speech too. Mother is worried and making sure he gets a thorough check-up. He's been putting it off, but now he's going to go."

Moira was finished with her packing and closed the pack. Byron helped her zip it up. He got up and helped Moira to her feet, drew her into his arms and hugged her. Nina got to her feet. Byron and Moira held each other tightly, neither saying a word. Moira drew back after a long moment and said, "I never thought that I'd agree so quickly to do something so serious. Is it just your charm that has beguiled me, or is it that you're so big and I'm so small that I knew it was useless to resist?" She smiled up into Byron's face.

Byron touched the tip of her nose gently with his finger and said, "Never you mind the how. I'd do anything that works to win you even if it were underhanded. The scoundrel always gets the fair lady." He picked Moira up and swirled her around and said, "Now I've got you where I want you, and I'll never let you down." This was too much for Nina. She jumped up against Byron's leg and started barking.

"You've got to, at least for right now. JD's Seven's get together is in about twenty minutes. It'll take us half that long to get to Eric's place. And Nina is going to eat you up."

"Well, if it must be, it must be." Byron lowered Moira to the floor, but still held her in his arms." Nina stopped barking and Byron leaned down and petted her. "Good girl, Nina. See, I didn't hurt our lassie. Let's go together on my scooter."

"Darling, you know that's illegal. The penalty is being grounded for three months."

"There is no penalty, sweet, unless you get caught." Byron lifted Moira into the air and swirled her around for the second time. "We'll fly like the wind. They will never catch us." This time Nina just watched, content that Moira was not in danger.

"You're impossible."

"That's by design."

"That's crazy."

"Also by design."

"I give up."

"See, it worked!"

"You big lug, why do I love you?"

"Let me count the ways."

"You're impossible."

"That's by design." Byron lowered Moira to the floor. They kissed and headed for the door followed closely by Nina.

CHAPTER 3

"Hey, there," Eric said, "I hereby perform a citizen's arrest for illegal scooter operation. You can't have two passengers on one scooter." Eric and the other members of JD's Seven were waiting outside of Eric's house when Byron and Moira arrived on his scooter. Eric held the scooter while Anastasia helped Moira get off.

As he was setting his scooter's kickstand, Byron said, "Eric, don't you know the difference between 'can't' and 'shouldn't'? We did have two passengers on one scooter. It can happen. It did happen."

"You English majors," Eric said. "Always trying to be one up on we illiterate."

"Don't take it personally, Eric," Moira said. "It happens to me all the time. The best defense is a good offence. Kick him in the balls, but not too hard."

"Good idea," said Jonathan Hearst. Jonathan was a member of the U.S. Olympic rifle team and had a famous family connection. He was the son of Wylie Randolph Hearst, the alternate U.S. delegate from California, who was related to the William Randolph Hearst. At twenty-three Jonathan was older than most in his classes. He had failed the final logic exam and had to repeat the class. Byron had helped him with his studies. He also told Jonathan that he would have to spend less time on the firing range and more time with the books.

Carlos Domingo gave a "thumbs up" to Jonathan's remark, and the others followed with the same gesture. Carlos's leadership extended to the frivolity of the group as well as its serious matters. His father, Miguel, had been a young Argentine cabinet member when his country was in a crisis in the first years of the century. During the round robin of Presidents, Miguel was kept in his position by each of them. Miguel remembered it as a time when Argentina was like a fragile sheet of metal receiving a daily dose of a strong acid that left lines of stress etched in Argentina's profile. Etched in Miguel's memory was his country's weakness. When world government offered financial aid to Argentina, Miguel was a willing adherent to trading independence for relief. Many other countries with like problems made the same trade.

The youngest member of JD's Seven, Kurt Kriger, welcomed Byron with a hand on his shoulder and gave Moira an affectionate hug. Kurt was seventeen and the son of Germany's delegate who constantly admonished his son not to make known his disagreement with the restrictions on personal freedom. Germany had been one of the last powerful countries to agree to join world government, but once it signed on, it urged tighter and tighter controls.

The group moved indoors to the media room in Eric's house. Many affluent families had media rooms complete with the latest telecommunications, recording and video equipment, but Eric's family had one extra capability that very few other media rooms possessed. As General Secretary of the Planet Council, Eric's father Roland was entitled to one of the few level fifty secure telecommunication lines. When the Planet Communications Act was passed in 2023, the Council recognized that certain of their officials should have the ability to communicate with any site in the world without the Internal Security Department or any other legal or illegal party listening in. Engineers from three leading telecommunications companies were given four months to design and install a system so complex and flexible that it could be constantly upgraded to keep one step ahead of the most skilled hackers. The seats in the media room were in rows like an auditorium. JD's Seven seated themselves in the first two rows.

"Any change in your father's condition?" Byron asked Eric.

Eric's despondency had become evident to close friends by a change in the look in his eyes and tone of his voice when references to his father were made. Somberly he said, "Aunt Marie said she could see some improvement, but none of the tests confirm it. She wants for Dad to recover so much, that she is trying to will it so. I'm trying to help Mom prepare for the inevitable."

"Anything we can do to help?" Carlos asked. "My mother would be glad to come talk with her. She went through this last year when her sister had a stroke."

"Thanks, Carlos and the rest of you," Eric said. "I appreciate all of your messages and support, but from here on out, I think it is a matter of remembering the great things he accomplished and being thankful we had him as many years as we did."

Eric stood up and turned to face the group. "Now, it's time to get down to our business. I have the addresses where you will be staying and who will meet you at the airport and take you there. Since all of you but Carlos and Kurt are on the same airbus, I'll be there to pick up most of you. Also, here is the password number to use to get in this house." Eric gave index cards to Anastasia to pass out. " No one will be in our house except our two cats, and we've made arrangements for them. Give this password to your parents so they can come over here to reach you, if necessary. As you probably know, our phone system has level fifty security. With what we have planned, this may come in handy."

Carlos stood up and said, "I'm speaking for Jonathan, Kurt and myself when I say I want our two brave couples to know we are behind them all the way. We are going to stay in Sweden an extra week to help out. We went in together to get you a little something." Carlos reached below his seat and withdrew two packages that he had hidden there. He went over to Byron and Moira and then Anastasia and Eric and gave each couple a package. Both packages were wrapped in wedding gift paper with silver bows.

The two couples unwrapped the presents. Moira uttered, "Oh, my, how nice; thank you so much," when she saw the two sterling silver chains each with seven links attached to a small engraved name tag that read "JD's Seven." "We can use these as a bracelet or choke necklace."

" Thank you all. It's beautiful. This way we will always be tied together," Anastasia said.

"Not tied, chained together. There's a difference," Jonathan said. Everyone laughed.

"I don't mean to run you off, but tomorrow's a big day, and I still have packing to do," Eric said.

The group stood up and in turn hugged each other. Tears were in the eyes of most of the group. Carlos ended the get together by saying "My country's Eva said, 'Don't cry for me Argentina,' when she fought for human rights. Let's not cry. Let's hope that what Moira, Anastasia, Byron and Eric are doing brings progress for humanity."

CHAPTER 4

"Do you think Byron is behaving strangely?" Laura asked Lawrence while they were eating breakfast at the dining counter. She took a sip of her coffee. Her blend was straight out of Brazil, and she was addicted to two cups in the morning.

Lawrence had just taken a large bite of toast. He finished it before answering. "Yes, I noticed it too. I expected he would blow sky-high when my resolution didn't pass, but he hasn't said a word about it to me. He probably has his mind on Moira and when they are going to apply for marriage probation, although he hasn't said anything to me about applying. Has he discussed it with you?"

"Not a word."

"I have been surprised by the lack of a reaction to the vote from Byron and the rest of JD's Seven. They also haven't shown much interest in the protest demonstrations. I'm concerned that the protests will cause the Council to impose new restrictions. The Council might even censor the press if critics continue to lambaste the Council and call for a change in its structure. In Australia there is a movement to end the Directorate and let majority rule on the Council. The Big Three will never agree to that without a fight, a military one." Lawrence finished his toast.

After a moment of silence Lawrence and Laura started speaking at the same time. Lawrence said, "Do you suppose. . . " as Laura said, "Byron and Moira may be."

"Together?" Lawrence said. "Are we thinking the same thing?"

"I think they've been 'together' long before this, but I meant considering something other than waiting six months to get married. I'm not sure what they could do, but Byron is not a patient person. Maybe they'll work it out when they're camping. How many tents do you think the group will be in? And who in which tent?" Laura was peeling an orange as she was speaking. A line in her forehead sharpened as she asked the questions.

"Those aren't really questions, are they? You know who will be in a tent with Byron. Maybe the pregnancy control in their body chips is a good thing after all." Lawrence smiled as he ate an extra piece of bacon--an unusual treat for him.

Laura looked displeased and said, "Don't joke about that, Lawrence. Marriage and having children is a serious thing. I'm glad they have the marriage probation period and training for parents. I hope Byron doesn't try to get around it some way. It would have helped us."

"Do you mean you weren't ready when we got married? As I remember it you moved the wedding date up two months because you were 'bored,' I think it was you said."

"Never you mind about that. We were talking about Byron and Moira. I hope they enjoy the trip and camping out."

"I'm sure they will," Lawrence said with a big smile. Laura picked up a piece of her toast and threw it at him.

Both Lawrence and Laura were surprised to have a message on their home phone the next morning from Byron. All their children always called them on their personal computer phone systems.

"Hi Mom and Dad; we arrived safely," the message started. "The funeral service for Roland has been postponed. Everyone is excited because he has had an unexpected increase in his medical condition rating to 109. We know that is a long way from the 130 rating needed to avoid euthanasia, but Marie is planning some special treatments in the hope he will recover fully. Since we don't know how long the delay will be, most of the JD's Seven are leaving today to go camping. We're turning off the phone feature on our computers, roughing it Anastasia says. When I turn mine on again, I'll call you. Know that I love you deeply and am grateful for your patience with me and all you have done for me. I especially appreciate your love of life and the way you both live it to the fullest possible. Bye, bye."

"What do you think of that, honey?" Laura said. "I can't imagine what that ending is all about."

"It's as if he were saying good-bye."

Merlin signaled an incoming call from John Browning.

"Lawrence, we just listened to a message from Moira over our home phone," John said over the phone. "Her message was unusual to say the least."

"Hold on while I switch you to our home speaker phone so Laura can hear it, too," Lawrence said. "Laura, its John Browning on the phone. He's heard from Moira. I'm switching on the speaker phone so you can hear."

"Hi, John. Is Peggy there, too?" Laura asked.

"I'm here," Peggy answered. "Moira left us a strange message from Sweden. Have you heard from Byron, yet?"

"We just listened to a message he left," Lawrence said. "His message was strange, too. What do you think is going on?"

"I don't know, but Moira's ending sounded as if she was going away and wouldn't be back for a while," John said. "Maybe, a long while."

"Same here with Byron," Laura said. "Lawrence and I were just talking about it. He said they were turning off their personal phones so we can't call them. I guess we could call Marie to see what's going on."

"I tried her, but her recorded message said she was in surgery and wouldn't be available for several hours," John said. "I left our number for her to call us. Who else could we call? I don't think we should call Roland's wife."

"Byron's message said Marie is giving Roland some special treatment," Laura said. "I don't know anyone else to call, but I'm worried. Something is going on in Sweden. I can feel it when there's danger. We've got to do something."

"Stay calm Laura, " Lawrence said as he put his hand on Laura's arm. "I'm sure there is a logical explanation. Our kids probably just wanted us to know they appreciate us now that they are planning to get married and will be moving out and on their own."

"I don't know, Lawrence," Peggy said. "The message from Moira was not like her. And she's never left a message on our home phone before. I think she wanted to avoid questions."

"That's probably why Byron didn't call us direct," Laura said. Her voice was loud and shrill.

"We'd better do some checking, Lawrence," John said. "I'm going to call our ambassador to Sweden and see what he can do. I'll let you know if I find out anything."

"I'll call Birgitta Borge, Lawrence said. "Even though she's just an advocate, she has connections high up over there. I'll call you as soon as I hear anything."

The Brownings disconnected. Lawrence started to ask Merlin to call Birgitta, but Merlin told him, "Agent Iago of Internal Security has been holding while your line was busy. Here he is." Laura moved closer to Lawrence so she could hear the conversation.

"Agent Iago, here. Is this delegate Lawrence Holmes?"

"Yes sir, what can I do for you," Lawrence answered in a measured, cautious voice.

"Good evening, sir. Sorry to bother you at home, but can you tell me the whereabouts of your son, Byron?" His voice was not threatening, but it carried authority.

"He's in Sweden," Lawrence said.

"Where in Sweden,"

"I don't know exactly, but why do you ask?"

"Excuse me for a minute, sir, while I put you on hold."

There was no answer for what seemed like a long time to Lawrence. "Why would Internal Security want to know where Byron is?" Laura asked.

"I don't know, love," Lawrence answered "Maybe his passport wasn't in order and they are checking on it." But Lawrence knew that wasn't the case. He surmised that Agent Iago was talking to his superior to find out how to answer Lawrence's question and if that was so, it wasn't good.

Iago came off hold and said, "The Body Functions Department couldn't access Byron for his regular monthly physical condition report. When they sent the signal to monitor his blood pressure, they got no response. They tried reaching him at the satellite phone number they had on file and received the person you are trying to reach is not available message."

Laura screamed!

"What was that?" Agent Iago demanded.

Lawrence put his arm around Laura to comfort her and in as calm a voice as he could manage said, "Just my wife, sir. Our cat tipped over boiling water on to herself. You may have heard the cat yelp, too. My wife is going to treat the cat's burn."

Lawrence knew that Agent Iago was lying when he said they had tried to access Byron's body chip. Byron's regular monitoring was a couple of days before he left for Sweden. Lawrence remembered Byron's saying that he had skipped his exercises for a few days and hoped his ratings were in line. That meant it should be more than twenty days before Byron's next monitoring.

"Can you tell me if he is having trouble with his body chip?" Iago asked.

Lawrence paused to give himself time to think, "Not that I know of. Byron didn't mention it before he left. Just when did the Body Functions Department try the monitoring? Was it today?"

After a short delay, Iago answered, "I don't have that information. The Department just contacts us if they can't access anyone's body chip. Can you tell me any way we can contact Byron?"

Suddenly, Lawrence realized that when he presented his resolution he was put on the Internal Surveillance list. That would probably mean that Byron and maybe even the rest of his family's movements were being monitored. When Byron passed through the airport security in New York, a report would automatically be transmitted to Internal Security that he was going to Sweden. Then it hit Lawrence like a ton of bricks: Byron had gotten someone to remove his body chip and he had gone underground. That was the reason for his "good-bye" message on the phone and why he hadn't been upset by the defeat of R-1948. Lawrence gasped, and then he coughed to try to cover it up in case Agent Iago heard it. Lawrence almost gasped again when he realized that Moira had done the same thing. It all figured. Before they left they had arranged to get their body chips removed in Sweden; most likely by Marie. They probably even decided to do it before the Council vote when they found out how old they would have to be before R-1948 applied to them.

"Uh, I don't know, sir," Lawrence said. "He planned to go camping somewhere while he was in Sweden. He's probably in a forest. While he went camping he was going to turn his personal computer-phone off."

"Have you heard from Byron since he arrived in Sweden?"

"Not directly, no sir, Lawrence said." And then another thought hit Lawrence. If I'm on the internal Surveillance List, my phone is being tapped. Lawrence remembered that a service man from the utility company had come by the house to check on what they said was "excessive water usage" a day or so after he introduced his resolution. They checked the whole house and said they couldn't find a problem. Since houses his size had their own water recycling equipment, their water usage was practically negligible. Lawrence guessed that the service man bugged his house. Internal security was probably listening in when Byron left his message on their home phone. Lawrence thought he had better not deny receiving any phone calls made lately.

"What do you mean by 'not directly,' Mr. Holmes?"

"I mean Byron left a message for us on our home phone, but I haven't talked to him since he left for Sweden." Lawrence decided to try and verify his theory that his phone was being tapped. "Would you like to hear the message Byron left, Agent Iago? I still have it recorded."

There was a pause and Lawrence could hear what sounded like a whispered question on the line. Then Iago said, "That won't be necessary, Mr. Holmes. We just want to know where Byron is. If he didn't give his location in the message he left, hearing it wouldn't help us. Where was Byron staying before he went camping?"

Lawrence thought, "They are tapping my line. They already have heard Byron's message. I'm glad I told them I had a message from Byron. I'd better be careful."

"Uh, I don't have the address here at home," Lawrence said. "I can get it for you when I go to the Council session tomorrow. The information is in my desk," Lawrence lied to delay while he thought about just what information to reveal.

There was another pause and another whisper in the background. "We'd like to have the information tonight. I'll send a car to take you to the Council Hall. It'll be there in about ten minutes. Better tell your wife that you may be gone for an hour or two. Hope your cat is O.K. And your wife, too. Good by."

Laura was beside herself. Lawrence took her by the hand, put his finger up to his mouth to indicate she shouldn't say anything and led her outside. "Love, I don't have much time. You've got to pull yourself together. Our house probably has been bugged."

Laura cried out, "Oh, no! I can't take this Lawrence."

"Laura, you've got to think of Byron. He's going to need help. Take your air scooter to the Brownings and tell them what's happened and that I think Byron and probably Moira have had their body chips removed and have gone underground. Go outside when you talk to the Brownings; their house might be bugged, too. Then go by Anne's and tell her the same thing and do it outside; her house may be bugged. Tell her to be very careful of what she says to anyone, especially those at the library; they will be questioning them. Then go tell the Gorbechevs. My guess is Eric and Anastasia are with Byron and Moira and may have had their chips removed. The Brownings and Gorbachevs may not know what's happened, so break it to them gently. If Anastasia has removed her body chip, her father is going to have some explaining to do. Being the delegate for Russia, he'll be under a lot of pressure. These kind of things are not supposed to happen to one of The Big Three. I know this will take time on your scooter even though the houses are in the same area, but we have to get the families involved informed. We're going to have to get organized."

Lawrence got the address of Eric's friend where Byron had been staying in Sweden from his home office and wrote it down on a card small enough that he could hide it in his hand.

Laura got away before the car from Internal Security arrived. Vehicular traffic was no longer a problem on the streets of New York or any of the cities in the world. Only a person's status or special condition qualified them for having personal ground vehicles. Large trucks still traveled on the interregional highways because of the economical savings of moving goods by truck, but only moving vans were allowed in residential areas. The air scooters were equipped with radar screens to avoid collisions and they flew above existing streets at different heights depending on the direction in which they were headed. To change directions, air scooters had to swing to the side of the street below them and make a gradual transition to their new height. Most accidents occurred when scooters were changing directions. Being at fault for an accident could lose the driver the use of their personal scooter for months during which they would have to pay for an air scooter taxis or do a lot of walking to commuter stations to get anywhere.

The Internal Security car that pulled up in front of Lawrence's house was one of their smaller ground vehicles. The driver checked Lawrence's body chip identification with his portable scan machine and opened the door for him to get in the back seat. The driver didn't look or act the part of a hard-nosed lieutenant. He was short and pudgy with a wide, thick-lipped mouth that spread into a big, toothy grin. He identified himself as O'Sheean. "But I like to be called Sugar Boy," he said in a friendly voice. "Iago will meet up with us at the Council Hall. He's awful impatient. Too much in a hurry for me, but I'm afraid I'll have to hurry you along. Sorry, sir."

"Fan of Robert Penn Warren or from the south?" Lawrence asked Sugar Boy.

"Both. Picked my name from his book after a friend of mine in the Department said I looked like him. My friend said Sugar Boy drove a big long Cadillac, and I had a job back in the old days and drove a Cad like the one in Warren's *All The Kings Men*. These little old cars like this one ain't worth hav'n."

Lawrence grinned and started to make a comment about Iago, but caught himself as he realized that Sugar Boy's jovial role was to contrast Iago's and encourage those he escorted to let their guard down. He probably wasn't a driver at all.

When Lawrence arrived at the Council Hall, Agent Iago was waiting for him at the check-in desk. "Your cat recovered?" Iago asked as Lawrence came up to him. Iago's expression wasn't a smirk, but it and Iago's slim frame reminded Lawrence of how Caesar described Cassius: "Yond' Cassius has a lean and hungry look; he thinks too much; such men are dangerous." Iago had that same look, was of medium height with hair clipped so short that it gave him a bald look.

Iago held up a special card to be scanned. "Admit" flashed on the screen so neither Iago or Lawrence had to undergo any screening.

As they headed for the down escalator, Lawrence asked casually, "Have you tried accessing Byron's body chip again?"

Iago hesitated and then answered, "No, Body Functions will try again tomorrow. We want to notify Byron tonight to have it checked in the morning. That's the main reason we need to reach him tonight." Lawrence didn't mention that in Sweden is was morning already.

When Lawrence and Iago reached the peoples' advocates section Lawrence pointed to the podium and said, "Ever notice how close my section is to the action?" When Iago shifted his eyes to look, Lawrence shifted the card with the Swedish address on it from his pocket to his right hand, which he pressed against his leg so Iago couldn't see it. When they reached Lawrence's desk, Lawrence pointed to his left and said, "That's James Anderson's desk there, the other U.S. advocate," as he pulled out the top drawer to his desk and reached in with his right hand. Lawrence withdrew his hand and gave the card to Iago. "Here is where Byron said he planned to stay until he went camping."

Iago took the card and looked at it. Lawrence worried that Iago might notice that there were no other cards in his desk drawer like the one with the address, so he casually slid the drawer closed. Iago watched Lawrence's maneuvers but didn't say anything. Lawrence felt relieved.

"Can you record phone conversations here at your desk?" Iago asked.

"Sure, do you want to try to call now?" Lawrence looked down at his watch and said, "Wonder just what time it is there now? My computer can tell me."

"Yes, let's call the number now."

Lawrence surmised that Iago still hadn't realized it was about 03:00 in Sweden or didn't care if he woke up Byron and the household where he was staying.

Lawrence leaned forward to block Iago's view as he entered his password to his desk computer/communications unit and said "Record call to Sweden, speakerphone, " and then spoke the phone number on the card.

Over the speaker phone they heard the dialing sounds followed by "There is no one available at this time. Please leave a message." The answering machine spoke good Unifren with a Swedish accent.

Iago had seated himself at Anderson's desk. He didn't move in his chair for some time. Lawrence thought he was trying to figure out what to do next. Lawrence guessed that he would have Carlos and the others located in Sweden through their body chips and have them picked up for questioning, unless all of JD's Seven had arranged for their body chips to be removed. Lawrence doubted that was the case, since he hadn't heard from the families of the others. Finally, Iago rose and said, "I'm going to stay here a while to make calls. Good night, Mr. Holmes."

As Lawrence walked back to the escalator to ride to the front entrance the thought crossed his mind that Iago was searching his desk. Since there was nothing in it that mattered except that there were no cards like the one he had given Iago, Lawrence wasn't worried. He thought he was probably making too much of insignificant details like the card thing, anyway. Lawrence wondered if criminals thought that way and spent their lives worrying about slip-ups that weren't slip-ups after all. Long ago when he was at the newspaper and had to keep his sources' names confidential, he had made a habit of placing a fine hair across the notebook in his desk so that if someone else moved it, he would know it. He had been careful in opening his desk earlier to not move his notebook. He wondered how well Iago had been trained and if Iago noted the hair on the notebook, would he look for the second one that was under the notebook in a groove in the bottom of his desk drawer?

"Was Iago satisfied with your cooperation?" Sugar Boy asked as Lawrence walked up to the check-out desk where Sugar Boy was lounging in a special chair reserved for the Council's Security chief who had a bad back. Sugar Boy had the chair rotated back farther than Lawrence had ever seen the Security Chief position it when he presided over the check-in and check-out desks during regular Council session hours.

"He didn't say," Lawrence said. It was the most non-committal answer Lawrence could think of.

"He sure likes to drag people away from their homes in the evening. I'm almost always late getting home."

"You might try to get promoted. If things worked out for you, you could be sending Iago out and you could stay in." Lawrence was surprised by the sharp look Sugar Boy gave him. Lawrence wondered why, since he was just trying to be friendly and avoid revealing anything damaging.

"Better be getting you home, sir," Sugar Boy said as he recovered his jovial manner.

CHAPTER ⌂

Laura arrived home before Lawrence. She poured herself a glass of Byron's Pouilly-Fuisse' chardonnay and flopped down in the media room on the couch. She was on her second glass when Lawrence returned.

"There's some cashews on the bar."

"Thanks, love," Lawrence said. "I'll get them in a minute. How are you?" Then he remembered the house might be bugged, and he put his finger over his lips to signal to Laura.

"Uh, fine." Laura didn't look fine. Her worry showed in her face as well as in the slump of her body. As Lawrence noted this, he imagined she had looked worse before having the wine.

Merlin announced, "Incoming from Carlos Domingo in Sweden."

"Hello, Carlos," Lawrence said. "I'm so glad to hear from you." Lawrence started to ask about Byron and then thought better. As he waited for Carlos's reply, he was worrying that Carlos would not know that their conversation might be bugged and how he could signal Carlos to be careful what he said.

"I'm calling to . . ." Carlos started when Lawrence broke in, "We've got a bad connection and I can hardly hear you. Give me a number to call. I've got a call I have to return first, but I'll call back later. Probably in fifteen minutes to half an hour." Carlos gave Lawrence a number to call.

Lawrence motioned for Laura to follow him outside. When they were in the yard he said, "Let's go to the Nilsson's so we can use their secure phone. Follow me on your scooter."

"Could I ride with you? It's dark and it's a short distance. No one will see us."

"O.K.," Lawrence said. He got his air scooter, climbed on and then helped Laura on to the back part of the seat. Lawrence had bought a larger than usual seat for the scooter just for this purpose. They were careful to ride double only at night to places where they wouldn't be seen.

On the way to the Nilssons, Laura said there had been several calls from the media wanting to talk to Lawrence about protest rallies throughout the world objecting to the defeat of R-1948. Lawrence said some had reached him, but he hadn't had a chance to prepare a statement, so he put them off.

"When is your doctor's appointment?" Laura asked.

"The nurse if going to call me with the first opening they have. There have been two emergencies and they have to get through them. Then, I'm next."

"Good. I'm afraid you have something serious. You just aren't the same."

"Well, if I'm not performing up to your expectations or needs, that is serious."

"That's not what I meant, you oaf," Laura said as she reached down and squeezed him between his legs."

"Yikes!" Lawrence exclaimed and then said, "Do it again."

When Lawrence and Laura were inside the Nilsson's media room Lawrence placed the call to Carlos in Sweden. Carlos answered on the first ring.

"Mr. Holmes, I see you are at the Nilsson's on their secure line." Carlos said, "I was hoping you would call from there. If you hadn't, I was going to hint that I was calling about something urgent and hope you would get the idea. Glad you were ahead of me. Byron, Moira, Eric and Anastasia have had their body chips removed."

"Laura's on the line with us," Lawrence said. "We knew Byron couldn't be contacted by the BBB, and I thought it likely that had happened and that the others probably had their chips removed, too. Did they have any problems with the operations?"

"No. They are all fine and in wonderful spirits. I don't think it is a good idea for me to tell you how it happened or where they are in case you are questioned, but they wanted you and their other parents to know they are safe and happy. But it will be a long time before any of the families hear directly from them. Probably be a year or more."

The Nilsson's two cats slunk into the room and looked Lawrence and Laura over. Then they found a place near the phone to lie down and watch what was going on.

Laura said, "Carlos, can't you tell us anything more? We've so worried. Are they in danger?"

"I've told you about all I can for now," Carlos said. "They have everything they need. A lot of planning went into the whole thing. Jonathan, Kurt and I are staying in Sweden for another week to help, if needed. After that, others will be available. The four of them will be together. Eric, as you know, is well along on his pre-med. and Anastasia knows a lot about nursing from her mother. They have rifles for hunting and Moira has often hunted with her brother and is a good shot. Byron is so smart that he can handle about anything that comes his way. Also, he told me to tell you that with your grandfather's Boy Scout manual, he is prepared. He said something about looking for a big switch and finding a bear, but I don't know if I got that right."

"You got it right," Lawrence said. I'll explain it when you get back."

"Marie operated on Roland. She said his immediate response was good. His capability rating rose to 115 in the first thirty minutes and he is resting comfortably. Everyone is elated and Eric thought it was all right for him to leave."

"Is there anything we should do?" Lawrence asked.

"If you will contact the Brownings for me, that will help. Also, tell them when they call, to call from the Nilsson's. I'll be available at this number from 19:00 to 21:00 New York time everyday until we leave. I will call the Gorbachevs direct since he has a level fifty system."

"I'll call the Brownings and the Gorbachevs to arrange to meet with them." Lawrence said. "Probably tomorrow at breakfast if they're available. Anything else?"

"Not for now, except, by the way, my guess is that you better start thinking about how it's going to be when you're grandparents."

"Oh, my!" Laura exclaimed.

"Well, you'll have plenty of time to get used to the idea," Carlos said.

"Thanks for everything," Lawrence said, and hung up.

The cats evidently noticed that the phone call was over, rose and left the room.

"What do you want to be called?" Laura asked. "Grandpa?"

"No, Grandfather," Lawrence said. "How about you?"

"Anything but Nana. I never liked that. What would you rather have? Boy or girl?"

"I'd prefer a boy be the first. Moira won't be able to go to a licensed obstetrician, so I guess they won't know ahead of time which it will be."

Laura's hand moved to her mouth as she exclaimed, "Lawrence, Moira won't be able to go to a hospital either! How will they be able to have it?"

"Same way as millions of others. And Eric will be there to deliver it. Also, Anastasia can help. Moira will be all right."

"When I told Anne that Byron couldn't be located by the BBB, she was upset. She's worried that may hurt her chances with the Pregnancy Committee. She is really going to throw a tizzy when she finds out he has gone underground, isn't she?"

"Yes, but she needs to know," Lawrence answered. "Go see her as soon as you can. I'll tell Kate."

"Do you think we should go over to Sweden and try to find Byron and Moira?"

"I don't think there is anything they need from us, and if we found them we might be followed and that would lead to their arrest. Besides, they are on a honeymoon of sorts. I don't imagine they want any parents around."

"You're right. I hope they are having a good time."

"You can count on it. It's sure good that Roland is doing better. I'll call the Brownings now."

Lawrence called the Brownings. John answered and Lawrence asked him if he could meet at the commuter station in the morning and go somewhere for breakfast. "I need for you to O.K. the final draft of our statement for the press. I changed your wording, and I'm not sure its what you intended," Lawrence said knowing that John would figure out that wasn't the real reason for meeting since John hadn't prepared any draft.

"Sure, Peggy will come, too. She's going with me to the Council Hall to meet a friend to go shopping," John said.

Lawrence had planned to try and arrange for Peggy to come, so he was glad John had understood that the wives were involved. " I'll meet you at 07:45," Lawrence said and disconnected. Then he called the Gorbachevs and got Boris on the line. He told Boris about the breakfast and asked if Klavdia would like to come, too, since Peggy and Laura were going shopping.

Boris said they both would be there. As one of The Big Three, Lawrence knew that Boris could obtain more details about the whole situation. He might even have friends in Internal Security who would pass on confidential information. Then the thought occurred to Lawrence that Internal Security might be watching Boris, too, and could enter Boris's house and disable his secure phone without Boris knowing it. Lawrence didn't know just how far Internal Security could go when one of The Big Three was involved. Probably the other two would have to sign off on such an action. They probably wouldn't agree to any of The Big Three losing their secure phone, because the tables could turn on them some day.

"Don't you think Kate ought to come with us tomorrow?" Laura asked.

"Definitely," Lawrence said. It was so late that Lawrence decided to wait until morning to ask Kate. "Now I'd better write my statement. The media will be after me for it tomorrow. Wouldn't they like to know Byron's body chip is gone? They'd have a field day with that."

"Do you think Internal Security will announce it?"

"Nope, not until they are ready to announce some action that they are going to take. I doubt if they have decided what to do. Maybe we should announce it, call for sympathy and try and put Internal Security on the defense. What do you think, love?"

"I'd ask Boris, first. He may have had experience with them."

"Good idea. I'm sure glad I have you. You're a keeper."

"How nice of you to say so. Don't be too long writing your statement. I might be asleep before long."

"Well, first things first," Lawrence said as he picked Laura up and headed for their sleeping boxes. "I'll finish the statement later."

"And I thought you put work before pleasure."

"Not if I have a choice."

Laura's hand was on the back of Lawrence's neck and her lips just below it.

CHAPTER 6

"Do you know how to run a hovercraft?" Eric asked Byron.

"Well, I'm not what you would call experienced," Byron said.

"That means he's never done it and doesn't know how, but I do," Moira said. "If you're Scottish, you know boating."

"And drinking and fighting and . . ., " Byron said with a smile as he put his arm around Moira's waist.

"Don't say it," Moira interrupted. "All men are like that. Not just Scots."

The two couples were walking down to the dock near the cottage Eric's family owned on the shore of the Gulf of Bothnia in Eastern Sweden north of Stockholm. At the dock was the Nilsson's six passenger high speed hovercraft built to travel over rough terrain. Their plan was to go north up the Gulf to the Ljusnan River. Then they were heading West on the river across Sweden to near Norway. The Nilsson's owned a hunting lodge two kilometers from the river on the Swedish side of the border that had been in the family since before disarmament. The lodge was in a remote, uninhabited area that Roland thought was safe enough from discovery that he stored rifles and shotguns so he and Eric could go hunting without having to go to one of the official hunting preserves. Roland knew he was risking an embarrassing situation if authorities discovered his illegal activity, but he chanced it thinking that, at worst, he would have to resign his position; he wouldn't be jailed.

"Byron is there anything you know that will be helpful camping out in the wilds of Norway?" Anastasia said.

"I can sing at our campfires," Byron said, "and I have this book about cooking a whole ox which will probably work for bears, too." Byron reached in his pack and removed his great grandfather's Boy Scout manual and showed it to the others. "I imagine there are more bears than oxen in Sweden and Norway."

Eric said, "And did your dad . . ., " and was interrupted by Byron's, "Tell me to carry a big stick when hunting bears? Yes, he did. But I love him anyway."

"Did you ever tell him that?" Moira asked.

"Not often, but I did before we left."

"I'm proud of you," Moira said. "I'll bet that was hard for you. In Scotland we think that shows character. As our Burns would say, 'A man's a man for a' that.'" Moira kissed Byron and said, "And I love you."

"Enough of that," Eric said. "We've got work to do and the sky looks dark."

The two couples reached the boat. As they loaded their packs and gear into the cabin, it started to rain. Eric checked the oil, ran the exhaust fan and started the motor and said to Anastasia, "Get the line and push us off, mate."

"Aye, aye, captain," Anastasia answered and jumped on board after giving the boat a push away from the dock. "See how I did that, Byron? You're third mate under your wife. You are at the bottom of the duty ladder."

"Does that mean I also have to clean the latrine?" Byron asked.

"Yes, and cook the meals and wash the deck, and aboard a boat, what you called the latrine is called the head," Moira said.

"Just so my duties include tucking my wife into bed or whatever they are called on boats," Byron said as he put his arm around Moira. "Did Moira tell you that I asked her dad for permission to marry her? My dad said I ought to do it the old fashioned way".

"You probably wanted to grab me by the hair and drag me into a cave," Moira said.

"Well, that's the way they do it in the Highland's, isn't it?" Byron said.

Moira jumped on Byron's back and said, "I'll show you what fathers do in the Highlands." She wrapped her arm around Byron's neck and drew her finger across his throat and said, "They slit the throat of anyone who touches their daughter, and then they cut off something else so no other lasses will be bothered."

Byron turned in circles, fell onto a seat and pulled Moira onto his lap and said, "That isn't what your father said when I asked for your hand. He said he had offered several lads a horse, a cow, and land if they would just carry you off, but he hadn't had any takers. He was thrilled when I said I'd take you for free."

Moira swung her arm to give Byron a belt saying, "I'll show you what you're getting for free." Byron caught her arm before the blow fell and kissed her while she pretended to struggle.

The rain stopped and the couples went above deck. As they were zipping along over the water, Eric asked Anastasia how she felt her father would handle the reproof he was bound to get over his daughter's body chip removal. Anastasia eyes were troubled as she said, "They will make it very hard for Dad. I'm worried, but he has always been able to come out on top when problems developed before. This is going to be tougher than other messes, though, because if you are a Big Three delegate, your family is not supposed to make any waves, not even small ones."

Eric was steering but took Anastasia's hand with his free hand and said, "Your dad wants you to be free and happy. He'd do the same as we did if he were in our shoes."

"I know you're right, but I don't like to cause anguish for my family."

"If things go right, we're going to be the cause of something they all are going to love. We can name him or her after your parents, if you'd like."

"Thanks, sweetheart, but I like either Eric or Erica. How about you?"

Eric lifted Anastasia's hand to his lips and said, "I'd lean towards Roland for a boy, but we've plenty of time to work it out."

The trip up Liusnan River to the turn-off to the Nilsson lodge took five hours. A creek flowed into the river from the east, which they followed for about 300 meters until it became too narrow. The lodge was located to the north of the creek about 800 meters through the woods. The path through the woods wound around large trees but was wide enough for the hovercraft. From the air it was not apparent that there even was a path. At each turn, Byron and Moira looked anxiously ahead to catch sight of the lodge. When it came into view as they rounded a sharp turn, it was about thirty meters in front of them. Byron let out a whoop and hugged Moira and said, "Behold, your castle awaits you, fair maiden."

Moira replied, "'This castle hath a pleasant seat; the air
Nimbly and sweetly recommends itself
Unto our gentle senses.'

Now, English scholar, who spoke those lines? And in what scene of what act?"

"Everybody knows Duncan's description of Macbeth's castle in Act I, scene VI," Byron said, "but if you know the response Banquo made, you go to the head of the class. More than that, whether or not you do know Banquo's response, these words of his evoke what I have in mind.

'This guest of summer,
The temple-haunting martlet, does approve,
By his loved mansionry, that the heaven's breath
Smells wooingly here: no jutty, frieze,
Buttress, nor coign of vantage, but this bird
Hath made his pendent bed and procreant cradle :
Where they most breed and haunt, I have observed,
The air is delicate.'"

"You rascal, you're always finding a line to help you bed me," Moira said as she gave Byron a push to the side.

Eric steered the hovercraft up to the lodge and cut off the motor. The group piled out and started unloading the gear as Eric unlocked the door. Anastasia said, "I'm famished. Let's eat first and unpack later." All agreed and they sat down at the only table in the lodge to eat the sandwiches and fruit they had brought. Byron uncorked a bottle of white wine and proposed a toast saying, "Here's to the freedom to choose where you bed and bed whom you choose at the time of your choosing."

Anastasia said, "Here, here, spoken like the horny poet we all know you are."

They clinked their thermos cups and drank. After eating, they moved their gear and supplies into the cabin and stored the perishables. When they finished, they returned to the table.

"Do you think they'll find the lodge if they suspect Marie removed our body chips?" Moira asked.

"I imagine they are already monitoring Aunt Marie's every move, but they probably don't know about this lodge," Eric said. "They probably do suspect Marie because who else would we know in Sweden to do it for us?"

"They might think you would know some other pre-med from your homeland who was qualified and sympathetic," Byron said. "A young person like that might be more suspect."

"I do know several pre-meds from Sweden, but none of them have access to an operating room," Eric said. "I think they'll focus on my aunt."

"Do you think she'll get caught?" Anastasia asked Eric. "There were several others in the operating room with us, so the word might get out what was going on."

"I'm sure Aunt Marie picked her assistants carefully," Eric said. "I think the key to our not being discovered is that she slipped us into the same operating room she used for Dad and did our removals just after Dad's operation."

"It's great that your dad's operation went so well and his capability rating rose so much," Byron said. "A brain transplant seems unbelievable."

"Aunt Marie didn't perform a complete transplant. She used only those parts of the donor Dad needed. She thinks Dad's personality will be the same, if he survives. This type of transplant has not been attempted on humans, ever. I'm still sorry I couldn't stay longer after the operation until he had a full recovery, but as you all know, when your mother is insistent, you might as well give in. She thought the authorities would not expect anything like what we did while Dad was in the hospital. Mom said she was sure he would have wanted us to escape while we could."

"Did your aunt have trouble when she told them she was postponing the euthanasia?" Moira asked. "What did she use as an excuse?"

"She didn't have any trouble," Eric answered. "She told them that some of the family couldn't get to Sweden in time for the funeral service, and she needed more time to set up the recipients of the organs Dad was donating. If you're a famous surgeon, you can get away with an amazing number of illegalities."

"Like our body chip removals," Byron said. "It's remarkable how she arranged it all. Also, I didn't expect that the operations would be as quick and easy on us as they were."

"Aunt Marie said it isn't such a difficult operation; it's just dangerous if you don't know what you're doing or your hand slips," Eric said.

"How come more people don't have their chips removed?" Anastasia asked Eric.

"They would have to have a skilled surgical team and a fully equipped operating room," Eric said. "Without those, the patient is likely to die. Not many doctors could arrange the operation secretly, and if they get caught, they lose their license and have to serve at very low pay in an emergency room for ten years. And any person caught having their chip removed has a special chip inserted in them that prevents their gaining access to airports, government buildings, major entertainment and sports events. They also have their occupation chosen by the authorities and twenty per cent of their income is deducted for twenty years as a penalty."

"That's a pretty limited life," Moira said.

"Like ours is going to be," Anastasia said. "We won't be able to fly anywhere or enter any building that screens for body chips. But it's worth it."

"Time for bed," Moira said.

"There are sheets and blankets in your room," Eric said as he picked Anastasia up in his arms and headed for their bedroom. "Byron, you're not the only one who carries beautiful maidens off."

"I'm glad you have come around to the Scottish way of courting," Byron said.

Moira quickly headed for the other bedroom and over her shoulder said, "I'm going to get there first and bolt the door."

But Byron was quicker.

CHAPTER 7

"Kate," Lawrence told her over the intercom early the next morning, "come outside; I want to show you something in our maple trees." Outside Lawrence said, "We have news about Byron from Sweden. He, Moira, Anastasia and Eric have had their body chips removed and have gone underground. We're meeting with the Brownings and Gorbachevs at breakfast and we'd like for you to come."

"Great! Hurray for Byron and the rest of them! I felt something was up, but I didn't think about anything quite that drastic," Kate answered with the bright cheery voice that only a morning person has. "I'll get dressed and be ready to leave for breakfast as soon as I finish in the cleansing chamber. No exercises this morning."

Lawrence, Laura and Kate mounted separate air scooters and headed for the commuter station. The Brownings and the Gorbachevs were already there when the Holmes family arrived. Lawrence told them that Agent Iago had called to find out why Byron was unavailable, and Carlos had called and said the two couples had arranged to have their body chips removed and had left Stockholm. The Gorbachevs had heard from Carlos, too, but not Iago. The Brownings were concerned for the safety of the couples but not surprised by what had happened.

The group decided they wanted to walk to someplace nearby for breakfast. Their choice was a popular throwback to the past, a diner with stools at a main counter and a few tables along the windows. Luckily, the diner wasn't crowded and a waitress pushed two tables together for the group. For a moment the group stood and looked at each other, unsure who should take the seat at the head of the table.

"Why don't you sit here," Lawrence said to Boris as he indicated the chair at the head of the tables.

Boris hesitated, smiled and said, "Does this mean I have to pay for every one? If so, I'll be glad to relinquish the honor."

"You keep the honor and I'll treat," Lawrence said. "My son is probably the one most responsible for what's happened, and I'm proud of that."

"Don't kid yourself, Dad," Kate said. "Two attractive young women are at the root of this. Byron and Eric just took advantage of a good opportunity to have families and not have to wait years to get started. I wish Mike and I could do the same, but we want our children to be educated in the States."

"Whatever their motivation, we need to do some planning," Lawrence said. "But let's order first."

The favorite menu item was Belgian waffles with blueberries, which Peggy, John and Laura selected. Kate and Boris had homemade biscuits with sausage, which Kate liked to drown with ketchup. Klavdia and Lawrence ordered homemade biscuits, gravy and crisp bacon.

"Bring us a large pitcher of fresh orange juice," Peggy added.

"Laura and I feel sure Internal Security will start a manhunt for our children, and if they're found, they'll be put on trial," Lawrence said. "The question is what can we do, if anything, to prevent the manhunt or help out if they are caught."

"You're right," Boris said. "Internal Security will go after them and may find them. To tell you quite frankly, I'm not sure how much I can assist publicly. My government is not going to like this. I believe I'm being watched already, and there's a chance my phone system is not secure. I doubt if Internal Security can get authority to deactivate my System Fifty, but I'm taking no chances."

"Do you know anything about this Iago, Boris?" Laura asked.

"He's from Italy," Boris said. "I was astonished that any parent would give their child such a hated name, but I found out that isn't his real name. When he was at the University in Milan, he played Iago in a performance that won him the highest award for acting at a competition in Rome. His classmates started calling him Iago as a compliment. He liked it. When recruits join the Internal Security Service, they have to select assumed names. Iago was what he picked. He uses it as his last name. He's no more a friend to us than his namesake was to Othello."

Boris saw that the waitress was bringing the coffee and orange juice, so he waited until she had left to continue. "I had to deal with Iago on a case when I was President. A scientist from Moscow didn't want to aid in developing an improved body chip, so they put him on the surveillance list. When they found out his sister was active in a protest group, Iago first tried to butter me up by saying we should work together for the good of Russia. He wanted me to have the scientist, his name was Bazarov, removed from his position, deported and switched to another kind of work. I told Iago he didn't have any proof that Bazarov had done anything illegal or even wrong. Iago's superior, a sneaky, short and stocky man whose name I don't remember, tried to go through the Directorate staff to overrule me, but they wouldn't do it. Iago will be happy to bring me down if he can. I'll get his superior's name. We may be dealing with him, too."

"What do you think about our announcing that our couples have had their body chips removed so as to get the jump on Internal Security?" Lawrence asked. "We could get those sympathetic to our cause to start a petition to the Council to let our couples be as they are not harming anyone and will, I'm sure, not try to enter any restricted areas. I believe we could get a lot of signatures and huge media coverage. It might even start a movement in at least Scotland, Russia, Sweden, and parts of the U.S. Those participating in protests on the rejection of R-1948 will probably help."

"Dad, I think it will work," Kate said. "And we could use that song *Let It Be* with the words changed to *Let Them Be* to popularize the idea. The group that recorded Byron's lyric poem could make it a hit. I guess we would have to get permission from the song's copywriters, but I bet we could."

"Brilliant idea, dear," Laura said. "And the proceeds from the sales could go to some cause related to young people."

"Or babies, " Lawrence interjected, "since we may have some on the way. I think our children would approve of that."

"At the hospital where I used to work, a charitable organization made funds available to aid handicapped young mothers who had trouble taking care of their babies," Klavdia said. "That might work."

"The petition and song together will be something concrete that our supporters and world wide opinion can latch onto," John said. "Kate can you get the song deal going while our wives work out the charity deal?"

"I'll get Mike to help," Kate said. "He'll know how to contact the song's publishers. I'll contact the recording group."

The waitress brought the orders and the entire group starting eating. The women talked to each other about the details of the charity group as Lawrence and John talked about the petition until Boris interrupted with, "I think our ideas may help, but we ought to prepare for what happens if they don't stop Internal Security. Songs or public opinion won't deter this Iago. He's probably on his way to Sweden already."

"Do you think we should go to Sweden too?" Laura asked.

"We may want to for a second reason," Boris said. "I learned early this morning that Roland died late last night after an operation to replace part of his brain. I'm not supposed to be telling you this, because it won't be announced until later today. Marie tried a partial brain transplant using the brain from a donor severely injured in a scooter crash. She was able to keep the donor's brain functioning throughout the operation and it went well. Roland's capability rating went up immediately and he was recovering better than expected. But several hours later the new brain evidently sent a signal to Roland's heart that caused it to speed up too fast, like a surcharge, and his heart couldn't handle it. The family will probably announce funeral arrangements the day after tomorrow. I'm sure many of the Council and staff will go. Council sessions will probably be suspended for several days."

The families talked over the situation. The Brownings and the Gorbachevs decided to go to Roland's services, but since Lawrence was still having some problems with his speech and walking, the Holmes decided to wait until after his doctor's appointment to decide. No one was sure what more to do than the petition and song. They finished their breakfast.

"John if you'll help me draft the petition, we can get it printed in the Council office and start distribution," Lawrence said.

"Lawrence, we skipped over your idea of announcing our children have had their body chips removed," Peggy said. "I think we should do that today."

"I think Peggy is right," Klavdia said. "Let's do it today. But I think it would be better for Boris if he didn't go to the news conference. They are sure to ask questions that it might be better for Anastasia if he didn't have to answer."

"Klavdia's right," John said. "You'll be more help, Boris, in the background rather than out front."

"O.K. I'll stay behind the scenes and find out what I can from some connections I have," Boris said.

"Do any of the rest of you want to join me at the news conference?" Lawrence asked. "I think there will be one today, because the media representatives have been after me to make a statement about the protests. I wrote one late last night so I'd be ready to meet with them today."

"Why don't we say Lawrence is going to be the spokesman for all three families?" Peggy said. "We could say it's to make it easier for the media to deal with one person rather than six."

"Is that all right with you, Lawrence?" Laura said,

"Yes," Lawrence said, "if it's all right with everyone else." The others nodded their approval.

"I'd keep the statement about the body chips completely confidential until you make the announcement," Boris said.

"Good idea," John said. "O.K. We're set. I'll pay half the bill, Lawrence."

"I've already made arrangements, but thanks," Lawrence said. "Let's think about the good side of this. Our kids are together and doing what we would want them to do. All we have is a little bit of orange juice, but how about a toast to them?"

The seven clinked glasses and John toasted, "To our Moira and your Byron, and your Anastasia and Roland's Eric. May they be happy in their freedom and here's to the time they have together. We'll hope for the best."

"Hear, hear," came from all seven. Laura and Peggy looked into each other's eyes and saw tears forming. Klavdia's eyes had that look of determination the same as Anastasia's when she was excited; Kate had the same look. Lawrence and John looked hopeful. Boris's eyes showed determination, but an element of worry diluted any confidence that the determination might indicate.

Lawrence asked the Brownings to stay a few minutes more. Boris, Klavdia and Kate left, and Lawrence and John walked outside while Laura and Peggy lingered behind to go to the restroom.

"Moira's so young and we're probably not going to be with her when she delivers," Peggy said to Laura.

"Peggy, don't worry," Laura responded. "Eric is pre-med and Klavdia is a nurse. I'm sure Anastasia learned a lot from her. Everything will work out fine."

"I'm so glad they had the guts to take control of their lives," Lawrence said to John outside of the diner. "I was afraid they might have not gotten approval by the birth control committee to have any children."

"They will make great parents. And with their genes, their child will be really something," John said.

"The four of them will make a great team in a situation like this," Lawrence said. "Also, Carlos, Kurt and Jonathan are staying in Sweden to help, if needed. I could tell that those three are determined that the two couples have children. If they can just evade being caught until after the babies come, I believe things will work out, and I think that's their plan. If they get caught before then, I'm worried about what powers a judge has. Our children may not have thought about that since people have almost forgotten about abortions. There haven't been any except for health reasons since pregnancy controls and stun guns have been instituted. But I suppose a judge could order a forced abortion. "

"I haven't said anything to Peggy, but that's what worries me too," John said.

Peggy and Laura came out from the diner and the group walked back to the commuter station together. Lawrence and John caught the melting pot travel unit to the Council Hall. Laura and Peggy mounted their scooters and flew back home.

"Did you notice that Boris didn't show much confidence in our plans to try and stop a manhunt?" John said as he and Lawrence waited for their travel unit.

"I did," Lawrence said. "And he probably has the best grasp of the situation in regard to Internal Security. But I can't think of anything else we can do."

"Me either," John said.

CHAPTER 8

"I wanted to come over as soon as I could," Anne said to Laura as she dismounted from her scooter. Anne had let herself inside her parents' home and then watched for her mother's return. "I'm really feeling badly. I've been so nasty about Byron and I'm sorry. He had one of my friends at the library give me this letter from him this morning when I went to work. He wrote it before he left for Sweden, but he didn't want me to read it until he had his chip removed. I have to go back to work, but I wanted you to see it right away." Anne handed her mother the letter:

Dear Sis,

You may know by now that I've had my body chip removed. If you haven't heard, I hope this is not too much of a shock for you and too upsetting. It was a tough decision for me to make, and Moira, too, because we know it will make life difficult for our families.

But this letter is for you; for you and Kenneth. I am sincerely concerned that my action will affect approval of your application for parenthood. I am hopeful that the esteem in which the Council and the whole world holds Dad will override any negatives I have created. But in the event your application is regretfully rejected, I have done the only thing I could think of to make it possible for you and Kenneth to have children. I have made arrangements for the deactivation of your pregnancy blocks in your and Kenneth's chips by a very good friend of mine. As you know, it does not require an operation; just an electronic signal. I have the utmost confidence in my friend's ability to do this, and no one will know. He says there have been accidental births from defective chips that have been covered up so the general populace does not know it can happen. My friend can arrange it so the birth of your child is listed as accidental and there will not be an inquiry. He says that once you have a family, it is unlikely they will reactivate your blocks, but if that does happen, he will deactivate them again. To contact him, place the message below on planetnet within a week after your parenthood rejection if it unfortunately happens. He will know if your application is rejected, but he will only get in touch with you when he sees your message on the planetnet. Also, he has a backup who knows the whole setup if something should happen to my friend. The message is: 'If you know the whereabouts of Kevin Montgomery Snider, formerly from Topeka, Kansas, please p-mail your reply to sniderm@ pol.com. My friend will set up this p-mail address if he sees that your application was rejected. Moira and I talked about going this route for the child we want to have. We decided we wanted our family to grow up in another atmosphere even if it means hiding out for years. Hope this helps.

By the way, we are planning to name our child John Law-rence if it's a boy and Mary Louise if it's a girl. Hope we didn't take names you were planning on, but I guess cousins can have the same names, anyway.

Love, Byron and Moira

"That was very thoughtful of your brother," Laura said.

"And I have been saying he only thinks of himself. I'm ashamed of myself. Will we be able to be in touch with him?"

"I doubt it. I think he and Moira want to stay hidden at least until their baby is born. I don't know what the authorities would do with a pregnant Moira if they found her before the baby came. That's not something I want to think about."

"What do you think Kenneth and my chances are with the pregnancy control now?"

"I believe you have a good chance. Neither of you have given any trouble, and you are eminently qualified to be parents. There would be a big stink if you were turned down, and the authorities don't want any more problems from the Holmes family right now."

"I admire Byron and Moira for their daring, but that's not the life for Kenneth and me. He has a good position and I do too. We just want to get along."

"You deserve a child or even twins, and I think you'll get your choice."

"I need to get back. Will you call Dad and tell him about the letter?"

"I'll wait until he gets home from the Council. We can't use the phone for anything that might cause problems."

"Glad you reminded me. I'll be careful and tell Kenneth, too." Anne hugged her mother and then mounted her scooter and waved as she flew off.

CHAPTER ♀

"Why is the Directorate proposing to spend 1.3 million dollars for a psychological study of level seven students?" Polish delegate Lech Wojtyla asked. The Council was considering the budget for fiscal 2042 when Lawrence and John entered the Council Hall. They had decided to check their desks for messages and then meet in the advocates' conference room.

"The birth control administrator desires to compare the attitudes of young people of differing parenthood," the education commission's executive secretary stated in answer to Wojtyla's question.

"Will the students' religious backgrounds be one of the parameters considered?" Wojtyla asked. The executive secretary said she did not know and would ask and report back later. "They're probably going to try and reduce the number of Catholics now," Wojtyla said to the delegate seated next to him. "Well, since they restricted India, Africa, and dark skins and even some Muslims, I guess Catholics are going to have their turn because of how vigorously we oppose the whole idea of the authorities deciding if and when couples can have children."

Lawrence opened his desk drawer carefully to check the position of the hairs he had placed inside. He found that both had been dislodged. Lawrence thought, "Iago's not as sharp as he thinks he is, unless he moved the hairs on purpose to try and intimidate me. I'll ask Boris what he thinks."

On the top of Lawrence's desk was a memo from the Council's public relations department director, Pierre Ballenger. Lawrence liked Pierre. He was from Brooklyn and had been a reporter for the Washington *Post* before being hired by the Directorate staff. They had been on many assignments together when Lawrence was with the St. Louis *Post Dispatch*. The memo said the news media had confronted Pierre this morning demanding that Lawrence appear at a news conference today. Pierre had hand-written a note at the bottom of the typed message pleading with Lawrence to let him have at least fifteen minutes to talk with him before the news conference. Lawrence could imagine the heat Pierre was taking. He sympathized with Pierre and called him and told him he could have as much time as he wanted before the conference and to set it up for 14:00. Lawrence started to tell Pierre that he had a surprise for the media, but decided not to mention it.

Then Lawrence and John met in the advocate's conference room. There were only two other delegates in the room who evidently were not as interested in the budget report as they were in taking a break. Lawrence and John greeted them and then seated themselves at a table as far away from the two as possible. Lawrence had already formulated the wording for the petition in his mind, so it only took about ten minutes to complete that draft. Then they drafted a statement about the two couples in Sweden to present at the news conference. John and Lawrence agreed to meet again in an hour for lunch to decide which delegates to ask to carry the petition. John took the drafts with him to get an original and fifty copies of each printed at the Council's administrative services office.

After finishing his meeting with John, Lawrence returned to his desk in the Council Hall. Discussion of the budget was still going on. James Anderson was at his desk and leaned over to say, "Lots of rumors are going around about Roland. Have you heard about the secret operation?"

Lawrence couldn't betray Boris's confidence, so he answered, "What's going on?"

James told him most of what Boris had told him earlier, but the story had grown into a full brain transplant of a younger man who was not like Roland at all. The word was that the donor was heavily tattooed, had been transferred three times to successively lower level work assignments and was no longer allowed a stun gun because he shot his sister with his. James asked if Lawrence and his family would be going to the service in Sweden. Lawrence said he hadn't decided.

"What are delegates saying about me?" Lawrence asked as he moved his chair closer to James.

James was surprised by the question. He looked puzzled and said, "Just admiration for a good effort that didn't succeed. Why did you ask?"

"It was because of your warning me a week or ten days ago to be careful."

"That was before your resolution lost. Is anyone giving you trouble?"

"I can't talk about it right now. I'll be making an announcement later today that will give you my situation. If you hear anything I should know, call me to meet you rather than talk over the phone."

James nodded, more puzzled than ever.

At 13:30, Pierre came by Lawrence's desk, and they went together to the staff's conference room. Pierre was universally described as "rotund with a round smile." His thinning hair was attributed to the stress of his occupation. Pierre prepared for news conferences, the most stressful events in his life, in the same way as Laura overcame her aversion to making verbal reports: he secretly had a glass of wine, usually red, and it worked for him, too. "Lawrence, old boy, you may be in for it this afternoon. The wolves are out and will be after you."

"And my blood?" Lawrence asked.

"No, it's just that they are tying you to this tremendous upheaval going on all over everywhere. Some are asking me if this is what you intended. Others want to know if you support it. And others want to know what it's going to lead to. They think you have the answers to all these and other questions. I thought you ought to have some warning before you entered their den."

"Pierre, you're a good man. Thanks for the advance notice. 'Fore warned is fore armed.' I have a copy here of the statement I am going to make. Want to see it?"

Lawrence held out one page. "Is that all there is?" Pierre asked.

"That's all there is about the international protests, but there will be a second statement about something different. The second statement is to be confidential until I give it out. You'll get your copy then."

"I'd rather see it ahead of time. I don't like surprises."

"Sorry I can't let you have it. Several persons are involved and that's the way we agreed to handle it. I can't go back on my pledge to them."

"Enough said. At least the Directorate can't blame me for something I didn't get to see. Let me see your first statement."

Lawrence handed it to Pierre who lowered his glasses, which had been perched on his forehead and read: "Gentlemen and Ladies, Ladies and Gentlemen: I have two statements to make. The first is as follows: on behalf of all those who supported R-1948, I wish to express appreciation for the intent of persons everywhere who have protested the Planet Council's rejection of R-1948. As much as we appreciate the intent, we deplore those protest actions which have resulted in injuries and property damages. It was not our purpose to incite inappropriate expressions of protest. We did not organize or participate in them; they are harmful to our cause. To those persons or organizations which are protesting improperly, we say, 'Stop it, stop it right now,' and we mean it. Violence is not the way to progress; deliberative debate followed by responsible decision making is. Our side did not prevail in its first initiative. In order to have another opportunity to advance our cause, we must conduct ourselves as the loyal opposition. We feel that time is on our side in the race for restoration of mankind's rights so long as we do not disqualify ourselves by violating the existing rights of the individual."

Pierre looked up from the paper and said, "Well said. If it doesn't scatter the wolves, it should hold them at bay."

"Thanks, Pierre. Are you ready to go?"

"Ready or not, here we go. Isn't that what you said before your speech?"

"Something like that."

Lawrence and Pierre walked together to the small auditorium where large news conferences were held. Nearly one hundred media representatives were set up with TV cameras, digital cameras and recorders in the room.

Pierre presented Lawrence and said that Lawrence was going to read two statements and questions should be held until both statements had been read.

As Lawrence finished the first statement, murmurs were heard throughout the auditorium. Having been a reporter himself, Lawrence was sure that the news media had been hoping for a dramatic rallying-of-the-forces calling for reversal of the rejection of R-1948. That would be news. Lawrence's statement was not going to do anything to sell newspapers or boost TV ratings.

Lawrence paused before starting his second statement. The seriousness of his expression and the curiosity of those assembled brought about a silence unusual for the normally unruly group. Only the quiet humming of the television cameras could be heard.

Lawrence looked up from the pages he held and said, "I have been selected as a spokesman for the families of Moira Browning, Anastasia Grobachev, and my son, Byron Holmes." Lawrence was once again aware of how unintentionally he was speaking slowly. It bothered him and he frowned.

"What I have to say is my best attempt to express the collective feelings of three families. Naturally, that cannot be done completely or even accurately. These families have chosen to have a spokesperson in an effort to simplify the communications between them and the media and to spare those family members unaccustomed to the rigors of news inquiries the anxiety that can accompany having to answer personal questions before an international audience."

Media representatives were all looking at each other wondering what in the world this was about? A quiet buzz became loud enough that Lawrence stopped and waited for it to die down. Then he continued, "The three young people just named have evidently had their body chips removed." A collective gasp was audible. "We were informed that the Body Functions Department has not been able to access their body chips for their monthly physical monitoring. None of the three families have been in direct contact with their children since they traveled to Sweden to attend the planned funeral services for Roland Nilsson. We do not know where they are or when they plan to return or be in contact with us next."

By this time the room was in motion with cameras and correspondents trying to get closer to the podium from which Lawrence was speaking, but at the same time be quiet enough not to miss a word.

Lawrence paused and looked up from the pages he held and rotated his head to look squarely into the cameras. "All families are firm in their support of their children. We know the action they have taken is not in accordance with the dictates of our government but is in accordance with the dictates of their hearts and in keeping with the spirit of all men and women to crave freedom. We appeal to the world--let them be. They wish no harm to anyone. They are no threat to anyone. They are fine, young adults who are a credit to their families and their countries. We love them and are proud to be the parents of such brave, daring and caring individuals that are worthy of the esteem of all mankind."

Lawrence folded the pages he was holding and slipped them into his pocket. Many news representatives were pushing forward to be in position to ask a question. Ten to twenty media representatives shouted out their questions at once. Pierre stepped forward to the microphone, raised his hands in the air and said in a loud voice so he could be heard above the shouting, "Ladies, gentlemen. Order please. Order. One question at a time. Mary Duval, your question."

Mary Duval was a reporter from the Chicago *Tribune* and had been assigned to Planet Council coverage for over 15 years. She was not the most senior media representative, but one of the most respected and most courteous. Pierre was doing Lawrence a favor by calling on her for the first question.

"Peoples' Advocate Holmes," Mary said, "I know that the families you are speaking in behalf of must be concerned about their children, how they came through the operations for removal of their body chips, if indeed that has occurred and if they are having any problems. How do you plan to get in touch with them?"

Lawrence paused before answering to consider just how far to go with his answer. Then he said, "We have no idea how to make a direct contact, but we are trying to get word from friends of theirs who traveled with them to Sweden to confirm what we think has happened. We expect some information, possibly as early as today. Our children know of the concerns you mentioned, and we are confident they will arrange some way of alleviating them, because they are considerate, loving persons."

The next ten or so questions included: why the three had gone to Sweden, where they had been staying, who went with them, how long had they planned to stay, were they joining with others of like mind, had they told what they planned to do before they left, were the couples married and even a question that subtly referred to the likelihood that the young women would soon be pregnant. Lawrence patiently answered all the questions truthfully including identifying Eric Nilsson as one of the friends they were with in Sweden. Most of the answers were that the parents didn't know in advance that anything but a trip to attend Roland's services and some camping afterward was planned. Then there were ten or so questions about the protest rallies, which included if Lawrence planned to attend or support any in the future, had any of the protest leaders been in touch with him and that in light of the many protests, did he expect the Council to reconsider R-1948? To each of these questions Lawrence answered "No." Then Pierre interrupted to say, "One more question. Gilbert Brell."

"To return to the probable actions of the three young persons and possibly Eric Nilsson as a fourth since it is public record and well known here at the Planet Council that he and Anastasia Gorbachev have applied for marriage approval, do you think removal of their body chips, if that has happened, was a direct result of the rejection of R-1948?" Brell asked.

Lawrence looked down, raised his hand to brush back his hair, looked up over the heads of the media representatives as if to seek help in answering a question he wasn't sure how to answer or that he wanted to answer. Then he looked directly into the cameras to say, "That question can, of course, only be answered by the individuals taking whatever actions they did. However, I do want to say this. I know that group was hopeful that my resolution would pass because they felt that all persons, but particularly the youth of this planet, deserve to live in a freer society. I know, also, that some of the group wanted a much shorter time frame for a transition to greater freedoms. I know the two couples involved were concerned about their chances for being approved for parenthood. Other than what I've told you, I can't add anything more other than this-- if I had been in their shoes when I was their age and in the same circumstances, I would have done the same thing, and I believe my Laura would have joined me."

The senior media representative said, "Thank you, Mr. Holmes, and, uh, well I shouldn't be saying this; I know it will surprise my colleagues, but I am retiring next month so I can't get into too much trouble. Anyway, and I'm only speaking for myself when I say the youngsters have my best wishes."

The rush of the representatives to file their stories drowned out Lawrence's "Thank you."

CHAPTER Λ∇

"Morning, sleepy heads," Anastasia said to Byron and Moira as they emerged from their bedroom. "We've been up for a long time." Anastasia was cooking bacon, and Eric was breaking eggs into a large bowl getting them ready to scramble.

"And you've been out cutting wood, killing a deer for dinner tonight and hauling water from the creek," Byron said.

"Ha, ha," Eric said. "Any more of your smart ass remarks, and we'll make you do all the wood splitting. There'll be a lot of that when we leave the lodge."

"How long do you think it's safe for us to stay here?" Moira asked.

Eric said, "Until tomorrow, and then we'll hike into Norway. It's about 10 kilometers to the border. After we stop there for a day or two, we'll go deeper into the forest. Today Byron and I will take the hovercraft up the creek a little way so we don't leave a trail, and then we'll go cross-country carrying the tents and heavier stuff to find our first campsite. That way we will have light packs for our hiking tomorrow. Moira, if you and Anastasia can set up the sound monitor around the cabin while we're gone, we can get away earlier tomorrow."

"Sure, tell us where you want it set up," Moira said.

"It should cover the backside of the lodge, but mostly ring the approach towards the creek where we came in," Eric said. "By the way, the signal from the sound monitor is how Marie will let us know that she wants to send us a message. When we hear the signal we are to turn on and tune our receiver to match the transmitter she will be using."

Byron said, "I take it that means this is our last day for 'home cooked' meals. Probably our last bacon and eggs?"

"Unless you find chickens and pigs in the forest," Anastasia said.

Moira said, "Well, let's eat. Byron and I'll clean up since you and Eric did the cooking."

They all sat down around the table. It was made of rough sawn planks. The top was uneven, but the table was plenty stable.

Byron asked Eric, "Did you make this table?"

"Dad and I did," Eric replied. "Any complaints?"

"No, no," Byron said. "I just figured that you built the lodge and everything in it without hauling anything in. That's commendable. I couldn't do it."

"We brought the electrical, plumbing and heating supplies in with the hovercraft, but anything wooden we got at the site. It was hard work, but fun. My brother and Marie came along to help, and she is very good with a power saw as well as a scalpel. She just doesn't like to sand. That's why the table top is a little rough."

"We've got to do something special for Marie," Moira said. "She risked a lot for us."

"She's so thrilled at what we are doing that she probably considers that reward enough," Eric said. "If she hadn't been operating on Dad, she probably would have had her chip removed when we did. You know she has never married. I wouldn't be surprised if she joined us later after Dad's fully recovered."

"We could use her help," Anastasia said as she looked at Moira. "Particularly with the deliveries. Or do you want to deliver your own baby, Eric?"

"I will, if necessary, but I'm going to try and get help when the time comes," Eric said. "Aunt Marie can probably arrange for one of her staff to come, if she can't."

"We should let our parents know that help will be there when the babies come," Moira said. "I'll bet they are very worried about that."

"Next time we're in touch with Carlos or Marie, I'll do that," Eric said. "It'd be nice if we had a safe but simpler way to make contact than for Marie to have to come to the lodge." He looked at Byron and said, "Can you figure a better way?"

"I'll work on it," Byron said." "My Boy Scout manual may have something about smoke signals. That's probably safe if our friends are the only ones in the area to notice them. Homing pigeons might be better. Can you train them if I find them, Moira?"

"The great thing about you, darling," Moira said, "is you always have an answer. And you certainly have been cheery. Aren't you worried?"

"No, sweet. I have a loaf of bread, a jug of wine and you beside me in the wilderness. What more could I ask for."

"A small army to defend us?" Anastasia said.

"Haven't you read what Wallace and a few good Scots did at Stirling Bridge?" Byron answered. "And we have Moira, too."

"In Scotland we say 'He that tholes, overcomes,' which means that he that endures overcomes," Moira said. "I think we can do it."

You're my lass," Byron said as he kissed Moira.

CHAPTER ΛΛ

"I'd like to call Carlos this evening," Lawrence told Laura when he arrived home the evening after his announcement about the body chip removals. "Let's go now and eat when we get back. We had better take separate scooters this time."

"In that case we can race. My thirty-five kilometers per hour will be faster than yours, I'm sure," Laura said.

At the Nilsson's they called the secure number in Sweden Carlos had given them and got him on the second ring.

"We have more questions," Lawrence said. "Did Byron and the others have any post operation problems?"

"No. They only had to rest for two hours after the operation, because it is a quick and easy procedure if you have the right surgeon and good facilities but dangerous and long if you don't."

"I won't ask you who did it," Laura said, "but it sounds as if there are only a few who fit that bill that would actually do it for someone else, so I feel better already."

"I, I, well, I think you are on the right track," Carlos said.

"I assume that no chip features are operating," Lawrence said. "The medical data is gone as well as the location coordinates?"

"You're right. Have you heard that Roland died?" Carlos said.

Lawrence said, "Boris told us confidentially this morning, and they announced it at a Council session in the afternoon. We don't know if we are going to the funeral service. In case of an emergency, is there a way to get word to Byron and the others?"

"There is, but it's difficult and it can only be initiated over here," Carlos said.

Laura asked, "Are they anxious about the future?"

"They were feeling great when they left. It's such a joy to see both couples so happy together enjoying their newfound freedom. It's the way it ought to be for everyone. If I had a girlfriend who would marry me, I'd be with them even though I know it's a big risk. When I find one, I'm going to do the same thing they did. I may seem as if I'm a pretty calm person to most people, but I'm willing to do what should be done if it's important enough. Marriage and children are important enough."

"We'll keep an eye out for a real sharp gal for you," Laura said. "Do you prefer blondes, brunettes or red heads?"

"That's not a matter of concern," Carlos said.

"Are Byron and the others still in Sweden?" Lawrence asked.

"No one knows their exact location," Carlos said. "They wanted it that way and want to keep it that way for at least nine months."

"Nine months, heh,"Lawrence said. "That's a well known time interval, isn't it?"

Laura said, "Do you know if they had any kind of ceremony before, before . . . "

Carlos broke in, "Yes they did. Marie arranged it with a Lutheran minister. He's the same one who now is going to conduct Roland's service. He's a very close friend of the family, and Marie knew she could trust him. Jonathan, Kurt and I stood up with them. It was a double service with double rings. Byron asked Moira what kind of ring she would like and had a former classmate of his make it. He just got it finished before they left for Sweden. It is a beautiful emerald cut diamond that Byron must have been saving up for. Moira was overwhelmed. The ring she gave Byron was made in Scotland of copper and gold. Moira has had it in her hope chest since she was a teenager. Byron really teased her about that saying she must have been awfully confident that someone would come along and ask her to marry him. Moira said in today's world a lassie didn't have to wait to be asked; she could pop the question to a laddie if she wanted. Eric's mother, sister and brother were there for the ceremony too. It was outdoors, and except for the light rain just before the service started, everything went off without a hitch. We have pictures we'll bring home with us."

"John Browning and I drafted a petition to the Planet Council calling for amnesty for both couples. Kate is going to get the group that recorded Byron's *Liberty* to work up a *Let Them Be* song to build support for not chasing them down. If Marie, and you and the others have any other ideas, let us know."

"Great ideas. I'll talk to Marie and let you know."

As Laura was asking Carlos what Moira and Anastasia wore to the wedding ceremony, Merlin announced, "Agent Iago is calling."

Lawrence moved into another room and said, "Good evening."

"Have you been in contact with Byron, yet?" Iago asked.

"No, I haven't," Lawrence answered. "Have you?"

Iago ignored the question and asked, "Have you been in contact with any others of the young group that went over with Byron? Carlos Domingo, Kurt Kriger, or Jonathan Hurst?"

"No, I haven't," Lawrence answered "Have you?"

Laura had disconnected with Carlos and joined Lawrence.

Again, Iago ignored Lawrence's question and said, "I'd like for you to come to our headquarters tomorrow. I'll have a car pick you up at 09:00. Bring your most recent color photo of Byron and any clothing that he wore recently with you.".

Laura was close enough to hear the conversation. She clasped her hand over her mouth and turned away so Iago couldn't hear her gasp.

"I have a doctor's appointment about an emergency condition at 09:30 tomorrow. I probably won't be through before 10:30 or 11:00. I'm having some tests run. I can come then."

The silence on Iago's end of the line lasted for ten seconds or more. Then Iago said, "We will pick you up at your doctor's office at 10:30. Is it at the clinic at the Council Hall?"

"Yes," Lawrence answered. "I'll tell my doctor to be through by then if at all possible."

In a sly, sinister voice Iago said, "This appointment have anything to do with your body chip?"

"Sorry, I didn't hear that," Lawrence said. "Must be trouble on the line."

"Perhaps so," Iago said, and he disconnected.

In a voice too loud and rising Laura said, "They'll hunt them down and kill them, won't they?"

"Don't get hysterical, love," Lawrence said. "They will try to find them, but they wouldn't dare injure them. They will want to bring them to trial."

"But Byron will resist. He'll use his stun gun and anything else he can. I know he will," Laura sobbed.

Lawrence put his arm around Laura and said quietly, "Byron won't do anything that would endanger Moira. If he resisted, she might get hurt. But the main thing they have going for them is that Iago may not find them. Eric and his dad have hunted all over Sweden. Eric will know where to go and how to cover their tracks. My guess is that they are deep in some forest where they can't be spotted from the air. It would take an army to search the wilderness. I bet they have a long-range sound monitor set up near their camp, so they'd know if trackers were in their area long before they got near. They used those monitors to locate the terrorists back in the 20's, because they can distinguish between human and other sounds."

"The search parties have an army and will have those sound monitors, too. What are we going to do?" Laura's sobs rose to crying and she slumped to the floor.

Lawrence lowered himself to be beside her. He drew her head to his shoulder and held her tightly. After a few minutes she relaxed and said, "I just need to be hugged every so often to settle down. Thanks, darling."

"Our youngsters are smarter than the authorities and Eric knows the area better. Remember, the branch of the army in Sweden cannot have any personnel from Sweden. And the Swedish government is not going to be sympathetic to any manhunt for two couples who have not done anything to harm anyone. They will probably restrict the amount of funds and personnel available for searching. I need to pull every string I can to get as many signatures on the petition to the Council. The protest movement that reacted so strongly to the defeat of R-1948 has to be channeled to demands for mercy for the four of them. I'm going by the Brownings and the Gorbachevs on my way home. You go by Anne's and tell her what Carlos said."

"Oh! How could I have forgotten to tell you? Byron wrote a letter to Anne before he left. He has arranged for she and Kenneth to have a child if the Parenthood Committee turns them down."

"I don't know how he did it, but that's marvelous. I'm not surprised that Byron was looking out for Anne. We are lucky to have a son who is sensitive to other's concerns even when he has a multitude of his own. I'd like to see the letter when we get back home."

As they flew off in different directions, Lawrence thought he saw a scooter by the side of a house two down from the Nilsson's. He flew down to the end of the block, paused, and then turned left at the maximum speed of his scooter and flew between the first and second house, maneuvered into a tight space between the house and a scooter storage building and turned off his ignition so his radar sender was inactive. Within a few seconds a scooter he recognized by its black color and large search light as being one of Internal Security's turned the same way he had and flew on down the block. It stopped midway down the block, reversed directions, and flew back by the houses he was between. After reaching the intersection, the Internal Security scooter flew away. Lawrence waited five minutes and then flew between houses away from the street he had been flying above and on to the Brownings.

Lawrence found John at home and told him about Iago's call. John had received a call, too, but he wasn't required to go to Internal Security's headquarters. Iago told John a car would come by to pick up Moira's clothes and photo.

Boris wasn't at home, but Klavdia was. She didn't think Boris had received a call from Iago. He hadn't mentioned it or the need to get any of Anastasia's clothes or a picture. Lawrence surmised that Iago had been told to treat the Gorbachevs differently, since Boris represented one of The Big Three.

As he flew home, Lawrence thought about his being followed by Internal Security. Since they could easily have called into headquarters and gotten a fix on his location between the houses through his body chip, he wondered why they hadn't resumed following him. Lawrence decided Iago wanted him to know he was tailing him just as he wanted him to know he had searched his desk. It was probably the recommended next step in a war of nerves.

CHAPTER Λ2

"I was surprised to hear from my nurse that you wanted an appointment," Dr. Rex Morton said to Lawrence as he came into the waiting room shortly after Morton's nurse had run a check on Lawrence's vital signs through his body chip and checked his blood count. "It's only been seven months since your annual check-up. My nurse said that you have been suffering from an unsteady gait and slowness of speech. She just told me that there are indications that your condition has changed drastically since your physical. You did the right thing to contact me."

Rex Morton was at Washington University Medical School doing his residency when Lawrence was assigned to do a feature article on the trials and tribulations of doctors during residences. Rex and Lawrence had hit it off from the start and when there was an opening for the head of staff position at the Planet Council clinic, Lawrence first convinced Rex to apply and then lobbied hard and helped get him the position.

"Preliminary indications are that you are one of the very few to have Wilson's disease," Rex told Lawrence. "My nurse is preparing a relatively new test that will tell us for sure if you do. Persons whose bodies don't rid themselves of copper at the right rates end up with a surplus that can cause severe problems, even death, if not diagnosed and treated promptly. If that's what you have, we've caught yours in time."

"When did I get it and how?"

"You've had it since birth; it's inherited. It just took a long time for the copper to build up in your system. Symptoms usually show up between the ages of four and forty. Yours were late. The unsteady gait and slowness of speech are two tip-offs."

"What are others?"

"A yellowing of the eyes and . . . "

Lawrence interrupted with "Is the yellowing a sure symptom?"

"It's important."

"Byron's friend Eric Nilsson noticed a yellowing of Byron's eyes. Byron said his eyes weren't bothering him and thought it might have been from the late hours he had been keeping. Does Byron have to go to a doctor's office to be tested?"

"No, the test is relatively simple now and can be done anywhere if you have the right stuff."

"Thank God. How soon must he be tested?"

"If that's the only symptom, he'll be all right for a week or two, possibly longer, but the sooner the better to prevent damage to his body."

"How about Anne and Kate?"

"Definitely should be tested. Have they had any of the symptoms we've talked about?"

"Not that I know of. I'll have both come in this afternoon if at all possible. Can you test them then?"

"My nurse will run the tests, but I'll be sure to check the results and prescribe the treatment if needed."

"Can you give me what I need for Byron? Evidently, you haven't heard the news."

"What news? I've been tied up for days. I haven't seen or heard anything."

Lawrence told Rex about what Byron had done and how it would be difficult to locate him. Rex said he would give Kate everything needed to test and treat Byron when she came in. Rex said Eric could easily do the testing and treatment. Lawrence told Rex that Kate wouldn't know about getting the things for Byron, so he would leave a note for her. On the way out of Rex's office Lawrence called Kate and told her quickly about Wilson's disease and asked her to call Anne and arrange for her testing too. He did not mention over the unsecured line the things Kate would be getting for Byron or the note he was leaving her which asked her to make reservations to fly to Sweden the next day.

After Lawrence's appointment with Rex, he hurried to the main entrance because he was ten minutes late. The Internal Security car was waiting just outside the entrance. Lawrence carried Byron's clothes and his picture in a dark green bag, which he used when he played tennis at the Council's indoor courts. Council members were used to seeing him with it, so no one had asked him about it. His mind was still on Wilson's disease. He was relieved that the treatments he received would stop any future problems, but he was angry with himself for not making an appointment with Rex when he first noticed his problems three or four months before. If he'd done that, he could have had Byron tested before he left for Sweden.

Sugar Boy was standing beside the car. Lawrence wondered if he had been on the scooter that followed him to the Nilsson's house the night before. Probably not, Lawrence surmised, because there was something about him that suggested he was more than a low-level assistant. He walked over to Sugar Boy, shook his hand and said, "I keep you busy. Do you have anyone else to escort around?"

Sugar Boy smiled but didn't answer. They walked together to the commuter station. Sugar Boy had made reservations for them on the relaxation unit. Lawrence was the first on when it arrived, and Sugar Boy took a seat in the row behind Lawrence. Lawrence decided to put on the headset and nap all the way downtown. He had so many things to think about that might keep him awake, that he was glad to have the headset's electrodes to help him get to sleep.

The headsets in the relaxation cars had four options for being awakened when you reached your programmed destination: soft music, gentle vibrations, a recording of your own voice to say whatever you chose or the recorded voice of Nicole Kidman, a famous movie star of the early part of the century, saying "Our time together is over, darling. Sorry to have to leave you, but it's been swell. I'll be waiting for you to dream with me again. " Kidman's message wasn't from a movie, it had been created by piecing together more than one recording. When it was introduced in 2024 in an attempt to add a light note to a world that was becoming increasingly regulated, three Baptist churches in New York City objected. But when the transportation department's record of the options chosen showed Kidman's recording was selected 80 % of the time, the department rejected the protests. Later, the most popular actresses at the time were substituted for Kidman, but many objections were received and her voice became a permanent fixture. On the few occasions he used the headsets to go to sleep, Lawrence selected Kidman, but today he opted for the music.

The commuter station stop for Internal Security was inside their headquarters building. This arrangement was to facilitate the transfer of prisoners into and out of the detention rooms. In order to disembark, passengers had to have a special pass or be checked in through a holding area. Sugar Boy had a pass, and he and Lawrence walked through the entrance down a hall for what was popularly known as the "peep show." All persons to be interrogated at the headquarters were subjected to a strip search, but the procedures were impersonal in that no persons conducted the search, just machines.

Lawrence had heard about the peep show, but neither he nor any of his acquaintances had ever been subjected to it. Sugar Boy took him to the door of the peep show room and told him to step inside and take off everything he had on. After that, Sugar Boy told him with a smile, "'Oz' will tell you what to do."

The peep show room was five meters square with no windows and bare of all furniture but a clothes rack and an elevated hospital bed. In the ceiling, along the walls and in the floor were slots through which beams of light and rays projected onto the bed. Persons being interrogated were not aware that their bone structure was X-rayed for identification purposes in case they had plastic surgery to hide their identity and that the rays installed an electronic residue, which could be detected for eight months from a distance of one thousand meters to facilitate the continuous tracking of their location.

Lawrence entered, took off his clothes and his watch, and stood by the bed. Oz commanded, "Take off your ring," in a voice that reminded Lawrence of the message a computer gives if it is turned off improperly. Lawrence took off his wedding ring and placed it on the bed. Oz said, "Lie on the bed on your back. Close your eyes and cover them with the mask that is on the bed." Lawrence did. The strong light that came on warmed his body. The light went off and Oz commanded, "Lie on your right side." After the light turned on and off, Oz had him turn on his left side and then stomach during which the light again turned on and off. "Put your clothes on, check to be sure you have all your possessions, and exit," Oz said.

Sugar Boy was waiting outside the door with the green bag Lawrence had brought. Sugar Boy led Lawrence down a long hallway and out through a door to a separate small stand-alone building. There was only one door into the building, which had ten rooms, each equipped with one desk and three chairs. Above the desk was a skylight, which provided ample illumination since it was late morning on a cloudless day. Iago was seated in one chair and a young man Lawrence thought was a stenographer in another with a court-reporter-like machine on his chair arm support. The machine had a keyboard, but it also had a lens that was aimed towards Lawrence. The young man looked disinterested as Lawrence came in and remained that way throughout the interrogation. Lawrence wondered why Iago needed a stenographer since he assumed the interrogation was being recorded;

probably so there was a human witness present Lawrence thought. The young man looked at Lawrence and typed for a minute or so. After that, he didn't type anything. Lawrence surmised that it was not a recorder he was operating; it was a wireless lie detector that monitored the brain during questioning. Lawrence knew the results from that type of lie detector could not be used in court, but it would help Iago nevertheless.

Lawrence handed Iago the green bag without comment. Iago placed it on the desk, took out the contents, looked at them briefly and said, "Is this the best picture you could find? I think we have a better one from the Cultural Development Bureau."

"Our family is not big on taking pictures," Lawrence said.

"I understand you are planning to travel to Sweden. You will have to go through a special security check at the Stockholm airport, by the way. Do you plan to make contact with your son while there?"

"I don't know if he is in Sweden. I don't have any devise to contact him where ever he is."

"Have you heard from any of your son's friends who went with him to Sweden?"

All three of the families of the two couples who went to Sweden had anticipated being asked this question, so Lawrence was ready with the answer they had agreed to give. "Yes, Carlos Domingo called Boris Gorbachev and told us that the children involved, that is Byron, Moira, Anastasia, and Eric, had gone camping near Stockholm. The two couples said they would be back in four days, but they haven't come back, yet. Carlos said he didn't know where they were, and he hadn't heard from them since they left."

"Why have you and your wife been going to the Nilsson home so often?"

Lawrence and the families were ready for this question too. "The Nilssons asked us, and by the way they asked the Brownings, too, to check on their house regularly since Roland's stroke was well publicized and buglers might target it. They also have two cats, "Bridget" and "Bardot" which are well trained, but if the power were to go out, the automatic litter cleansing box would need emptying while they were gone. They also said their phone system had much better connections with Sweden, and we were welcome to call from their house."

Iago looked frustrated. He paused, then he said, "Mr. Holmes, you are a clever man. Through your newspaper career you are experienced in the ways of the world and your participation in the Planet Council has most likely increased your understanding of the danger your son and his companions have placed themselves in. If you want to lessen the consequences of their unlawful actions, you had best help us find them."

Lawrence was not prepared for this threat. He had been looking to the side during the interrogation so he could hide any involuntary facial reaction to the questions from Iago. He paused before turning his head to look directly into Iago's eyes. Then he said, "Agent Iago, you are correct that my newspaper career has been beneficial in teaching me important lessons, and being a member of the most powerful legislative body of this day or any time in the past has refined that learning process. What I have learned is that the pen is more powerful than the sword.

Please write these words into your memory. 'Do not let harm come to my son or any of his companions.' To do so is to imperil you and all those you represent."

Iago stared back at Lawrence. Lawrence didn't flinch. After a long moment, Iago looked to the side and said, "You're dismissed."

Sugar Boy was waiting for Lawrence outside the interrogation room. He escorted Lawrence to the commuter stop inside the Internal Security headquarters and told the attendant Lawrence was to have a reserved seat on the next travel unit of his choice. Lawrence selected the melting pot to the commuter station nearest his home.

Laura was eating lunch and surprised to see him home so early in the day. "What are you doing home so early?" she asked. "Had lunch, yet?"

"No," Lawrence said. "It's nice out. Let's eat on the patio," he said as he held his finger to his lips to remind Laura to be careful what she said.

Laura fixed Lawrence a smoked ham and Swiss cheese on seven grain bread. He liked lots of mayonnaise on both sides of the meat and cheese. She had tried to find the best substitute for the Miracle Whip dressing that Lawrence loved. The company making it had gone out of business in 2029. The company that bought the rights to continue with the name just couldn't get it right somehow. When Miracle Whip devotees complained about it, the company said they were using the exact same recipe and equipment. Lawrence said his mother would have said the employees making it weren't holding their mouths right.

On the patio Lawrence and Laura sat down to eat. Laura started to ask, "How did your doctor's . . .," as Lawrence started to say, "I've got something important . . ."

Laura stopped. Looking frightened, she took Lawrence's hand. "Are you all right?"

"I'm going to be," Lawrence said. "But I wasn't and the kids may not be either. I've got Wilson's disease, which is caused by a build-up of copper in your body. The diagnosis and treatment are simple, but untreated the disease is fatal. It's hereditary. It's possible it contributed to my dad's death without anyone knowing it, since his death was thought to be accidental and there was no autopsy. I've arranged for Anne and Kate to be tested today.

"Remember how I have been unsteady on my feet and have had difficulty speaking? Those are both symptoms of Wilson's disease. None of our children have had those symptoms that I know of, but I'm worried about Byron. Before he left he told me that Eric noticed he had a slight yellowing of his eyes, which I've found out is also a symptom. I hadn't noticed it, but that might be because it develops slowly and seeing him almost every day, I didn't pick up slight changes. Eric's medical training made him more alert to anything that looked abnormal. We've got to get Byron tested soon and treated, if necessary. It's not an emergency situation, but he can't go weeks without treatment, if he has it. We need to go to Sweden and take testing equipment and the antidote for the disease. Kate has made reservations for us to leave tomorrow. I'm going to the Nilsson's this evening and call Carlos. I think you had better stay home and pack. Kate is going to Sweden with us. She wants to help us find Byron. Anne offered to go, too, but I told her she didn't need to go."

Laura hung her head. Her hand was still in Lawrence's. He squeezed it. She looked up. "What if we can't find Byron? And if we do, what if they follow us and find them?"

"We'll find them, I'm sure. And we'll have to find a way to do it secretly."

"They'll be watching us. And Carlos and Marie, too. I wish you had never thought of your damned resolution."

"I feel the same way sometimes too, love, but we can't go back. We've got to move ahead. We've been through worse."

"When has it ever been this bad?"

"When Byron wouldn't take your milk. That could have been disastrous. Friends helped us then. They will now. Carlos, Jonathan and Kurt would do anything for the two couples. I believe they would even risk their lives for them."

"It always seems to have been Byron who has been the one in trouble. Why is that?"

"There is no rhyme or reason to a lot of things. But remember the choices you were talking about that I have made? There are only a few real choices a person has that aren't greatly affected by factors he can't control. But you do get to choose to marry or not. No one can force you to marry. And, no one can force you to marry someone you don't want to. When we got married, we could choose to have children or not have children on our own schedule. I made those choices, and I don't regret for a moment the consequences. Having you, Byron, Anne and Kate have been worth everything that has gone before and whatever happens ahead."

Laura moved into Lawrence's arms and stayed there for a long time.

Later that evening, Lawrence called Carlos from the Nilsson's and told him the plan to fly to Sweden the next day and about the need to have Byron tested and possibly treated for Wilson's disease. Carlos said he would meet them at the airport and tell them about contacting Byron. Lawrence gave Carlos his flight schedule and told him about the interrogation with Internal Security. Carlos said the Swedish branch of Internal Security had questioned Jonathan, Kurt, Marie, and him, and they were being followed. Carlos ended the conversation with, "Keep up your spirits. Marie has a lot of connections over here, and the Swedish government is on our side. The Peoples' Advocate from Sweden, your friend Briggita Borge, called and is here to help however she can."

CHAPTER Λ3

"Byron, you are the one we can most afford to lose, you bring up the rear," Eric said as he led the way through the woods. He followed the route he and Byron had taken when they hauled supplies to the campsite where they planned to be for a few days. Anastasia was close behind Eric as second in command, then Moira and, as directed, Byron was last. The packs they carried were relatively light, the sun shone brightly through the tall pines of the forest and everyone was feeling so cheerful that they began to sing. Each hiker selected a song starting with Anastasia.

"I choose Waltzing Matilda ," Anastasia said. "When I was a teenager a member of the Australian figure skating team taught it to me. We became friends, and later when I withdrew from the Olympic trials, she sent me a dozen of my favorite flowers, yellow tulips." Everyone sang Waltzing Matida twice in English, except for Eric who had to sing in Unifren.

Moira chose Bonnie Boy. Eric knew it in English and his tenor voice was so melancholy that Moira shed a tear after the last refrain. "Your tear is worth a thousand words of praise," Byron said to Moira as he wiped it away with his hand.

"I hated marching in my physical training camp, but at least we sang while we marched and the dumbest song was Straw Foot, Hay Foot ," Eric said. Our instructor said it came from the U.S., and it was created to help farm boys who didn't know their right foot from their left learn to march. They tied hay to the left foot and straw to the right foot and sang out the foot to use in time with marching. Is there any truth to that story, Byron?"

"Absolutely, but I was told it didn't work in Scotland because they didn't know the difference between hay and straw or their right foot and their left," Byron said.

"I'll show you the difference between my right to your jaw and a left jab to your stomach," Moira said as she turned and swung as best she could with a pack on her back.

Byron avoided both blows, picked her up, and as he set her down on her left foot, said, "This is your left foot. Now keep in step and move along."

"No fighting in the ranks," Eric said and started his song. The others joined in, but they sang it only one time in Unifren.

Byron's turn to pick a song caused a problem. He wanted time to think of just the right song for his choice. After more than a half-hour he announced, "We are now going to sing the choral from Beethoven's Ninth Symphony which should be sung in German. But I'll agree to have it sung in Unifren in the interests of camaraderie."

"In the interests of your safety and well being, you can sing a solo," Anastasia said and Moira and Eric gave a thumbs up signal. Byron's rendition of his chosen song was so well done that he received enthusiastic applause.

Shortly before noon they came to where Eric and Byron had left the supplies the day before. Since the hovercraft had matted the grass where Eric lowered it to the ground to unload the supplies, they decided to eat first and then hike farther to another location to camp, so it wouldn't be obvious they had been at this place in the forest.

"Dinner is served; you may be seated ladies and gentleman," Anastasia announced in her best imitation of a maitre de. Moira and Anastasia had packed a lunch of sandwiches, apples, raw carrots, red wine and Hershey bars. They all gathered around a fallen tree trunk with their four portable campstools. A discussion ensued as to whether or not lunch could properly be called dinner. Anastasia insisted it could. Eric said, "No way, dinner was the evening meal." Moira said when she was a child you ate "Din, din" morning, noon and night. No one would give in.

Byron pulled out his pocket dictionary, which was too large to go in anyone's pocket, out of his pack and recited, "Dinner, the chief meal of the day, eaten at the noon hour or in the evening." Another argument ensued as to whether or not this was going to be the "chief meal."

Anastasia wanted something more "chief" in the evening to eat and said she had been mistaken in saying, "Dinner is served." She agreed that she should have announced "Lunch is served."

Eric said he hoped she would be more careful in the future and Anastasia pushed him off his stool.

They were all hungry and as they were eating rather than talking, it became quiet. Moira broke the silence. "I'm worried about what happens if we get caught."

No one answered right away. It was as if they didn't want to think or talk about it.

"What's our battle plan if they find us?" Moira asked.

"The main thing is that Moira and Anastasia and what we hope is growing inside them are not hurt," Byron said. "I think the best thing to do is not resist. If they find us, there will be more of them equipped better than we are, so we won't be able to overcome them."

No one responded to Byron right away. Then Eric said, "Much as it hurts to just give up, you're right. We shouldn't even use our stun guns."

"As difficult as it may be, I think we should not show that we are frightened or upset," Anastasia said. "This may turn out to be a political battle, and we want them to know we have strong connections and support to help us."

"I don't know if I can fake it," Moira said.

"They probably will treat us more carefully, if we act like we know the whole world is on our side and we expect to win out in the end," Eric said.

"My guess is that they will be under orders to be very lenient with the children of Council delegates, particularly the daughter of a Big Three delegate," Byron said.

Anastasia and Moira looked at each other as if to ask which one of them was to say what was on both of their minds. Moira did. "I'm proud of you two for the way you have thought this thing through. It takes courage to do what most would consider unmanly. It's not the macho thing. She raised her cup and toasted, "Here's to two fine, brave men who will subdue their natural instincts for the good of their mates."

Anastasia said, "Hear, hear." They clinked their cups to each other's as best insulated cups can be clinked.

After they finished their lunch, they raked the area they had matted down as best they could with tree branches and strapped on their packs. Eric used his compass to lead the way towards Norway. A discussion ensued as to how the group would know when they passed from Sweden into Norway.

"We will know immediately because the large beautiful trees of my homeland will give way to smaller, scrubby imitations of Swedish trees, " Eric said.

"No, we'll know because the air will be cooler than the hot air that we have just been subjected to," Anastasia said.

"It doesn't matter if we've reached Norway, because neither Sweden or Norway can compare with the Highlands," Moira said.

"Geographical boundaries are of no consequence to the spirit of mankind-- the soul of the forest is universal," Byron said.

"A philosopher," Moira said. "Just what we need in the wilderness."

Late in the afternoon Eric and Byron stopped and studied the topographical maps of Norway and Sweden that Marie had provided. Marie had urged them to hide out in Norway, because she thought the authorities would assume they would stay in Sweden where Eric had friends and better knowledge of the land. After crossing into Norway, the plan was to move every two to three weeks to a new campsite traveling in creeks to avoid being tracked. Eric felt sure that they had crossed into Norway, so they began to look for a suitable campsite. Soon they came to a swiftly flowing creek that had formed a basin where it splashed against a cliff. The basin was deep enough to bath in and would make a good place to store anything they needed to keep cool. They pitched their tents at the top of a slight incline above the creek not too far from but out of sight of the basin.

Eric and Byron carried the tents and supplies they had hauled in with the hovercraft, so their packs were heavy. They were tired. Anastasia and Moira pulled off their mates' boots and massaged their feet. Then Anastasia opened a bottle of wine, one of six they had left, sliced a hunk of sharp cheddar cheese and passed around Swedish stone wheat crackers. Byron asked where the bread was and why the wine wasn't in a jug. Moira hit him over the head with his boot spilling a little of his wine. Byron held up his hands in surrender and said, "He that blaws in the stoor fills his air een. I learned that the hard way in Edinburgh."

"That means, ' He that stirs up trouble, finds himself in it,'" Moira said. "Who should know that better than my laddie?"

Anastasia said she was too tired to fix a "chief" meal. Moira felt the same. Eric said he had enough cheese and crackers for a meal, but how about dessert? Byron passed out Hershey bars. Arm in arm the couples headed for their tents.

CHAPTER ∧4

"Have you seen all the news reports since your statements at the Council news conference?" Kate asked Lawrence. She was seated in the window seat of the air bus flight from New York City to Stockholm. Lawrence was in the center seat and Laura in the aisle seat, which she preferred, because she got up frequently during the two and a half-hour flight.

"No. Did anyone pay any attention to anything but the body chip removals?" Lawrence asked.

"One line from your statement calling for an end to violence was included right at the end of one report I saw on TV, but most of the broadcasts were about the two couples and their parents. All the families received sympathetic treatment. Eric's probably the most because of his father. Most of the comments about the Gorbachevs focused on the difficulties of any official from one of The Big Three when a family member did something unlawful or unethical. One account compared it to the troubles former President Clinton and Hilary had; it even included negative information about Hilary's brothers and something about pardons. I hadn't heard about the pardons mess."

The refreshment inquiry beep sounded. On the screen above their seats the choices for the day were displayed. "Orange juice, blueberry muffin, butter," Kate said.

"Coffee, wheat bread toast, butter, ham, and inquire again in five minutes," Lawrence said.

"They had a nice picture of you and Mom," Kate continued. "They showed Anne and Kenneth's wedding picture and there was mention in the New York *Times* that they had applied to start a family. The article hinted at the possibility that Byron's misdeeds might have an affect on their application. The picture of me was from a horse show. The horse looked better than I did." Both Laura and Lawrence smiled.

"How's the *Let Them Be* song coming along?" Lawrence asked.

"Real well. It was to be recorded today. We got permission from the Beatles' copyright holder without any fees attached. The group recording it has good connections with the recording industry. They think it will get lots of play. The proceeds are going to the fund Klavdia Gorbachev suggested. Oh! Also on TV there was a report about the petition you and John Browning wrote. It's getting tremendous support, not only in the Council but all over the place. Copies of it have been made and are being signed at universities, by church groups, at sporting events and even in shopping centers. Or you can sign up on planetnet on a new web site someone started. One religious channel proposed asking the Pope to endorse the movement. "

"You've been busy."

"Not any more than you."

Laura rose from her seat and headed down the aisle towards the restroom.

"Has Mom calmed down any?" Kate asked.

"Outwardly only. I'm worried about her. She had rather I'd just kept writing for the St. Louis *Post Dispatch* than what I've gotten into. I can hardly blame her. Byron would probably still be safe at home in the U.S. if I hadn't introduced my resolution."

"It's more likely that Byron would have taken off sooner. You didn't cause him to do it. And as you said in your statement, you would have done the same thing."

"Thanks, sweetheart."

The plane landed in Stockholm on time. When Lawrence, Laura and Kate went to the counter marked, "Foreign Passengers Screening" a slender, dark-haired man with a deeply tanned face met them. Lawrence thought "I'm not sure what his native country is, but it isn't Sweden. He's probably with Internal Security from Iago's branch."

The man held a sign "Holmes family." Lawrence walked up to the man with the sign and stood in front of him but didn't speak.

"Mr. Holmes?" the man with the sign said to Lawrence.

"Yes, that's me. How do you do Mr. . . . .?" Lawrence said.

"Cortez. Come with me, please," Cortez said. And, as obviously an after-thought, "Er, welcome to Sweden. Since your son Byron is now listed as a category 'C' missing person, I am to escort you through a special security scanning."

As they started off behind Cortez, Lawrence said, "And how do you like it here in Sweden?"

Cortez looked aggravated and answered, "This is not my home. I'm here on special assignment."

Lawrence, Laura and Kate followed Cortez down a long corridor to a room with an "Authorized Personnel Only" sign on the door. Cortez inserted a card from his pocket into the top slot of two above the doorknob. A green light came on and Cortez opened the door. Lawrence wondered what the second slot was for, but he never found out. Cortez held the door for the others and they went in. Two areas were partitioned off with walls made of Walsul, a relatively new sound proof material seven centimeters thick that could be cut with an ordinary carpenter's saw but had the strength of a six centimeter thick sheet of steel. Swedish engineers developed Walsul by using nuclear energy to rearrange the molecular structure of cardboard.

One area was marked "Women" and the other "Men." "Ladies" and "Gentle-men" had been banned for official use in 2021 after a bitter debate at the Planet Council. Women's rights organization had argued that the use of "ladies" implied that females' influence depended on their physical attributes rather than their mental capacities. The male Council delegates agreed to the ban on the use of "ladies" but wanted to continue the use of "gentlemen." A majority of the female delegates threatened to walk out of the Council Hall if "gentlemen" was not banned also. The male delegate from Italy said, "Let the women have their way. We have to keep peace in the family," and the Council agreed. Lawrence continued his use of ladies and gentlemen.

Cortez said that Laura and Kate should step inside the Women's partitioned areas and take off their shoes, jackets and jewelry, including watches, and place them and any pocket items on the small table inside the room. Then they should step inside the partitioned area and wait for instructions. Lawrence was told to do the same in the area marked "Men." When Lawrence got inside the "Men" area he saw an attendant and slots in the walls and ceiling floor similar to those in the peep show in the New York Internal Security headquarters. The only furniture was a clothes rack and the small table. The attendant showed Lawrence where to stand and told him to remove his shirt and coat. Lawrence noticed that the attendant was examining the items on the table while Lawrence was getting the same kind of strong light treatment that he had gotten in the peep show room. He found out later that neither Laura nor Kate had to remove their clothing. He didn't find out that a tiny receiver was being inserted in his wristwatch that provided for the constant monitoring of his location and the same insert had been placed in Laura's and Kate's watches.

After the security check was over, Cortez showed them the way to the baggage claim area where Carlos was waiting for them. Carlos helped load the luggage into Marie's eight-seat air van, one of the largest air vehicles allowed private citizens. They climbed aboard and headed for Marie's house. Laura said, "When those lights came on, did you feel something getting on your skin? I did."

"Mother, that was an electronic beam, Kate said. "You probably felt the warmth, although I didn't."

"I want to get into a cleansing chamber as soon as I can and take one of Lawrence's showers if Marie has a shower. I itch all over."

Marie lived on the outskirts of Stockholm on a large estate not far from Roland's home. Carlos, Jonathan and Kurt were staying nearby with friends of the Nilsson family. Marie was not at home when Carlos dropped the Holmes family off, but her butler met them at the door, took them to their rooms and served them a delightful smorgasbord of Swedish fish, meats and cheese and a Swedish sauvignon blanc. After finishing the meal, Lawrence and Laura took a nap and Kate walked around the estate and looked in on the horses in the sixteen-stall barn.

Marie arrived home about 18:00 Swedish time. Marie had invited Carlos to come and he arrived shortly afterwards. Laura had spent an extra fifteen minutes in the cleansing chamber. Marie did not have a shower, so Laura rinsed herself at the basin, but she said she still itched. Lawrence thought it was nerves and was hoping another glass or two of wine would relieve the itching. Marie motioned for her guests to join her outdoors in the gazebo. In the center of the gazebo was a large bar-height round table with bar stools all around except where a lift up section allowed access to the inside of the table. Marie thought that her house might have been bugged after her speech to the Planet Council calling for R-1948 to be passed. In order to have a safe place to have a conversation, she had made sure no outsiders had been left alone in the gazebo.

When Marie had Byron and the rest of JD's Seven over for dinner, Marie found out what Byron's family liked to drink, so on the table was Beefeaters Gin, Noilly Prat French dry vermouth, lemon twists, olives, Georgia pecans and a choice of two Chardonnays, one of which was a Pouilly-Fuisse' for Laura, gin and tonic for Kate and a German ale for Carlos. Marie raised the section of the table and moved into the center to mix and serve drinks. She asked Lawrence to mix a martini the way he liked it, and said she would have one, too, because Roland had told her that Lawrence mixed the best martini he had ever had. Most noticeable were the napkins printed with "Ye may tak drink oot o a burn when ye canna tak a bite oot o the brae." Lawrence and Laura already knew the translation. Moira had brought the napkins with her and left them as a gift along with a bottle of Macallan Scotch Whiskey, a single Highland malt. Lawrence held up a napkin and in his best imitation of John Browning's brogue, spit out the words on the napkin followed by, "Or, many died of starvation in old Scotland, nobody of thirst."

Lawrence was glad for the lightheartedness because it helped relieve Laura's tension at least for the moment. He cracked a pecan and while he used a pick to remove the meat he said, "Marie, it was nice of you to arrange for this warm weather. We expected highs of 14 degrees and it was 20 at the airport. Seriously, thanks for everything you've done. We heartily approve of Byron's and the rest of the group's actions.

"Did you hear that we had to take some of Byron's clothing and his picture to Internal Security?" Laura asked. "I wanted to have a dog piss all over the things before I took them, but Lawrence said I'd better not do that."

"I talked to the Brownings," Carlos said. "They had to provide Moira's clothes too, so Mrs. Browning bleached them first to try and remove the scent."

"Wish I'd thought of that," Laura said.

Lawrence whispered to Kate to tell her mother she wanted to show her the horse barn. Kate did. She and Laura took their drinks with them and left.

"I know Carlos has told you that Byron may have Wilson's disease," Lawrence said to Marie. "How can we get the test equipment and antidote to Byron?" Lawrence put down his drink.

Marie placed her drink on the bar and said, "Some one has to take it to my hunting lodge to trip the sound monitor Eric placed in a ring around the near-by area. When the monitor shows someone is at the lodge, Eric will set his radio receiver to a certain low power wavelength that we don't think the authorities will be able to pick up. Whoever goes to the cabin will take a low power transmitter and receiver to send and receive coded messages. Once Eric has verified the sender's identity, he will arrange a place to meet up with his contact, if they need to meet."

Marie finished her martini and ate the olive before continuing. "The problem is finding someone to go to the lodge who is not known in this area or being watched by Internal Security. We know they are watching all my employees and me. I think we can transport someone within seventy-five kilometers or so of where the couples are. Internal Security could follow us that far, but they wouldn't be able to track a hiker going mostly cross-country the rest of the way. It will be a long and tough hike overland only partly along trails and unpaved roads. The last part of the hike will be through a deeply wooded area."

"Hike or ride?" Lawrence asked. "Kate wanted to come to help in meeting up with Byron, because she thought she would not be watched as closely as I would. And she can ride. She just needs a good horse."

"I've got that. She can have her pick of sixteen Arabians. Two of my stallions are high spirited, but they are the fastest and have the most endurance."

"She's been looking them over, already. I think Kate can handle your stallions."

Carlos said, "I think I should go. I'm a good rider."

"Thanks, Carlos," Lawrence said, "but I'm sure they are watching you, Jonathan and Kurt like a hawk."

"Like a what?" Marie said. Lawrence's Unifren pronunciation was very good, but some words didn't translate well.

Carlos translated to Marie who said, "Oh, yes we have hawks here, too. They are watching Carlos, Jonathan and Kurt that way, I'm sure.

"I think Kate is our best bet," Lawrence said. "We need a plan to get her away with a horse."

"There are equitation competitions every week in Arbra this time of the year, and that's on the route to the lodge," Marie said. "Arabian horse shows are a relatively new thing in this part of Sweden. Someone happened to notice that the grass near here is good for them. A trainer from the U.S. moved here about 15 years ago and started breeding. He got the first horse shows set up so he could sell his horses. It worked and now we have lots of Arabian owners. From Arbra it's a long way to the lodge. The show classes end late in the afternoon, so Kate could enter a few of them and instead of coming back to Stockholm, take off on the horse before they knew she was gone. One of my grooms could slip away and show her to a trail. There are some good trails and rural roads that she could follow and cover 70 or more kilometers in a day. The last 20 kilometers or so to the hunting lodge she will be following a creek instead of on a trail and that will go slowly. There are some small towns on the way, but we found a really secluded area for our lodge. From the lodge it won't be far to where the couples are camped. They plan to keep moving every few days until they get all the way into a remote part of Norway, but they haven't had time to go very far, yet ."

"Sounds like a good plan to me." Lawrence said.

"It's as good as I can think of," Marie answered. "How much time do we have before Byron needs to be tested?"

"Three or four days or even a week more won't make a difference," Lawrence answered.

"I'll check on the schedule of equitation competition in the morning."

"I don't want you to say anything about this to Laura, yet," Lawrence said. "She's worried that something bad is going to happen to Byron. I don't think they will hurt the couples, if they find them. But if Kate were to get caught, too, Laura would go bananas."

Marie saw that Laura and Kate were returning. As they came up to the gazebo, she said, "What do you think of those stallions, Kate?"

"Two of them were about to knock down the stables over a mare," Kate answered. "I liked the chestnut, best."

"That's Wasa, named after Sweden's King in the 1500's," Marie said. "You spell it with a 'V,' but we spell it with a 'W.' He thinks he's the King."

"Does he jump?" Kate asked.

"He wants to even when he's not supposed to," Marie said. "But when he finds that his rider is experienced, he behaves pretty well. He won't give Kate any trouble."

"I'll just have to learn to cuss in Swedish," Kate said. "I assume he wasn't trained in Unifren."

"You're right; we only use Unifren when we have to," Marie said. "And never with the horses."

Lawrence said, "It's been a long day. Do you have breakfast before you leave in the morning, Marie?"

"Bright and early at 06:00. Care to join me?"

"I will," Lawrence said. "Don't you want to sleep in, Laura?"

"Absolutely," Laura answered covering a yawn with her hand.

"I want to take a ride," Kate said. "I'll even get up early and join you for breakfast."

"Good night all," Marie said. Everyone headed for bed.

CHAPTER ∧◌

"I'm going to tell your mother when we have lunch that you're taking the test equipment to Byron," Lawrence told Kate as they were eating breakfast the next morning. "She said she was going to sleep in and skip breakfast. Be prepared for an outburst."

"Let's do it together," Kate suggested. "I want Mom to know that I insisted on doing it; you didn't talk me into it."

Lawrence took a bite of toast and chewed it slowly while considering Kate's offer. His eyes were cast downward. He was so deep in thought and took so long in answering, Kate would have wondered why he was not responding if she hadn't witnessed this scene many times before. Lawrence looked up and turned to face Kate. "I want you to know how proud of you I am. You do so much for me so often. And here I am letting you take a great risk that I should be taking. I would make the trip if there were any way I could think of to get to Byron without being followed. I know they suspect I will try to contact him. And now you are making it easier for me to tell your mother what will be terrifying to her. I love you, Kate."

"Dad, I know that, but it's special to hear it from someone who doesn't often open up that way. I'll be thinking about how to tell Mother that I'm going to find Byron."

Later in the morning Marie called from her office and related the schedule for the equestrian competition in Arbra. There were a few classes that Kate could enter, and the last one started at 15:00 the day after tomorrow.

Kate had a good ride on Wasa and worked with Marie's trainer to become familiar with the equitation rules for the classes she was going to enter. She studied a map Marie had left that showed how to get to the hunting lodge. Kate packed the equipment and supplies she would need on her trip to meet Byron. Then she met with the groom who was going to take her to the trail where she would start her trip. They went over their plan for leaving the horse show grounds.

Then Kate joined her father and mother who were seated in the gazebo having lunch. Kate decided to have a glass of Chardonnay to fortify herself for what she knew was going to be a trying encounter. Lawrence was having wine, but Laura wasn't. As Lawrence was filing Kate's glass, Kate said, "Mother, I know this Swedish Chardonnay, it's really good. Won't you have a glass?"

Kate and Lawrence were disappointed when Laura answered, "No, I drank more than I should have yesterday. I'm being careful today, at least until dinner."

"Laura, love," Lawrence, said. "Kate and I have something to talk to you about. It's something that must be done. It's important. We wish there was some other way to do it than what we have planned, but we've not been able to find a better way."

Laura stiffened. She looked from Lawrence to Kate and back again. "What is it?"

Lawrence started to answer, but Kate spoke up and said, "I'm going to take the test equipment and antidote to Byron. It has to be done on horseback. The authorities are watching Dad, JD's Seven and Marie's employees, and there is no one else we can trust, so I'm going."

Lawrence was glad that he had given Laura a warning that something bad was coming. That was probably why she didn't scream. She groaned. It was a low groan. The kind of groan caused by pain rather than shock. The groan continued. Laura's head was bent over her chest. Her eyes were closed. Her fists were clinched. When the groan finally died out, she sobbed softly.

Lawrence moved quickly to Laura's side and placed his arms around her.

Laura looked up at Lawrence. Horror was in her eyes. "How can you do this to me?" she said as she pulled away from him. "I can't take any more. Byron is gone and now you are taking Kate. No! No! You can't do it." Her sobbing became crying.

Kate moved to her mother's side. She was thinking of the fear her mother had been living with ever since Lawrence had gone up against powerful adversaries. A fear heightened greatly by Byron's flight into the unknown. Kate took her mother in her arms and held her tightly for a long moment. Then Kate released her hold and said, "Mother, we have to save Byron. You know you would risk your life for him, Dad, Anne or me without hesitation. Byron would do the same for any of us. Byron's best chance for survival is for me to go. I promise you that I will come back. Now, buck up like that hardheaded woman that Elvis sings about and we love. Dad needs your support. He has been going through hell too. Hug him."

Laura looked up into Kate's eyes. Laura's eyes cleared. She turned to Lawrence and held out her arms and then reached out to Kate to come into her embrace. They held each other for a long while. Then, Laura stood up and said, "Let me help you pack. I'll give you my stun gun so you can be a two-gun gunslinger."

CHAPTER ∧6

At 05:30 the next morning Marie helped load two stallions, one mare and two geldings into the horse trailer. She had entered her horses in twelve classes in the horse show so that there would be a lot of coming and going around their stalls at the show. She hoped that with all the activity, Kate's departure would not be noticed. Three more classes ridden in by other riders from Marie's barn would follow the last class that Kate was riding in. Marie was riding in one of those classes herself on her favorite horse, a stallion named Eskkort. Kate was going to return to Wasa's stall after her last class, change into casual riding clothes, and walk Wasa with a groom and one of the geldings towards an exercise ring to cool down their horses. After their horses were cooled down, they were going to head for the trail.

Kate was pleased with the second and third place ribbons she won. Everything worked as planned. At 15:35 Kate and the groom galloped away from the horse show grounds. They rode hard for about an hour before they reached the trail where Kate would take off alone. Kate thanked the groom and headed down the trail.

As the number of horses being ridden in this part of Sweden had grown in recent years, new trails were established, which were well marked and cleared of undergrowth. Kate rode until dusk and estimated she had traveled about twenty kilometers. Although she had a high-powered light that attached to her riding helmet, she thought Wasa needed to rest. She decided to make camp for the night rather than ride after dark,

On the many endurance rides Kate had taken along trails in upper New York State, she had slept in a horse trailer bunk complete with a thick mattress, heat and water from the storage tank. Many trailers even had showers and some, which were used for large horse shows in major cities, had small cleansing chambers. Sleeping on the ground in a sleeping bag under the stars was a novel experience, and she liked it. She decided to make a campfire, although she didn't need one for cooking since she had a portable-cooking stove powered by a portable generator that used lightweight stored power units. Kate just thought that a campfire was what a person ought to have on the trail. She didn't drop off to sleep quickly. She was reminded of the account in *Memoirs of Hadrian* of Hadrian lying on his back "abandoning for some hours every human concern," watching the movement of the heavenly bodies in accordance with the system the astronomer Theron of Rhodes had explained to him. From nightfall to dawn Hadrian gazed at a world of "crystal and flame . . . that was the most glorious of all my voyages." Kate wanted to watch the stars move across the sky and forget all her family's concerns too. After about ten minutes, she fell asleep.

The next morning Kate rose at daybreak, ate a quick breakfast while Wasa was having his oats, and headed out again. The trail was steep for long stretches, and fallen tree trunks blocked it in some places requiring a detour off the trail. Evidently, there had been a storm a day or two before in the area. She traveled part of the way along roads and crossed others. She came near enough to two small towns that she saw people at a distance. Several pick-up trucks passed by on the roads. Fortunately, she didn't come close enough to anyone that it was likely they would be able to describe in detail what she looked like.

In the late afternoon when Kate stopped to water Wasa at a shallow stream, she thought she heard the drone of a small airplane. To her it sounded like one of the combination helicopter/single engine planes, called Heliwings, being manufactured in Germany, because the motor sound changed from that of a normal plane to a chopper and then back again. She walked Wasa off the trail into the woods until the sound was gone.

When she camped for the second night, she started to make a campfire, but changed her mind. Hearing an airplane made her think that her campfire might be spotted, and she didn't want to take a chance on that happening. Clouds had moved in and the sky was overcast at dusk. "No stars to watch tonight," Kate thought.

The next morning a light drizzle started about an hour after she resumed her ride on the trail. It was still warm, so she took off everything but her bra and shorts when she donned her rain gear. The rain continued, and she had to trot more slowly to prevent Wasa from slipping. Within two hours the rain stopped and the sun came out just as she came to a creek. From Marie's description, she was sure this was the creek that led to the lodge. She walked Wasa in the creek for about 800 meters to prevent being tracked and then climbed up onto the bank. She followed the creek until she spotted the large tree with a double trunk at a sharp bend where Marie had told her to turn off to go to the hunting lodge. It was mid-afternoon when she had found the lodge. Kate wasn't able to spot the sound monitor wire, because Moira and Anastasia had hidden it in the leaves. She moved very slowly on the way to the lodge and banged on the metal fastener of her saddlebags to make a lot of noise. She yelled out "Ship ahoy," to make a human sound. She had decided on "Ship ahoy" because she couldn't think of anything else that was called out over long distances to attract attention. She wished Byron were available to give her a battle cry or something more dramatic to yell, because he knew about things like that.

Kate tied up Wasa under a tree and found the key to the lodge on the bottom side of the cover over the woodpile where Marie said it would be. She carried her pack and saddlebags into the lodge. Then she took the transmitter and receiver outside to the lodge porch and sent the planned signal to Eric.

CHAPTER ∧7

The first full day they were at their campsite, Byron suggested that he and Moira take a hike around the area to "see what's here." It was sunny and warm, much warmer than Byron had expected. What Byron really had in mind was trying to get Moira to go skinny-dipping in the basin part of the creek near their campsite. The basin's water would be warmer than the flowing creek, but he knew getting Moira to even step into the freezing water of the creek was going to be a challenge. After climbing to the top of the cliff above the basin, he looked down over the edge and told Moira, "I believe that's deep enough for me to dive."

"You crazy nut," Moira said, clearly exasperated. "That water's not over a meter deep. You'll break your neck if you dive in."

"I'll bet you it's at least two meters. What do you want to bet?"

"I'll bet you a punch in your belly."

"And if I win, you have to come in with me. O.K.?"

"You're on. I'm going to enjoy this. You don't know how hard I can belt you."

Byron took off his shirt as he ran around the side of the cliff down to the basin. By the time Moira got there, he had all his clothes off and plunged into the water and was splashing through the creek to the far side of the basin near the cliff where leaves mostly covered the water surface. By the time he got to the cliff, his head was barely above the water level. The basin was about ten meters wide so that with the leaves covering him, Moira couldn't see that he was on his knees.

"See here. I'm about to drown. It's even deeper over here," he said as he pointed to the right. "Come on in. You lose."

"I don't believe you, you scoundrel."

"Watch then. I'll prove it."

Moira watched Byron move to his right and his head go under water. He bobbed up raising his arm up with one finger and then went under the water again. When he came up the second time with two fingers raised, he called out, "I'm about to drown. You lose. Come on in."

Moira took off her clothes and started walking in the water towards Byron holding her arms around herself to try to keep warm. When she got all the way over to where Byron was kneeling and the water wasn't even up to her waist, she lunged at him and grabbed his head to push it under saying, "You snake in the grass. You tricked me."

"So I did. And your nipples are most enticing when they stick out like that. Is it the cold water or that you're so mad."

"I'll show you what I'm going to do to what's sticking out on you."

Moira reached under the water and grabbed Byron's penis. He put his arms around her and held her close and said, "More, more, squeeze tighter."

Moira opened her mouth to say something, but Byron was kissing her by then.

After they came out of the water, Moira and Byron lay side by side in the sun to dry. Byron started to roll over onto Moira when they heard Eric calling for them. Reluctantly, they put their clothes on and returned to the campsite.

"Kate's at the lodge. She set off the sound monitor, so when I got the signal from it, I was ready with the receiver. She gave the code words, so I knew it was a friend. She must meet up with you, Byron. Your dad has found out that he has something rare called Wilson's disease. There is a chance you have it, too, because it's hereditary. If so, you have to be treated soon with an antidote she has with her. Wilson's disease can be fatal. She came on one of Marie's Arabians."

Moira grabbed Byron's arm and said, "Go, go. Hurry."

There's not that much urgency," Eric said. "He just needs to be checked and treated in the next few days, but the sooner the better."

"Then sooner," Moira said. "Is Kate coming here?"

"I think the best plan is for Byron to meet Kate somewhere on the way to the Lodge. She can come on horseback, so Byron probably won't have to hike so far." Eric said.

"Then I'm going with him," Moira said. "He might get lost on the way."

"But I can take my Boy Scout manual and a compass," Byron said.

"This isn't funny, Byron," Moira said. "I've just gotten you for a husband, and I'm not taking any chances on losing you. And that manual of yours is so old it wouldn't help. Get your pack. We're leaving now."

"Hold it, hold it, Moira," Eric said. "We need to work out a few things. And you need to eat before you start a long hike. Let's talk it over while we eat. I'll call Kate and tell her to eat while we are. You're right that Byron needs a keeper. I'm glad you're going with him."

"I'm glad, too, but for a different reason," Byron said. "We might have to spend the night on the trail."

"One track mind he has, doesn't he," Anastasia said.

Byron and Moira went to their tent to get their packs ready while Anastasia and Eric fixed lunch. "Do you think there is a chance that Kate was followed?" Moira asked Byron.

"I think we should assume that. She still has her body chip. If they have all my family under surveillance, they know that Kate is not in Stockholm with my parents."

"We've got to get the test equipment and antidote from her."

"True, but we don't have to meet up with her. Eric can do the tests and give shots or whatever is needed for the antidote. Since Kate has been to the lodge, the authorities may know that location. I don't think we had better go close to it or have Kate come close to where we are now. We shouldn't even go to a place Kate has been."

"So we couldn't even have Kate take it to a safe drop-off place ?"

"No, but we could use a safe carrier."

"What do you mean, carrier?"

"The horse. Horses don't have body chips."

"You're so damn smart. How do you think of these things?"

"There is a chance that Marie may lose a horse, but that's better than if I lose you or the baby."

Byron patted Moira's stomach gently. Moira put her hand over his and smiled.

"Let's talk to Eric and Anastasia."

Moira and Byron explained their ideas to Eric and Anastasia who hadn't thought about the chance Kate was under surveillance. Eric said that there was an abandoned fishing camp on the Ljusnan River that was close to the lodge and, therefore, not too far from where they were camped. At the camp was a fenced garden. Eric thought a horse would be safe there even if left over night. The problem was how to get the horse to the fishing camp without Kate taking it.

"I hate to involve another person who isn't part of our group, but there is a hunting guide fairly near the fishing camp who could be hired to come to the lodge to pick up the horse and take it to the fishing camp," Eric said. "Kate would have to have a believable reason for wanting to leave a horse at an abandoned fishing camp for the guide to agree to come."

"Because the horse is injured and needs to have a fenced in place to stay, possibly even over night, while Kate goes for help," Byron said. "And she doesn't have the time to walk the horse to the fishing camp because she needs to leave right away in the hovercraft."

"Authors have to be able to make up stories, don't they?" Anastasia said.

"How do we get in touch with the guide?" Moira asked.

"I've got his computer-cell phone number," Eric said.

"Do you think the guide will buy that story?" Moira asked.

"If Kate is frantic, pays him well and rushes off, he may not have time to think it through," Eric said. "This guide is smart about some things, but not in other ways. Also, he will want to help a good looking girl get out of trouble."

"Is that the way you are, too?" Anastasia asked.

"Oh no," Eric answered. "As you know, I want to get a special good-looking girl into trouble."

"It's not trouble if you're married, you dummy," Anastasia said as she boxed Eric's ears.

"Byron, don't you dare say, 'Oh, its not you, Anastasia, he's talking about, "Eric said. "I'll flat out kill you."

"Let's get back on the subject, " Moira said. "We need to call Kate."

Eric called Kate and told her the plan and told her where the fishing camp was located. Kate wasn't sure how she would make it look as if Wasa was injured. Byron said "hello" to Kate and suggested using ketchup or killing a rabbit to smear what looked like blood on Wasa's leg and then bandage it. He wondered what you could do to make a horse limp slightly without hurting the horse. Maybe add weight to one leg and cover it up with a bandage? Kate said she would call the guide, work on a fake injury for Wasa and call back when she had answers.

Eric said, "Do you suppose Anastasia and I should go with you and do the tests at the fishing camp?"

"Let's talk about that," Byron said. "On the one hand, you know where the

Brink Hudlee

place is. If you come with us, we would be sure to get to the right place and get there quicker. Also, you could test and treat me right away. On the other hand, four people near the river might be spotted more easily than two and cause someone to mention it to others. And to look at the worst scenario, if Moira and I get caught, you will get caught, too."

"Haven't you read The Three Musketeers?" Anastasia asked. "One for all and all for one."

"I think we should stay together," Eric said. "If there is trouble, we will have a better chance of getting out of it with all four of us."

"What do you think, Moira?" Byron asked.

"I think we should all go, but when we get near the fishing camp, Eric and Anastasia should stay hidden until Byron and I get the horse. If Byron and I get caught, than they should take off."

"I agree," Byron said. "That's a good plan."

Eric and Anastasia left to get their packs ready. Eric decided to leave the tents and extra supplies at their campsite to make hiking easier. He knew that they could find shelter at the fishing camp and spend the night there before returning to their campsite. Then he changed his mind and decided to pack their sleeping bags in case something didn't work out. Byron said to Moira, "Don't you think we could make do with one sleeping bag?"

"If you weren't big as a house we could," Moira said. "I think I'd better take my own."

They decided to bed down early and start at sunrise the next morning. As they were finishing their evening meal around the tree trunk, which they had made their table, Byron said to Eric and Anastasia, "What do you plan to do after your baby comes?"

Eric and Anastasia looked at each other and then Anastasia replied, "We think we will have Marie arrange for plastic surgeons to alter our appearance. We know we can't fly anywhere or live in big cities, but Eric could be a doctor in a remote rural area, and I could be his nurse. Eric has enough money to tide us over for a few years, if we live simply. We plan to ask for cash for his services; or maybe use a barter system. How about you and Moira?"

"We hadn't thought about plastic surgery, but I hope to get a novel published using a different name," Byron said. "I'm not sure how we could get income transferred to us without a planet ID number."

"We may have to live off the land, big guy," Moira said. "I'm a good shot so we'll always have enough to eat."

"I'm worried about our child's education and social life," Byron said. "I can teach her or him languages and literature, but what if he or she wants to be an engineer?"

"Whatever our child wants to be, he or she will be better off in a free world," Moira said. "I'm not afraid as long as I have my man. I do want you for our doctor, Eric. Guess we will have to stay near wherever you practice."

"Well, we have about nine months to work it out," Eric said. "Time to hit the sack." The two couples headed for their tents holding hands.

Early the next morning they ate a quick breakfast and headed for the River

ᏞᎾᏮ

Ljusnan instead of going cross-country to the fishing camp. Eric's plan was to hike along the riverbank and arrive at the camp after the hunting guide had delivered Wasa and left.

The hike to the river was made easier when they came across a stream flowing towards the river. They followed it and reached the river about noontime and had lunch. After lunch they hiked until about 16:00 hours when Eric said he recognized the bend in the river where the fishing camp was located. Byron and Moira carefully approached the fishing camp. They spotted the cabin and then the enclosed area where they could see a horse. They crept up moving from tree to tree to stay out of sight until they got to the cabin.

The cabin was made of logs with a stone chimney. It looked deserted, but Byron crawled by himself around to the back and listened for sounds of life for five minutes. When he didn't see or hear anything, he motioned for Moira to join him. The cabin had two small windows that were covered with grime. Byron wiped enough of the grime off to be able to see inside. There was one large room partitioned off at one end by a curtain that was drawn back. Byron could see that no one was inside. He and Moira went to the one door and tried it. It opened easily. They went in. There were four cots, a wooden table, and four wooden chairs. Byron said, "Looks like we have a place to eat and spend the night."

"I'm glad," Moira said. "Sleeping outdoors without a tent is no good if it rains."

Byron said, "Go get Eric and Anastasia. I'll get the supplies off the horse."

Eric, Anastasia and Moira came back together and joined Byron inside the fenced garden where he was rubbing Wasa's mane. He had removed the saddlebags from Wasa and hung them over the fence enclosure.

"That's Wasa," Eric said. "He's one of Aunt Marie's best stallions. Kate must be a really good rider to have handled him. I tried to ride him once and could hardly stay on. Of course, Wasa knew I wasn't an experienced rider."

The two couples' attention was focused on the horse, so they were startled to hear, "Stand where you are, do not move and raise your hands." Agent Iago was loud and authoritative and he moved quickly from behind them to confront them. Instinctively Moira moved closer to Byron. She leaned against him to conceal that she was trembling. Eric put his arm around Anastasia and pulled her to him. The two couples looked around to see how many man were with Iago. Eric seemed to be sizing up the situation; his fisted were clenched. Anastasia's face was fixed with a look of defiance.

"Take it easy, Eric," Byron whispered.

Six armed men moved inside the fenced area to surround the two couples. The men had crept up silently from the wooded area behind the couples. "We will not hurt you if you do not resist," Iago said. "We are members of the Internal Security Department with authority to return Byron Holmes, Eric Nilsson, Anastasia Gorbachev, and Moira Browning to the United States. Do you acknowledge you are those individuals?"

Anastasia was more angry than scared. She slipped out of Eric's arms and walked boldly up to Iago and said, "I'd like to see your credentials before I answer any questions."

"Certainly, Ms. Gorbachev," Iago said. "Here are my credentials and a copy of an order from the Director of Internal Security authorizing the actions I described." Iago handed his badge and a thick envelope to Anastasia.

Byron took Moira's hand, which was still shaking, and moved to where they could see what Iago had given Anastasia. Eric moved up behind Anastasia so he could read the documents over her shoulder. Byron said, "We'd like to discuss this matter in private. We'll stay inside the fenced area where you can keep an eye on us."

Iago hesitated. Just as he started to speak, Anastasia said, "All citizens have the right to assemble in peace so long as they are not a threat to the public, and we are no such threat."

The two couples moved to one side of the fenced area and gathered closely together so that they couldn't be overheard. "I think they have us," Byron said. "One of the armed men has a portable scanner that will verify that we don't have body chips. Even without a written order they can detain us for that. I think we might as well agree who we are and cooperate."

"If that will help us with the testing of Byron and his treatment, I agree," Moira said. Her face was pale. Her voice was unsteady. She held on to Byron.

Eric was obviously upset but didn't say anything.

"We've got to keep Kate in the clear if we can," Byron said. "The order didn't include her. I'm glad we haven't met with her, so she might be all right."

"I think that Eric ought to say that there is a medical concern with Byron that needs to be taken care of immediately," Moira said.

"Tell them after the medical treatment is done, we will go peacefully," Anastasia said to Eric and Byron. "While you are involved with that, I'll contact Kate by telling them I have to go to the outhouse and taking the radio with me. Moira, you will have to distract them so they won't hear me using the radio. Can you handle that?"

Moira bit her lip and with a determination she hadn't shown before and said, "I'll do it."

"Iago and his men must have come by river," Byron said. "Anastasia, tell Kate to hide out on the bank of the river where the creek to the lodge flows into the river. When they take us back, I'll be on the side of the boat towards the creek with my cap on if it's safe for her to pick up Wasa. If my cap is off, she should take the hovercraft back, get help and return for Wasa."

While Eric and Byron were talking to Iago, Anastasia told one of the guards that she was going to the outhouse and needed her pack. Instead of her pack, she picked up Eric's, which contained the transmitter covered up by his clothes and not visible to the guard watching her. Moira stayed with the guards and asked them questions as Anastasia went to the outhouse. The guards didn't answer her questions, but she kept asking anyway.

Anastasia reached Kate on the radio easily. Kate was dumbfounded and worried that the two couples had been apprehended. She said she didn't think she had been followed and wondered how Internal Security knew where Wasa was.

"I don't know how they found us," Anastasia said, "but we want to be sure they have no grounds to arrest you." Anastasia told Kate the plan for signaling her.

"I'll be at the river, but surely, there must be some way I can help the four of you right now," Kate said.

"We may need your help later," Anastasia said. "If you are in their hands, you can't do anything."

"I hate it if my coming is how they found you, but that's bound to be what happened."

"You had to come. Byron had to have help. We're all appreciative of the risk you took to get the testing equipment and treatment to us. Byron is very grateful, and he doesn't want anything bad to happen to you."

"Tell Byron not to worry about me. I'm not in custody. You are the ones in trouble. When I get back to Stockholm, we'll get everyone together and work out something."

Anastasia put the radio equipment back in Eric's pack and rejoined Moira on the porch of the cabin. Soon Eric and Byron joined them on the porch. Iago and the guards watched from the yard, but were too far away to overhear. "We acknowledged to Iago who we are, and he agreed to let me test and treat Byron," Eric said. "Byron does have Wilson's disease, but I've already given him the first doze of the antidote, so he is going to be O.K. Iago didn't say anything about Kate, but someway or other they must have followed her without her knowing it. It wasn't by latitude and longitude coordinates from her body chip, because in a dense forest that doesn't help much. Anyway, they didn't indicate they are charging anyone but us. Their portable scanner showed that Byron and I don't have body chips. That's the chief violation they are charging us with. They have a boat coming within an hour or so to take us back."

Anastasia told Byron and Eric what Kate had said. "Damn it, I'm sorry my having a rare disease messed everything up," Byron said.

"The main thing is that your dad found out what he had and got the treatment to you," Moira said.

Byron pulled Moira around so she faced him. He looked in her eyes and lifted a finger to gently touch her nose. "'As ae door shuts anither opens,'" Byron said.

"In Scotland that means you are never left entirely without hope," Moira said as she took Byron's hand in hers, raised herself up onto her toes and kissed him.

Iago came over to the porch and said, "While we are waiting for the boat, I'm going to test you two women for body chips.

"What happens to us next?" Anastasia asked.

Iago stared at her for a moment wondering how much he should tell them. Remembering O'Sheean's instructions, he decided he could answer her question. 'We are taking you back to New York. You will be tried in a court and a judge will decide your case."

"What has happened to others whose chips were removed?" Eric asked.

"We've never apprehended a person who had their chip removed," Iago said. "Three men died when a veterinarian tried to remove their body chips, but if anyone succeeded we don't know about it. Some persons have just disappeared. They might have succeeded."

Iago ran the tests on Moira and Anastasia and confirmed they did not have body chips. He called the two couples together and said, "Since you four do not have body chips, the law provides that a temporary, locked identification bracelet be secured to your wrist or ankle, which you must wear at all times. I see you all have bracelets on your wrists; that's an unusual design. Do you want your ID bracelet attached to your ankles?"

All four selected ankle bracelets.

The boat that Iago said was coming arrived. It was the largest boat that could navigate on the Ljusman River. Iago asked if the horse was to be taken aboard.

Eric said, "No." He started to say more, but decided that the less said, the better.

Iago escorted the two couples aboard the boat and it took off.

Byron checked and found that all the guards were on the boat with Iago. When the boat passed the creek that led to the Nilsson's lodge, Byron was in place on the side of the boat towards the shore where Kate was to be watching. He looked for her, but didn't see her. He had pulled his cap down tightly to withstand the stiff breeze generated by the swift movement of the boat.

CHAPTER ∧8

Sixty-three delegates from the Planet Council including John Browning and Boris Gorbachev were in Stockholm for Roland Nilsson's funeral services. In addition to the delegates, prime ministers and official representatives from thirty countries assembled in the Riddarhuset, the seat of the Swedish parliament, for the services. The Nilsson family selected the Riddarhuset, because Roland's career started there, and it was the best place available to accommodate the large group of mourners that were expected.

The Nilsson family had anticipated that Roland would be euthanatized, so they had prepared for a combined funeral and commemorative service. The advent of frequent euthanasia orders had brought about this new type of service. If the individual designated for euthanasia was able to participate, and had accepted his or her fate, a last visit with family and friends was often included. Cynics said this had come about and even gained popularity because the survivors did not have the cost of traveling to both a deathbed visit and the funeral service. Also, the date for the combined service was scheduled in advance, which made the whole affair much easier for the survivors to arrange to be present. Many services were held late on Saturday afternoons or Sundays so the families would not miss work.

The chance to have one last visit with a relative or friend and tell them in person how much they had loved them came to be thought of as a beneficial feature that helped with the grieving process. The great amount of attention, admiration and sympathy for the one in whose honor the last visit was being held was for some the only time in many years that they had felt appreciated.

The Nilsson family, Lawrence, Laura, John, Peggy, Boris and Klavdia were assembled at Marie's house to go together to the service, which was to begin at 10:00. Marie had arranged a continental breakfast for the group. Just as they finished eating and were seated around the coffee table, the butler whispered in Marie's ear that there was an urgent call on their residential line. Marie left to take the call.

The expression on Marie's face when she returned was one that the group had not seen before. Marie was often agitated, excited, pleased, disappointed or even saddened and it showed. When she returned, Marie was clearly shaken. Her shoulders were slumped. She labored just to walk. Her head was down. She came into the room and went to Nilsson's widow and took her hand. Tears were in Marie's eyes. In a choking voice she said, "Our children have been captured. An agent of the Internal Service, his name is Diego or something like that, is bringing them to Stockholm under arrest."

"No, no, no dear God. Do they have Kate too?" Laura cried out.

"I don't know about Kate," Marie said. "I got my information from the head of Internal Security here in Sweden. He took a risk in calling me, but I have helped his department with medical emergencies and we've been friends for a long time.

He's not the typical Internal Security type. I asked where the children will be held in Stockholm. Since they gave no resistance, he thought they would be taken to a safe house rather than police headquarters.. They probably aren't handcuffed or anything like that."

Mrs. Nilsson's body stiffened. A look of fierce determination locked her features into stony rigidity. Quietly, but firmly, she said, "Any one from a country that voted against Lawrence's resolution will not be allowed into Roland's service. I won't have it. Marie, I want you to tell the ushers who will be permitted to attend and who will not. If we have to move it to another place, we will. I don't want to see the faces of those responsible for preventing my Eric from having his freedom. Roland wouldn't want them there. It's his service."

"Everybody, let's try and keep calm," Lawrence said. Everyone sat down.

Klavdia grabbed Boris's arm and said, "Can you get Dulles to intervene? Is there a chance he would?"

"Dulles is here for the service," Boris said. "I think Klavdia is right that I should try to get his assistance."

"John, do you and Lawrence think you or maybe all of us should tell Dulles we want to meet with him?" Peggy asked.

"Boris, you know Dulles better than we do because of Big Three connections," John said. "What do you advise?"

"Dulles doesn't like to be put on the spot," Boris said. "Probably better that I approach him first. The best way to avoid embarrassing him would be for me to tell him he won't be welcome at Roland's service, and that if I demand to meet with him while it's being held, he will have an excuse for not being there. The Secretary of State from the U.S. is here too representing his President. He may welcome an excuse as well. I think I should suggest to Dulles that the three of us meet at the 10:00. Do any of you have a problem with this?"

"Anything that will help our children, I'm for," Laura said. The rest nodded their approval.

"By the way, did you find out the name of Iago's superior?" Lawrence asked Boris.

"Yes," Boris said, "its O'Sheean. I don't know his first name. I had trouble finding out anything much about him."

"O'Sheean; O'Sheean," Lawrence said. "I think that's the name of the guy that they had pick me up, Sugar Boy. I thought something was funny. Now I understand."

Boris left to call Dulles. The rest of the group finished their coffee in silence.

CHAPTER ∧♀

The Internal Security boat for the trip to Stockholm was the new shallow-draft luxury model Water King made by Bass Pro of Springfield, Missouri, USA. It was capable of speeds up to 80 km/hr, but on this trip it was traveling at 55 km/hr to make for a smoother ride. Iago allowed the two couples to go below to the cabin and be by themselves.

"Do you think they will separate me from Anastasia when they incarcerate us?" Eric asked.

"That will be a tough one for them to handle," Byron said. "When they find out we were married in a chapel, there will be a lot of international pressure to let a man and his wife be together, particularly if the wife is pregnant."

"International pressure to let us go our own way was building before we took off," Anastasia said. "It doesn't seem to have done us much good. They came after us with a vengeance."

"It was Internal Security that tracked us down," Moira said. "They operate outside the political realm. Governments have other considerations."

"And one of those considerations is to enforce the law," Anastasia said. "I think they will throw the book at us. They can't let well-known families with influence get away with something as drastic as what we did."

"When do you think they will reinsert our body chips?" Moira asked.

"I don't think they can until we have our trial," Byron said. "But like Iago said, this is new territory for the authorities. They may not know what they can do."

"I'm worried about Aunt Marie," Eric said. "If . . ."

"She will just have to handle our being in custody," Byron interrupted with his finger to his mouth when it suddenly occurred to him that the boat might be bugged.

Moira took the clue and said, "Could we lighten up and talk about something other than what's going to happen to us? I'd like to get it out of my mind for just a little while."

"Yes, I understand," Byron said. "I know you are worried, darling. How about me telling you that this boat was made near where I grew up. Well, within a couple of hundred miles of St. Louis, anyway, in Springfield. My dad interviewed the owner of Bass Pro, the boat manufacturer, and I got to go along because we were going to meet him at a place where there was a water slide. He gave me a Bass Pro T-shirt, which I wore when I went down the slide."

"Your childhood was really fascinating, Byron," Anastasia said with a sly smile and a wink to Moira. "But I'm hungry. Iago said there was food and beverages down here for us. Let's eat."

"Well, since you've had enough of my story-telling, I'll cook instead. You ladies shouldn't have to do it every time," Byron said.

Eric and Anastasia gave Moira a questioning look. "Does Byron even know how to make sandwiches?" Anastasia asked Moira.

"What an insult," Byron said. "Give me a wok and I can make world class cashew chicken."

"He's right," Moira said. "I've had it and it was awesome. Just don't offer to clean up after him, especially if he's having wine while he's concocting the sauce."

Byron prepared sandwiches. They opened two bottles of a Toscana Pinot Grigio/Chardonnay combination they had never heard of, but it turned out to be good wine.

"This may be our last wine for awhile," Anastasia said.

"Just so it isn't our last meal," Moira said.

Above deck Iago was reporting to O'Sheean in New York. "They gave up peacefully, and as you instructed, I have let them be alone at times and have been agreeable. I didn't have an opportunity to bug the fishing cabin, but I have the cabin on our boat bugged. I'll review their conversations when we arrive in Stockholm and let you know if they revealed anything important."

"How did they take being captured?" O'Sheean asked.

"They are a spunky group and obviously had anticipated that they might be apprehended. They don't wring their hands or complain that it isn't fair what's happened. Except for the Browning girl, they act as if they expect to beat this thing. They even kid each other and try to seem almost carefree. I thought they would be frightened, but they may not have thought of some of the consequences of having your chip removed. We should be in Stockholm within three hours, and I'll take them to the safe house on Kommakargatan. I'm looking forward to calling the parents in, particularly the Gorbachevs, but as you instructed, I won't make any sarcastic remarks."

CHAPTER 2∇

"I'm disappointed at being banned from Roland's services," Dulles said as he greeted Boris at the door to his hotel suite." Dulles had agreed that he and the Secretary of State, Daniel Jay, would meet with Boris at 10:00 at their hotel in downtown Stockholm. Because of the heavy demand for air taxis to attend Roland's service, Boris was late arriving for the meeting.

Dulles voice was pleasant enough, but the sour expression on his face revealed how displeased he was. "I appreciate your warning me so that Daniel and I were not turned away at the door. That would have been unfortunate. I imagine many other delegates and officials are going to be angry." Dulles walked Boris into the suite's large parlor where Jay was waiting. "Would you like coffee or something else?" Dulles asked. His offer sounded more perfunctory than genuine.

"No thank you," Boris said and took a seat on a sofa between the chair where Jay was seated and the chair where Dulles sat down. Boris turned towards Dulles and said, "I am glad you are here in Stockholm. I am sure you have been informed that my daughter, her husband and two children of delegates have been tracked down by Internal Security and are being brought to Stockholm under arrest."

"Yes, we were informed," Dulles said as he picked up a cup of coffee.

"I'm very disappointed that I wasn't informed by Internal Security, but that is another matter I intend to pursue later," Boris said keeping his agitation under control. "Has Kate Holmes been detained?"

"No," Dulles said. "She evidently made radio contact with the two couples, but since she did not meet with them, she has violated no law. She is probably on horseback on her way back to Stockholm. No one is following her."

"I'm here to get your assistance in having the two couples released immediately into the custody of their parents, all of whom are here in Stockholm." Boris turned towards Jay to include him in his appeal. "The parents will, of course, guarantee their appearance at whatever subsequent proceedings occur."

Dulles and Jay looked at each other as if to ask which of the two was going to answer Boris's request. Jay turned to Boris and said, "I'm afraid that will not be possible. Internal Security has confirmed that they do not have body chips and under the law, they must be detained until the judicial procedures are concluded."

Boris turned abruptly to Dulles and said, "Bill, surely in light of the positions of John, Lawrence and myself an exception can be made. The Directorate can issue a special order providing for us to be responsible for the availability of our own children. I'm positive that the Directorate would do that." Boris spoke confidently, but he didn't look confident.

"I'm sorry, Boris, but Daniel cleared this with our President as soon as it was known that your children illegally removed their body chips," Dulles said. "What they did undermines our whole security system. She decided that if they were apprehended, they would be detained until a trial is held. My hands are tied." Dulles looked away from Boris and sipped his coffee.

"But if the Directorate voted for it, the one vote of the U.S. could not veto their action." Boris reached out his arms towards Dulles as if to pull out of him the help he sought. Dulles put down his coffee and looked towards Jay.

"Have you talked to your government since your daughter went underground, Boris?" Jay asked.

"No, not directly," Boris said as he dropped his arms to his side and his voice dropped. "I sent a message to the office of my President saying that I was sorry for any embarrassment that Anastasia's actions might have caused to Russia, but I included I was supporting my daughter and her friends' position, regardless." Boris's tone was firm.

"I'm sure you are aware of the response throughout Russia to your daughter's rash conduct," Dulles said as his voice rose. "Your daughter was a heroine before. This has made her a courageous martyr defying the law. If you seek to get the Directorate to take a stand, I have been told that you will be replaced. My government would do the same if it were my daughter or son. If you weren't representing one of The Big Three, it might be different. But we, like Caesar's wife, have a different standard to meet."

"And I used to be President of Russia," Boris said. He paused and then said, "I could cause a lot of trouble over this at home."

"Would that help your daughter if you are replaced on the Directorate?" Jay said quietly without showing resentment at Boris's threat. "You'll have more influence over the outcome if you keep quiet and work behind the scenes to get as light a sentence for her as possible. If you don't cause trouble, you might get her off with just having her chip replaced. She might even get to choose her occupation. If you fight it and lose, they may make an example of Anastasia. Big powers don't like upsetting issues like this. We want a quick trial and hope that the whole thing will die down."

"We've been through a lot together, Boris," Dulles said in the false sympathetic voice Boris knew well. "I'd like to help, but Daniel is right. The best I can do for you is urge that the court be lenient because they are so young."

Boris stood up, looked Dulles in the eye, and said forcefully, "We have been through a lot together, and I've stuck my neck out for you many times, even when it might have gotten cut off. I expected better of you. Damn you all to hell. You don't need to show me out," he said as he walked towards the door. "You've shown me enough already."

Boris caught an air taxi to the Riddarhuset and arrived while Marie was delivering the eulogy for Roland's funeral services. Boris took a seat on the back row of the auditorium so as not to make a disturbance. Marie was at the podium and was gesturing towards a beautiful ceramic urn on a table to her left that was in the center of the auditorium's speaker's platform. The urn was decorated with a small replica of the Swedish flag in a grove of trees native to Sweden. In front of the grove was a body of water on which a tiny sailboat was floating.

"A part of Roland's ashes will be taken from his urn and spread on the Gulf of Bothnia," Marie said. "The Swedish parliament has requested that the urn with the remainder of his ashes be placed in a special new memorial alcove that will constructed in his honor in this building. The Nilsson family has agreed to their request. We are indebted to Greta Milles for the design and creation of this magnificent urn. She is a long-time friend of our family and we appreciate having Sweden's leading artist play such a significant role in the commemoration of Roland's life.

"As you know, Roland was a modest man. Several years ago when he had a mini-stroke, he gave me instructions as what to say and what not to say at any service held in his memory. He actually said, 'If a service is held.' I am honoring his wishes by not relating his many accomplishments or extolling his many virtues. He wanted me to acknowledge the love and support of his family. He wanted me to say he had high hopes for the future. He said he did not want me to interject any of my personal views; he said that he and the rest of the world had heard enough of them during his lifetime.

"So, I have been severely restricted today in what I could say. I did receive his blessing to recite these words of Euripides:

'Humility, a sense of reverence before
the sons of heaven--
of all the prizes that a mortal man
might win,
these, I say, are wisest; these are best.'
Good bye, good Roland."

Marie bowed towards the urn and returned to her seat with the Nilsson family.

Boris joined Klavdia after the service to go to Marie's home where she had arranged for friends of her family to gather outdoors around the gazebo. Before other guests arrived, he told the Nilssons, Holmes and Brownings about his meeting with William Dulles and Daniel Jay. They were disappointed but not surprised.

"We've got to utilize the outpouring of sympathy for our children to force the authorities to release them," Laura said. "This is power politics."

"I think we should make our focus an appeal to students to organize demonstrations," Peggy said. "Many changes in government and reforms have started on the campus. The schools are still in session, so large numbers of students are available at specific locations where they can mobilize."

"How about the churches?" John asked. "They meet every week."

"They can help, but after the Sunday services, church members go back to work," Lawrence said. "I think that Laura and Peggy have the right idea. Students will even miss classes if they are stirred up. Kate will be back soon and can help us contact student leaders. With all the universities and colleges in New York, we can stage a massive protest. Peggy is right that students can ignite the population."

"Don't forget Carlos, Jonathan and Kurt," Marie said. "They are still here and will do anything to get the two couples freed, now and during the trial."

"We don't want them to do anything overt that might get violent," Lawrence said. "Someone might get hurt, or even killed. We don't want anyone to die over this."

"Do you think I should resign as Russia's delegate and member of the Directorate before they replace me?" Boris asked. "How do you feel Klavdia? You know

Russia as well as I do; will that help or hurt?"

"Boris, dear," Klavdia said, "I thank you for asking, but as Laura said, this is power politics. You, John and Lawrence can best answer that question."

"I'm not so sure that this will be a Council matter as much as one of the people," Lawrence said. "In regard to the people, you, Laura, Peggy, Marie and Kate may better know the reaction to a member of the Directorate giving up his powerful position to fight for his daughter."

"All right," Laura said. "I'm for Boris announcing today that there will be a news conference tomorrow so that all the media representatives here for Roland's service will stay over. I think we should all appear at the news conference, Boris announce his resignation, and then all of us denounce the authorities for not releasing our children. It's time to go to war."

"Bravo!" Peggy said. "I'm going to call for a sympathy strike in every city and town on the planet. And if husbands won't stay home from work, wives will know exactly what to do, or rather what not to do."

"I'll stay home from work, " Lawrence said quickly.

Everyone smiled, grateful for the brief relief from the tense mood.

"The strike is a good idea, " Boris said, "but I think it would be better if someone else initiated it. Maybe someone from a country without a direct interest. We also need to collect contributions for legal expenses. Marie will you get us a post office box set up?"

"First thing tomorrow morning," Marie said.

"If we all are agreed to have the news conference, my aide for public relations is here and he can set it up," Boris said. "I am going to contact the office of Russia's President to give him advance notice of my resignation. I would expect the same if I were still President. It's the right way to do it."

Everyone agreed to the news conference plan and gathered around the gazebo table where the food had been placed. John gave a toast to Roland. Other guests arrived and the Nilssons left the gazebo to greet them.

CHAPTER 2∧

Boris's aide arranged a news conference for 10:30 at the pressroom of the Riddarhuset where Roland's service was held. The news conference garnered so much interest that all major networks set up to telecast it throughout the world. The word of the telecast spread quickly, so although it was 04:30 when the telecast started in parts of the United States, millions of American men, women and even children had their sets on and tuned to watch. For one hour preceding the news conference, the networks showed background information complete with pictures and biographical information about all the principal persons involved. Midway through the one-hour buildup, a bulletin announced that an unidentified but reliable source reported that Byron Holmes, Moira Browning, Anastasia Gorbachev and Eric Nilsson had been found in a wooded area of Sweden near the Ljusnan River and were in the custody of Internal Security. Their current whereabouts was unknown.

A friend of Marie got word of the planned news conference to the two couples. When their request to watch it was initially denied, Lawrence called Brigitta Borg. She used a connection she had in the Swedish branch of Internal Security to get the denial reversed.

The safe house on Kammakargatan had a media room complete with a large screen for television, computer transmissions and training videos. Two armed guards escorted the two couples to the media room to watch the telecast. When the two guards made a point that they were allowing the couples to watch by themselves, the couples surmised that the room was surely bugged. Byron passed around a note suggesting that they act as if they were not unduly concerned about the trouble they were in.

The room was furnished with chairs to which computer keyboards were attached for interactive responses to the screen presentations. Although the computers responded to audio entries, the keyboards could be used so individual's responses could be registered without being overheard by others in the room. The couples found they could send each other private messages through the keyboards.

"That's not my best side," Anastasia said when her picture came on screen.

"Darling, you don't have a bad side," Eric informed Anastasia with his keyboard. Anastasia blew him a kiss.

"I didn't know that you were that famous, big guy," Moira said as she nudged Byron with her elbow while his literary career was being reviewed. "Aren't I privileged to know '…a brilliant intellectual that has been mentioned as a likely poet laureate of the world?'"

Byron reached over to pinch her sharply on the hip and sent a keyboard message: "No one likes a smart ass."

"Takes one to know one," Moira responded on her keyboard. "And stop your physical abuse, you brute," she said out loud so the others could hear.

"Quiet, quiet, you two," Anastasia said. "My dad's come on camera."

"My fellow citizens of the planet," Boris said. "There is trouble here in Sweden. It is serious trouble that has consequences for you as well as for me, my wife Klavdia, my daughter Anastasia, her husband Eric Nilsson, my friends the Holmes and Brownings who are here with me in the studio and their children Moira Browning and Byron Holmes who are in the custody of the Internal Services Department.

"'These are the times that try men's souls,' Thomas Paine would say. He would be right today. My precious daughter, her husband and their companions have been tracked down, captured and arrested. They have not threatened any one, and they have not harmed any one. They have voluntarily relinquished many privileges and opportunities in order to determine their own destiny. They have done what I would like to do. I suspect most of you would like to do the same. They have sacrificed much. They have shown us the way.

"Yesterday I submitted my resignation as the delegate for Russia at the Planet Council. The motivation for my resignation has two rootstocks. One is in response to my request on behalf of the families involved that our children be released to our custody, while this matter is being resolved. My request was denied and I am resigning in protest. The second is to make my time and energies available to assist in the legal defense of my daughter and her companions. By resigning I avoid any conflict of interest that might develop. The Holmes, Brownings, Nilssons and my family have formed a joint fund for the common defense of our children. I have been asked to be the treasurer with the responsibility of procuring contributions sufficient to obtain the best legal counsel available. I am honored to accept such an important assignment. Now, each of the parents of the children being detained would like to make statements. My wife, Klavdia, is the first. Klavdia."

"I'm proud to be the mother of Anastasia. My daughter has spirit and moral conviction. She first proved it when she gave up a chance for her life-long dream going to the Olympics. Now, she has done it again in risking much for what she believes is her right and should be the right of all individuals."

Klavdia was followed by John and Peggy who emphasized how appropriate Moira's yearning for freedom represented the heritage of courageous Scots. Marie spoke for the Nilsson family. She said she hoped Roland's long years of service in behalf of a better world were not in vain. "My brother would be at Eric's side today doing everything he could to free him if he were alive to be here with us."

Lawrence spoke briefly saying he had expressed his feelings numerous times before. "I stand behind my son, his wife and their companions and will do everything in my power on their behalf."

Laura stood up and walked resolutely towards the single microphone. The single microphone did the job of the numerous ones used in the past by transmitting the speaker's words to built-in receivers in the TV cameras. "Today do not read me as an hysterical mother, although I have been and can be one. Do not read me as a helpless woman fighting against impossible odds, although I know the task I face is difficult. Do not read me as kind and merciful when I get my dander up; although I fight fair. Read me as a hardheaded woman who is going into battle to win. I'll conclude with what may cause innocent people some trouble, and I'm sorry if that is what happens. But our side does not have the power and resources that our opposition does, so we have to take advantages of whatever opportunities come our way. So here goes; listen carefully and get your pencils ready. We need money. Send it to post office box 1984, Stockholm, Sweden and write or p-mail your delegate and . . ." Laura's last words were cut off.

The studio's event manager had passed his fingers across his throat to signal the sound engineer to cut Laura off when she said, "We need money." The sound engineer should have been able to do that before she said where to send the money, but he seemed to fumble around momentarily as he reached for the cut-off switch on the control board in front of him. He happened to have a daughter seeking approval for parenthood. She had been waiting four months for a decision.

"Jesus Christ, she shouldn't have done that," the event manager exclaimed. "We are going to get hell from the Planet Communications Commission. That's against PCC rules. How come you were so slow with the switch?"

"Just couldn't get my hand moving," the sound engineer said. "Guess it's my arthritis."

"You never mentioned having arthritis before."

"It came on suddenly," the sound engineer said as he turned to the side so the event manager wouldn't see his smile of satisfaction.

Laura had astounded the media representatives. She had been at news conferences with Lawrence before, but she had never participated in them. Her remarks quickly replaced those of Boris or Lawrence as the lead story.

"Imagine that," Byron said to the others in the media room. "Mom's a real tiger when she has a microphone."

"That one sentence with the post office box number will probably be worth, well, maybe even a million," Anastasia said. "I thought my dad was good at taking advantage of the media, but your mother topped anything he ever did, Byron."

"Everybody has been saying how proud they are of us; I think it should be how proud we are of them," Moira said.

CHAPTER 22

"But actually over a million people have demonstrated on our behalf and over a hundred thousand of them made donations to our defense fund," Anastasia said. "The whole concept of being forced to have body chips is being questioned. Doesn't that mean anything?"

Anastasia and Eric were sitting on one side of a long wooden table and Moira and Byron were on the other side. Their legal counsel, David Webster, was at the end. The members of the New York State Bar Association had persuaded the New York State judicial administrator that wooden tables, this one was made of red oak, were more conductive to negotiation, counseling and mediation than steel tables. Webster hoped it was true when he arranged for his meeting with the two couples in an eighth floor conference room in the New York State Court Complex. Attorneys using the room were guaranteed that their conversations with their clients were not being recorded. A guard was stationed outside the only door leading into the room.

"If this were a jury trial, it might," Webster said. "But your offense calls for trial by one judge who will decide if you are guilty or not, and the judge is only supposed to consider evidence, not sentiment. The law in regard to removal of body chips is explicit, and you have violated it without question. I advise you to plead guilty and present the best character witnesses you can and hope for leniency by the judge."

The trial of the two couples was set to start in two weeks on 02, Sixth month, 2040 at 09:00. The members of the New York State Bar Association did not vote on which attorney was best qualified to represent individuals who were charged with violating Planet law in regard to body chips, but if they had, David Webster would have been their choice. Webster was not only experienced, he was personally interested in cases involving civil liberties. He was also high priced, but the parents of the two couples received more than enough contributions from their TV appeal to engage him. John and Lawrence were personal friends of Webster's and had worked together to counter the many proposals made over the years to restrict civil rights.

"Will it make any difference if it is known I'm pregnant?" Anastasia asked.

David looked up quickly at Anastasia and asked, "Are you?"

"Yes, and Moira, too," Moira said. "We used the self-testing kits we took with us when we left for Norway, and we both tested positive."

"That won't change whether or not you are guilty, but it will drastically affect another matter," David said as he slumped in his chair. He dreaded being the messenger of what might be devastating news to these fine young children of his friends. All four saw the anguished look on David's face and instantly knew they were about to be confronted with a terrible disclosure. "Your pregnancies are illegal," David said, "and therefore subject to, to . . . reversal."

The four were struck dumb. Finally, Byron said, "That's murder. I won't submit to the murder of my child. They will have to murder me first."

"Is that the law or subject to a judge's decision?" Anastasia cried out.

"The law doesn't require forced abortions, but the court has the power to order whatever actions are necessary to abate the consequences of an illegal action," Webster said. "To my knowledge there is no precedent in a case of an illegal pregnancy. There haven't been any known abortions since pregnancy controls were instituted except for legally married women whose lives were threatened. Consequently, there haven't been any legal actions concerning abortions. Since there is no precedent, a judge might not require an abortion."

"But we can't count on it?" Eric asked.

"No, you can't count on it, and a judge's decision to not abort would be subject to appeal by the prosecution," Webster said.

The two couples looked at each other. Their common depression flowed through their eyes back and forth to create an invisible but discernable link. That link was like a heavy chain that immobilized all four. None of them moved or spoke. Their eyes sought some sign of hope from one another. None showed through. They sank.

After a long silence, Webster said, "I think it would be good if your pregnancies become publicly known. The tremendous universal support you have received calling for your release and the end of body chips that reveal your location might possibly be transferred to protests to forced abortion that possibly could influence a judge's decision, because children are involved. With the petition at the Planet Council and that song *Let Them Be* playing again and again on the radio, it seems like that's all you can get when you tune in, you are international celebrities. The threat of taking away your motherhood will stimulate thousands, maybe millions to cry out for mercy. It's possible that the prosecutor will exclude a charge of consummating an illegal pregnancy at your arraignment."

"Do you know the prosecutor well?" Byron asked. "What kind of person is he?"

"Ambitious, mainly," Webster answered. "His name is Fred Dewey. He has won a lot of cases and is fairly high up on the ladder in judicial politics. Since state prosecutors are elected, Dewey might be wary of being a part of a forced abortion, which could cost him votes in the next election. On the other hand, his campaigns have emphasized that he strongly enforces the law."

"How do you two feel?" Byron asked Moira and Anastasia.

"I want my baby," Moira said. "I'm not going to let them operate on me. We've got to find a way to escape."

"My dad will kill someone before they take my baby," Anastasia said. "He fought the Mafia in Russia, and he brought them under control. He's used to rough stuff."

"I can't participate in this kind of discussion," Webster said. "And you may be the ones who get hurt if you try to resist with force. I think we should concentrate on ways to persuade the court to not seek abortions."

"I don't think we can rely on the court system, but I agree with David that the first thing we ought to do is let the world know you two are pregnant and appeal for mercy," Eric said to Moira and Anastasia.

"I don't have a problem with telling everyone I'm pregnant, and I agree we shouldn't rely on that getting us off," Moira said. "Is that O.K. with you Anastasia?"

"I feel the same as you do, Moira," Anastasia said. "But I still want to talk to my dad."

Webster said he would draw up a statement for the two couples to approve that acknowledged their pregnancies and hopefully would ignite a movement calling for their being allowed to have their children.

CHAPTER 23

"The Catholic Church has protested the laws of the Planet Council that have deprived families from having children at the time of their own choosing since they were first enacted, but today we are not just protesting, we are demanding that the Planet Council modify the law to prohibit forced abortions," Pope Paul O' Sheridan announced in a special news bulletin released in Rome. Pope Paul had initiated many new practices including using his family name and permitting priests to marry, so he was not adverse to the idea of holding a live press conference to deliver his statement. His closest advisors pointed out a live conference might lead to questions the Pope might not want to answer. Pope Paul asked "What questions?"

"Since you have indicated support for the two couples who arranged the illegal removal of their body chips and are asking that an exception be made in their case, you might be asked what other violations you think qualify for exceptions," his advisors answered. "And the media can always misinterpret your spoken word. If you put it in writing, there is less chance of that happening." Pope Paul reluctantly agreed to use the written bulletin format. The bulletin was carried by all newspapers and included in news broadcasts repeatedly.

"I'm traveling to New York City to make this demand in person on behalf not only of the Catholic Church, but all citizens of the planet," the bulletin continued. "Our liaison to the Planet Council has drafted a resolution to make the modification I call for that will be presented by the Irish delegate to the Council tomorrow. I have requested permission to address the Council on behalf of this resolution. I also will join in the defense of the two couples at their trial and call for their immediate release. The Catholic Church does not condone or encourage the illegal removal of body chips, which might lead to the loss of lives because it requires a very dangerous operation. However, this is a special, unprecedented case in that two mothers-to-be are involved. I think an exception should be made when the birth and rearing of babies is at stake.

"I am pleased that several outstanding libertarians are also offering to appear on behalf of the two couples. Perhaps the discussion this event has generated will lead to greater freedoms for the planet. I support reconsideration of Lawrence Holmes's resolution R-1948.

"Judges are placed in positions of responsibility and charged with making decisions because they have demonstrated their commitment to bringing about justice. Justice will be served if those babies are allowed to be born and not be born in a jailhouse. I have ordered that a special mass be held to pray for the two couples and their unborn children in every Catholic Church. While in New York City I will be attending as many of those masses as possible. I call on all of the members of the church who cannot attend one of these masses to say a special prayer at their home."

The Pope being a part of the defense team was significant not only because of his position, but because he had been the legal counsel for the Catholic Church before being elected Pope. He was willing to get personally involved in legal actions when he thought an injustice might occur. He was also well known for his Irish temper and fighting spirit.

CHAPTER 24

"I'm not sure what you should do," Montgomery Cotton answered Fred Dewey. Cotton was Dewey's chief assistant and had done most of the work preparing the case against Byron, Moira, Eric and Anastasia. "If you charge them with illegal pregnancies, everyone will blame you if the judge decides on forced abortions. If you don't charge them, your next opponent when you run for reelection or another position, will accuse you of being soft in enforcing the law."

"That's the way I see it too," Dewey answered.

Dewey was standing and looking out his eighth floor window. He could see the Planet Council's site two blocks away. He also could see the thousands of protesters gathered in the mall area below. Many had large, hand-made signs with large lettering so they could be easily read when they appeared on television newscasts. "Forced Abortion is Murder," was the most prevalent sign, but "Pregnant Mothers Should Not Be in Jail," signs were in abundance, also. The mall had become one of the most familiar locations in New York City. In addition to protest rallies, free concerts were held there each Sunday evening during Seventh and Eighth months.

Cotton rose from his chair in front of Dewey's desk to join Dewey at the window. "Lots of votes out there," he said.

"Not all from New York, though," Dewey responded. "Those for strict law enforcement don't take to the streets to protest. But they do contribute well, and that's where most of my campaign funds come from."

"Well, you still have three days before the trial starts."

Dewey turned away from the window and seated himself behind his large, oak desk. Cotton returned to his chair and waited as Dewey silently rubbed his jaw, deep in thought.

"The Pope could give us an out," Dewey said. "Consider this scenario: I charge the couples with bringing about illegal pregnancies. After the Pope calls for lenience, I say that in consideration of his appeal and due to the extraordinary and unprecedented circumstances, I have decided to withdraw the illegal pregnancy charge and only pursue charges for removal of body chips."

Cotton thought it over for a short while. "I think that's as good a plan as you are likely to come up with in the time you have left. After the trial is over, I would leak that you were pressured by an unnamed White House official to drop the charges because the President was already getting a lot of flak. Ever since it became known that she had blocked letting the couples out on bail, her poll ratings have dropped."

"Prepare a statement for me explaining dropping the charges, so I can have it ready in case I need to use it earlier than planned. Also, leak that I am getting pressure from all sides of the issue, and that I am struggling with the decisions I have to make. Include that I have sought the advice of several women including my wife. I'll be sure to tell Janice so she will know what to expect."

Cotton paused and then said, "You might just actually ask Janice what she thinks. There are a lot more women voters than men."

"Good idea. I'll do it."

CHAPTER 2⌂

"Do you think the Pope will persuade the Council to prohibit forced abortions?" Kurt asked. Carlos, Jonathan and Kurt were having breakfast together at Jonathan's apartment in New York City. All three had on the newest fad in blue jeans, heavily starched and sharply creased dark gray jeans worn with elaborate chains as belts. The jeans were also so tight that their stun gun's shape was clearly visible.

"No," Carlos said as he attached his wrist tube to his nutrient supply. "I think the delegates will listen, but they wouldn't pass R-1948, and it was much less controversial. In any case there is not time for the Council to pass anything before the trial starts day after tomorrow. We can't count on any change in time to help Anastasia and Moira."

"Don't you think all the public support they are getting will influence the judge?" Jonathan asked. He toyed with a muffin. None of the three had much of an appetite.

"Public support has grown much larger than before they were caught, but there was a lot of public pressure against tracking them down and bringing them back," Carlos said. "Internal Security ignored it all and captured them. The judge will say that it's the law and that it is his duty to uphold the law even if most people happen to disagree with it." He detached his wrist tube and picked up a glass of orange juice.

"Well, it's up to us, then," Kurt said. "The parents have done the best they could. It didn't help. They have the best legal counsel money can buy, but he couldn't even get them released on bail."

"What can we do?" Jonathan said. He pushed the plate with his muffin aside.

"We've got to find a way to prevent the forced abortions," Carlos said. "We can't let that happen. It's time for us to take action." As he brought his hand down hard on the table to emphasize his point, his empty orange juice glass bounced and fell over, but none of the three seemed to notice.

Jonathan and Kurt nodded. "Count me in," Jonathan said

"Me, too," Kurt said.

"I have an idea," Carlos said. "It's dangerous. We may get hurt. But we need to take advantage of the fact that none of them have a body chip right now."

"They've got those ankle bracelets," Kurt said.

"They can be removed," Carlos said. "Here's my plan."

CHAPTER 26

"What will happen today at the trial?" Laura asked. Lawrence was finishing breakfast at the serving bar. Laura was seated on the stool next to him.

"The Judge will issue some formal instructions and the two sides will make opening statements," Lawrence said. "Then they will probably adjourn for lunch. Would you like a cup of coffee?"

Laura ran her hand through her hair and closed her eyes. "I don't feel like having anything. I couldn't sleep last night and I know you didn't either. Will the Pope be there today?"

"I doubt it. He's been consulting with David Webster, but security will have to be beefed up so much for his appearance that he probably won't appear at the trial very often. The Pope most likely will speak after the prosecution presents evidence and that will probably take a day or two at least." Lawrence moved from the serving bar to a leather lounging chair and slumped down. Laura moved to a straight-backed chair next to his. Her body was rigid. She clenched and unclenched her fists seemingly without knowing she was doing it.

Lawrence's voice was low and dreary as he continued, "The Pope's representatives will attend all sessions and he'll watch the proceedings on television, but when he is there, I imagine they will have to clear the courtroom of all spectators and allow only a pool representative for the media."

"Do you think the trial will turn into another debate on body chips and personal freedoms?" Laura turned in her chair and focused her eyes steadfastly on Lawrence as if to will him to look at her.

"It could." Lawrence glanced at Laura and then dropped his eyes. His shoulders sloped and he folded his arms over each other. "The defense team will have several outstanding speakers who will seize the opportunity to be on stage before a world-wide audience."

"Are you going to go on stage too?" Laura asked anxiously as she set up even straighter in her chair.

Lawrence closed his eyes and paused before he answered. "If I do, it won't be for the sake of my resolution. It will be to help Byron and the others. I'll do anything to help them." Lawrence's head dropped into his hands and he closed his eyes again.

"Arguing for the point of your resolution is arguing for Byron's right to have a child and for his release."

Lawrence looked up briefly. "If Daniel Webster thinks that will help, I'll speak at the trial or at a news conference or anywhere. " Lawrence closed his eyes again.

Laura reached over and took Lawrence's hand in hers. "Had you rather not talk about it, darling?"

Lawrence looked up at Laura. "I know you are terribly worried. I am too. What we have tried doesn't seem to have worked. I don't know what more to do."

Laura and Lawrence sat quietly. Lawrence leaned back in his chair. He stroked his forehead gently. Laura still held his hand.

After a few moments, Laura released her grip on Lawrence's hand and asked, "Did you see that there was another break-in at a hunting camp last night? This time just north of the City."

Lawrence leaned forward and said, "I did. When the first ones started occurring several months ago, I inquired as to how they can happen with all the security precautions in force." Lawrence rose to his feet and walked slowly around not looking at anything in particular. "The camp managers say the problem is that there are many camps and they are in wooded areas. They say it is difficult to guard each and every lodge twenty-four hours a day. In all break-ins up to now, the guns have been left leaned up against the doors. The break-ins have been a form of protest. Since no guns were taken in the past, no one has been too concerned. The break-in last night was different; guns are missing."

Laura stood up and walked over to Lawrence. "Is Kate going with us or with Mike to the trial?"

At the mention of Kate, Lawrence's eyes brightened. "She and Mike are going to meet us there."

"Will we have to fly separate air scooters or did you call for a private vehicle?"

"I have the vehicle coming. It will help when the session is over, since there'll be a lot of congestion."

"Good. How much longer before we need to leave?"

"Twenty minutes."

"I'm so worried. You are right. Everything we tried doesn't seem to have made any difference."

"David Webster hopes the Pope's appearance will make a difference. It gives the authorities a way out."

"A way out is what our children need."

Lawrence leaned over to Laura and lifted her face to kiss her. "We'll hope for the best."

CHAPTER 27

"Give me the details of the break-in at the hunting camp," O'Sheean said to Iago. "This may be trouble for us." The two of them were in O'Sheean's fifth floor office at the New York City headquarters of Internal Security. O'Sheean was seated behind a standard gray desk in a large upholstered leather swivel chair. Iago was seated so rigidly in a straight chair that he looked as if he were at attention.

"The entry was just after dusk," Iago said. "Footprints indicate three males were involved. The break-in was similar to most of those which have been oc-curring in that nothing was damaged except the locks on the buildings where the weapons are stored, but this time three shotguns and ammunition were stolen."

"And that was all? No handguns?"

"No other weapons were taken, although there were many in the building readily accessible."

O'Sheean swiveled around to look out the window behind his desk. The view from the fifth floor was of the scooter-garage roof. Four Internal Security scooters were positioned for departure as one was coming in for a landing. O'Sheean had been looking out his window in sixth month, 2038 when a departing scooter had collided with an incoming scooter causing the death of both pilots. Each time O'Sheean watched scooter landings he remembered the collision and couldn't help having a feeling of expectation that something similar was about to happen. "I think the break-in could be related to the trial. There are three young male friends of the two couples we have in custody who might do something like steal weapons and try to free them."

Iago could see the scooters in the air above the garage roof and knew about the collision O'Sheean had witnessed. He had noticed that each time O'Sheean watched the scooter landings his shoulders seemed to tighten. Iago had a strange feelings that O'Sheean was not worried that another collision might occur, but for some weird, disturbing reason he actually hoped there would be one. "Even if those three are the ones, how would they slip the shotguns past the security at the judicial complex? Everyone admitted to the trial has to pass through a screening at the entrance into the building."

"They would have to get into the building at night when no screening is being done and stash the weapons inside where they could retrieve them later. When is the Pope going to appear at the trial?"

"I don't know, but I doubt if it will be today. This is the first day of the trial and only preliminary proceedings will be going on."

O'Sheean swiveled around to face Iago. "I think you're right. The Pope won't be there today. If I were those three young friends of our prisoners, I would make my move when the Pope is there. Report to me what days that it is possible the Pope will be in attendance, because I want to be in the courtroom every day the

Pope is."

"But wouldn't that be the worst time to try a rescue when security will be at its highest?" Iago asked in as gentle a way as he could. He didn't like to question his superior's judgement.

"You think a lot, but young radicals are not so rational. They might guess that having the Pope there would assure that no violent action would be used to stop them, but they would be wrong. Matter of fact, it wouldn't be bad if one of those boys got a scare—maybe a flesh wound. We sure wouldn't want to do anything to hurt a pregnant girl, but the boys are fair game. I want you to locate the three friends and put a tail on them." O'Sheean pointed his finger at Iago to emphasize his orders.

"Should we pick them up and bring them in?"

O'Sheean thought for a moment before answering. "No, we've upset enough delegates already and they are sons of delegates. But let me know where they are staying. Also, have a special detail watch the judicial complex every night before the Pope is to be there. The local authorities may not have twenty-four hour surveillance of a courtroom. They probably wouldn't even think to notify us if someone broke in at night and didn't take anything."

"I'll send you a p-mail with the information you want as soon as I can get it." Iago rose from his chair and stood at attention waiting to be dismissed. "Anything else?"

O'Sheean tilted his heavy body back in his chair and rocked back and forward slowly with his eyes closed. "No," he said as he swiveled back around to watch the scooter landings.

CHAPTER 28

"Because of the extreme interest in these proceedings, we have moved this trial to this auditorium from the usual chambers in order to accommodate the large number of attendees expected when certain witnesses for the defense are scheduled to appear," Judge Henry Cartwright announced to begin the proceedings at the trial of Moira, Byron, Anastasia and Eric.

Judge Cartwright had been on the bench for thirty-two years and was the most experienced judge currently serving in the state of New York, but he didn't look the part of a member of the judiciary; he looked more like a prizefighter in training. Even his judicial robe didn't hide his massive shoulders; his bull-like neck swelled above the top of his robe; his large head barely allowed enough room for his wide jaw, thick lips and a huge nose; bushy black eyebrows punctuated a pronounced forehead. Yet, incongruously, he spoke in a soft voice, slowly and with careful enunciation.

The room arrangement for the trial placed Judge Cartwright in the center of a large stage, the jury just to his left, and tables for the prosecution and defense on his right. The families of the defendants were also on the stage and seated two to three meters behind the table for the defense. A thick, gray curtain hung across the back of the stage. Judge Cartwright gave instructions to the legal counsels and called for the prosecution to make its opening statement.

"The defendants have violated several laws including those relating to body chip removal and illegal pregnancy," Fred Dewey, the prosecutor, said as he faced the judge giving scant attention to those in the auditorium seats. "They should be subject to the prescribed penalties for the violation of those laws." Tall, well tanned, forty-four years old and favored by dark, wavy hair streaked with silver, Dewey could have been a poster figure for prosecutors wanting to portray a spirited crusader.

"The violation of important laws in itself makes this an important legal deliberation," Dewey continued. "But in addition, the unprecedented actions of these four persons has generated international attention, which has raised the importance of this trial to the highest level of judicial proceedings. We must prevent the undermining of the foundations of our society by confirming that no man or woman is above the law. In this case there is no question that the defendants knew the consequences of their unlawful actions. They fled and hid to escape being held accountable, an admission of guilt in itself. The allegations I have just made will be proven by the testimony of several officials I will be calling as witnesses for the prosecution. They will detail the defendants' illegal actions and those evasive maneuvers they took in order to circumvent conscientious authorities who were trying to carry out their duties."

Dewey turned to the audience to say, "I have both a son and a daughter who will soon be the ages of the four defendants. My children wish that they could do whatever they want to do regardless of anything else. But such permissiveness invites lawlessness. No civilized society can operate without a system for order."

Dewey turned away from the audience to face the judge again, as if to acknowledge that his final words should be directed to the one person with the power to decide the case. "Our system has been developed over many decades. It has been refined to meet the needs of the time. It has worked, and it will continue to work so long as it is upheld. That is what must be done. The law must be upheld." He took his seat.

David Webster rose slowly and took a position at the front of the stage from which he could address both the judge and the audience. The set of his jaw and the intent in his eyes signaled that not only was this trial about a serious matter, but that he was deadly serious himself. Sixty-eight years of age, slightly portly but solid and stately, well groomed but not glamorous, and courtly in his manner, the impression he gave could be summed up in one word, distinguished.

"I will prove that the defendants have done no harm to any person or institution and are deserving of an appropriate return to the conditions they voluntarily left temporarily," Webster said. "I have been overwhelmed by the significant offers to provide assistance to me in my efforts for the defendants. I am honored to relate to you the names of those who will be testifying for the defense. First and foremost, the most reverent Pope Paul O' Sheridan who has traveled from Rome to appear before the Planet Council and at this trial; Sigmund Demetri from the Institute for Philosophic Solutions in Athens, which is known for its outstanding student body as well as its renowned faculty of leading philosophers; C. S. Lewiston, has come from London interrupting his writing on Christianity to support the defendants; Lady Gregory Joyce, the Irish dramatist who has traveled from Dublin to join us; Lucius Alighieri, the Italian poet from Florence has come to assist and Patrick Salle, the former Prime Minister of India has traveled from Bangalore to support us.

"Fred Dewey is right about one thing. This is an important trial; important not only as a trial of the four defendants, but also as a trial of our system. This planet's populace is watching to see if justice will be served. We cannot disappoint them."

As Webster took his seat, Judge Cartwright struck his gavel and announced, "We are recessed until 13:00." All on stage and in the audience rose when the judge stood up and walked to the back of the stage to exit through an opening in the curtain on the right side. An aide of his was awaiting him there, and Judge Cartwright stopped to talk with her. The audience remained standing. Soon conversations began all over the auditorium. Those attendees who came alone even started conversations with neighboring strangers. The topics ranged from which defendant looked like which parent to the likelihood that forced abortions would actually be ordered if the defendants were found guilty, which almost everyone assumed was going to be the case.

The parents of the defendants moved forward to the table for the defense to speak to their children. A guard was at either end of the table watching carefully, but they did not intercept the parents. All of the children moved away from their table to gather in four, separate, family-related groups. Some in the audience moved towards the stage to be closer to the defendants and their parents, as if to show support for them. With the four famous families on stage and the judge leaving the scene, the setting was more like a ceremony recognizing the young men and women for their achievements than like a trial. But the seriousness of the potential outcome caused everyone to speak in low murmurs.

Laura moved quickly up to Byron to give him a hug and whispered something in his ear. Byron held Laura in his arms for a long time. Lawrence was a step or two behind Laura and patted Byron on the shoulder before he walked over to speak to David Webster. When Byron stepped back from Laura, he kept one arm around her and said, "How does Dad think the trial will turn out? He won't tell me much of anything."

"He told me that he's hopeful that the Pope's intervention will give the prosecution a political way out to let your baby be born. But as you know, your father never wants to raise hopes that may turn out to be false and cause even greater disappointment than if he hadn't said anything. I think he really expects what he is hoping for to happen, but don't tell him I told you."

Moira and her parents were nearby, but talking among themselves. "Are they feeding you well?" Peggy asked Moira.

"Of course, Mother," Moira, answered. "How do you think it would look if the government starved a pregnant woman?" Before Peggy could respond, Moira rushed into her arms saying, "I'm sorry. I didn't mean to be rude to you. I'm just nervous." Moira was almost sobbing as John joined them and put his arms around the two of them.

Eric's mother was the only one of his family allowed on stage. She and Eric talked in low tones. Somber by nature, she looked as if she had already accepted that there would be forced abortions and she must do the best she could to bear up under the circumstances. Eric looked defiant and said, "It won't be politic for the prosecutor to demand abortions. We're going to beat this, I'm sure."

Anastasia and Boris were engaged in a serious discussion while Klavdia looked on. "What are they saying in Moscow?" Anastasia asked. "Is the media on our side?"

"Definitely, " Boris answered. "But more than that, the public is up in arms. Rallies are being held. A large delegation of our people is planning a demonstration tomorrow in front of the auditorium. Our President is apparently having second thoughts about accepting my resignation, according to a friend of mine in his cabinet. I'm not sure how I should respond if they ask me to return to the Planet Council. I'll want to discuss that with the rest of our group, if it happens."

"You should tell them to 'go to Hell' I think," Klavdia interjected.

"Now, now, dear," Boris said. "We've got to think what will be the best for the children."

Lawrence brought David Webster along with him as he returned to Byron's side to talk with him. "David wants to know how you and Moira would feel about a plea bargain admitting a violation and accepting a short sentence for you and Eric in return for no abortions and Moira and Anastasia going free. Of, course, all of you will have body chips reinserted."

"I'd have to talk it over with all the others," Byron said. "We are in this together all the way."

No one was looking towards the back of the stage. Just as Judge Cartwright exited on the right end of the curtain, Carlos emerged from the left end of the curtain carrying a shotgun and a portable loud speaker. Jonathan and Kurt followed along behind Carlos and they were also holding shotguns. Even the guards didn't see the three of them until they heard the "Do not panic," Carlos said into his speaker. "These weapons are not to harm you. We are here to secure the release of the two couples on trial, because we feel that forced abortions are murder. Stay where you are and do not make sudden moves. We are wearing bullet-proof vests and our weapons are fully loaded." Jonathan and Kurt took positions facing towards the auditorium and behind the guards who were on stage. Carlos walked behind the table for the defense and trained his gun on the guard closest to him.

The audience and those on stage were so shocked that a strange silence of awe broke off all conversations and everyone stared at the three young men and their weapons. The guards made no move.

Lawrence moved quickly to Carlos's side and said, "Carlos, I know you mean well, but this is not the way."

Carlos turned towards Lawrence and started to answer when Byron interrupted him with, "Dad, let us handle this,"

Byron took Moira by the hand and led her towards where Carlos and Lawrence were standing. "This is the only way. They will kill our children. We'd rather take our chances on the run. Eric and Anastasia, let's go."

As Eric and Anastasia started towards Byron, Eric saw that Judge Cartwright had emerged from behind the curtain on the run to subdue Carlos from behind. "Carlos, look out behind you!" he shouted just as Judge Cartwright reached Carlos with his arms outstretched to grab his weapon.

Carlos turned around as Judge Cartwright charged into him. The impact caused Carlos's gun to fire to the side. Several screamed. The guards rushed Carlos and wrestled his gun away from him. Other guards came onto the stage and disarmed Kurt and Jonathan who had not known what to do, so they had not fired their weapons.

"Are you all right?" Byron asked Moira as he turned towards her.

"I'm all right," Moira said. "Oh, no!" she screamed. "Your father!"

"Dad, Dad, you've been hit," Byron cried out when he turned towards Lawrence and saw him staggering and holding his hands over a spreading dark spot in the chest area of his body cover. Merlin was in the process of calling "922," the emergency number for injuries involving heart functions. Two seconds after Lawrence was struck by the gun's blast his body chip signaled to Merlin that Lawrence had suffered a massive malfunction of his heart, brain, and lungs. Merlin was programmed to send a return signal to the body chip to release a newly developed chemical to counteract massive bleeding and then call "922." Byron reached out and caught Lawrence in his arms to keep him from falling.

"Laura, Laura, where are you?" Lawrence said in a choked, feeble voice as he collapsed into Byron's arms. Laura screamed and rushed towards Lawrence. Lawrence lifted his head when he heard the scream and tried to focus his eyes, but he couldn't.

As Byron lifted Lawrence erect, Lawrence's eyes cleared momentarily. He recognized Byron and tried to reach out to him with his arms, but he was not able to raise them. His eyes lost their focus; he gasped for breath and with as much voice as he could muster said, "Son, son, I love you. I love you as . . ." Lawrence died before he could finish his thought just as Laura reached his side crying, "No, no, no! You said nothing would happen. You said you would be all right."

Laura slipped her body inside Byron's arms to press against Lawrence as if to try and stop the bleeding. Lawrence's blood soaked into Laura's body cover turning the front of it the same color as its red stripes that designated her occupation and security status. Her sobs were deep and gasping as she pleaded, "Merlin, Merlin, save him. Please, God, let him save him."

EPILOGUE

The trial was telecast live internationally. Surveys after the telecast indicated that seventy-nine per cent of those adults with the capability to receive the telecast were watching or recording the trial--many on their own "Merlin." The interactive response to the shooting was immediate and an overwhelming condemnation of the Planet Council, the leaders of those countries that had voted against R-1984 and the individual members of the Council who cast the dissenting votes. Patrick Henry clubs throughout the world, international service organizations, church leaders and presidents of educational institutions called for a universal protest strike starting on the following Firstday and continuing until the Planet Council reconsidered and passed R-1984. Many of the same organizations and institutions demanded the freedom of the two couples and their safe return to Norway without having body chips reinserted. At noon on the day after the shooting, the Planet Council held an emergency session at which they acquiesced to both public demands without a dissenting vote.

Lawrence's funeral service was held in the new performing arts center in New York City on the second day after his death. It was the largest auditorium in the city, but it was totally inadequate to accommodate the immense crowd that had gathered to attend. The Pope and all the speakers who had come for the trial spoke and paid tribute to Lawrence.

Printed in the United States
35663LVS00002B/79-207